M000160244

YOU
AGAIN?

YOU AGAIN?

NICK SPALDING

LAKE UNION
PUBLISHING

Text copyright © 2021 by Nick Spalding
All rights reserved.

Published by Lake Union Publishing, Seattle

www.apub.com

Amazon, the Amazon logo, and Lake Union Publishing are are trademarks of Amazon.com, Inc., or its affiliates.

ISBN-13: 9781542032087
ISBN-10: 1542032083

Cover design and illustration by Ghost Design

Printed in the United States of America

YOU AGAIN?

Monday

JOEL – COINCIDENCE

There is a cocktail.

A most *magnificent* cocktail.

Let me tell you about it . . .

It is called a Sin City, and is, for all intents and purposes, simply an espresso martini. It contains vodka, espresso, coffee liqueur and sugar syrup, and is made in bars and lounges the world over. But there is one place on Earth – a place that I have only visited once before – that makes a Sin City like nowhere else.

None of the ingredients are any different. I know. I've *checked*.

But the Sin City made in the Reef Bar, on the tiny Maldivian island of Wimbufushi, is the single greatest thing I've ever had in my mouth.

For some reason, the bartender, whose name is Tarkan (it's vitally important to remember the names of all the people in the world who bring such joy), mixes an espresso martini so glorious, I kept waiting for the angelic wings to spring out of his back as he handed it over to me.

It has been six long years since I last had one of Tarkan's Sin Cities. But this is a massive oversight I shall be rectifying in the next eighteen hours or so – once the two portly Germans in front of me sort their tickets out, that is.

The self-service machines at Heathrow are supposed to cut the amount of time it takes you to check in your luggage by a considerable amount. This would be true, if it weren't for the fact that said machines can be right pernickety little bastards to operate. The two portly German gentlemen are having severe issues getting the machine they are using to recognise their passports, while the machine next to them is currently surrounded by an Asian family comprised of three thousand children, and a very harassed-looking mother and father at the centre of the throng. They are trying their hardest not to suffer a mental breakdown as they attempt to print off multiple luggage labels.

It's a bloody good job Cara and I have got three hours before our flight leaves, otherwise my stress levels would probably be rising right about now. As it is, I'm more than content to wait as long as necessary for a machine to become available. I'm going on holiday to where the best Sin City is, you see. With a beautiful woman who I am very probably in love with. Nothing is going to shatter my happy mood.

Absolutely nothing.

'Should we give them a hand?' Cara asks, as she looks on at the Germans and their struggle with Great British machinery.

'Probably best to let the staff handle it,' I reply. 'There's every chance I'll be as useless at operating the damn thing as they are and will only make matters worse.'

Cara rolls her eyes and gives me a playful punch on the arm. 'You're a lot more capable than you think, mister. Remember what we've talked about? You certainly sorted my iPad out for me, didn't you?'

'Well, yes. But I did also need counselling for six weeks afterwards.'

Cara chuckles, and goes back to watching the large gentlemen as they continue to grapple with the recalcitrant ticket machine. She also snakes an arm around my waist, standing a little closer to me as she does so.

Given that every single one of the ten ticket machines is currently being used (this is what happens when you're flying on a Monday morning), I elect to drop back into my idle Sin City fantasy, basking in the glorious memories of being sat at the Reef Bar, sipping my wonderful espresso martini.

The daydream is somewhat ruined when I'm forced to recall my companion at the time, who was invariably sat next to me, sucking down her third Bellini in a row.

Amy didn't like the Sin City. She didn't like it *at all*.

'It's too rich,' she used to say, turning her nose up at Tarkan's excellent efforts, before ordering yet another Bellini.

I bet Cara will like the Sin City. I bet she will like it *just fine*.

I look at my gorgeous girlfriend, which is a much happier thing to do than picture the *wicked harpy* in my mind's eye. I'm very much looking forward to creating *new* memories with Cara on Wimbufushi – the first of which will involve that cocktail, and the second of which will hopefully involve the tiny bikini she bought on ASOS a week ago. It's got these little twirly tassel things at the hips, and sequined bits right on top of her—

AMY.

The shock runs through my body, like one of the airport security guards has decided to try out their new taser on me. I feel my legs go weak, and my vision go wonky. My heart starts to pound.

As the blood drains from my face, I blink rapidly, trying to unsee what I think I've just seen.

It must be a hallucination.

3

One triggered by all the recent stress I've been under at work.

And I was just daydreaming about my Sin City, wasn't I?

Which made me think about Amy, didn't it?

Yes. That's it. I didn't really just see her walking towards passport control in a floaty blue dress, pushing a suitcase, alongside a tall man in a Hawaiian shirt – her hair up in that side ponytail she always liked to drape back over her left shoulder.

For a moment, I'm convinced that I did hallucinate the whole thing, because Amy has disappeared. But then she re-emerges from behind a gaggle of excited tourists, and I can see that I'm not hallucinating at all.

My ex-wife Amy is here at the airport. *Right now.*

'Joel? Are you okay?' Cara asks, putting her hand on my arm.

I can't let her know what I've seen.

This is supposed to be a happy, exciting day. I don't want to ruin it for her by revealing that I've just seen my evil ex-wife, less than fifty yards away from us, heading airside with a man who also seems *very* familiar to me for some reason.

'Yeah, yeah, I'm fine,' I lie, trying my hardest to will the blood back into my cheeks. 'Just feeling a bit tired, is all. Looking forward to getting away.'

Cara nods and squeezes me tight. She knows how stressed I've been at work in the past few months. It's more than believable I'd be a bit peaky.

The portly German gentlemen appear to have sorted out their issues with the ticket machine and are moving on, giving Cara and me the chance to (hopefully) get our luggage labels printed out and stuck around our suitcase handles a lot quicker than them.

As we trundle our suitcases over to it, I glance back at where I saw Amy. There's no sign of her. And Heathrow is a *very* big airport. The chances of us running into one another while we're here are probably pretty small, aren't they?

Yeah. I'm sure it'll be fine. *Absolutely* sure.

We don't have anything like the issues with the luggage labels that the Germans did. There's a tricky moment when I inadvertently stick mine briefly to my knee, but I manage to pull it off without removing too much leg hair, and get the label on to the suitcase without much more trouble.

Having done that, Cara and I pull our suitcases over to the check-in desk, where we have to queue for another ten minutes, before finally getting rid of the heavy things.

Normally, as I watch my suitcase disappear into the bowels of the airport via the conveyor belt, I feel a great sense of relief to have got shot of such a cumbersome object. Not today, though. Not when I know that somewhere ahead of me is my ex-wife and her Hawaiian-shirt-wearing partner.

. . . who I'm *sure* I've seen before somewhere. I'm *sure* of it.

'Okay, Joel?' Cara says, snapping me out of my worried reverie.

'Yes!' I reply, a little too loudly.

'Great. Let's get through security then. I really need a coffee.'

'Okay,' I agree, feeling my heart race. On the other side of security is Amy, and I've never felt less secure in my life.

I am made to feel slightly better when Cara slides her hand into mine as we walk away from the check-in desk. She has a habit of performing these small, surprising acts of intimacy that I'm really not used to. It gives me a strange, but wholly marvellous feeling of security. And she's been doing it ever since we got together a few months ago. I feel like I've been saved.

As we follow the giant glowing yellow signs pointing us in the direction of the customs and passport check, I begin to get myself under control.

Even if we did bump into Amy, it wouldn't be the end of the world. I haven't seen her now for nearly two years, and there would been no reason to do anything other than give her a curt nod if we met, and move on with my life.

My *excellent* life with Cara.

Oh God.

What if Cara sees her? What will she do? Will she want to say hello? They do know each other – even though they probably only met a handful of times at the agency. It'd probably upset Cara, though, I know that. She knows all about what Amy did to me after we split.

Blast.

Maybe I should have just fessed up and told Cara I saw Amy earlier? Then she'd have a warning. But I can't do that now, otherwise Cara might wonder why I chose to keep it a secret.

Aaargh!

I pull the toiletries out of my rucksack and place them in a see-through bag, and I curse myself for not being more forthright.

While I empty out my pockets into the grey plastic tray and pull out my iPad, I can't help but picture a scenario where we bump into Amy and her bloke in the most awkward of situations. In the queue at Costa, for instance. Would Amy try to spark up a conversation in such a circumstance? Would Cara? I know I bloody *wouldn't*. What would I have to say? '*Oh hi, Amy. Are you going to be paying for your coffee with all the money you bled out of me in the divorce?*'

Aaargh!

'These things are always nerve wracking to go through, aren't they?' Cara says, as she sticks her rucksack into another one of the battered plastic trays. She's misinterpreted the reason why I look so perturbed. She thinks I'm nervous about security – but I don't have the headspace to be stressed about that, because Amy is in here . . . *somewhere.*

Damn it. I should have bloody *said* something!

I send my belongings off to be x-rayed and look around to see if the metal detector is free to walk through. The distressed look on my face must be quite obvious, as the security guy takes one look at me and indicates that I should come over to be checked out in the full body scanner.

Oh joy. I hate these things. You feel like a right pillock standing there with your arms up, as the whole thing whirs around you, getting a really good image of your penis for the staff to all laugh at.

I wonder if Amy had to go through this thing as well . . .

She could have stood right where I am mere minutes ago. Or maybe her Hawaiian-shirted partner had to do it, with his arms up, and the machine getting a picture of his penis with its x-rays.

Rays.

Ray.

His name is *Ray*!

Ray Holland.

He was . . . he was a bloody *client* of ours, wasn't he?

Yes, that's bloody right!

Back when Amy and I were the power couple at Rowntree Land & Home, we sold Ray Holland a rather elegant five-bedroom place in Sevenoaks.

Bloody hell! She's now with a guy she met while *we were still together.*

'Fuck me!' I blurt out with sudden rage, within the confines of the scanner.

'Are you alright, sir?' the security guy asks, looking suspicious all of a sudden.

Oh, *shit.*

I've just displayed a random act of aggression while going through security. I'd better assure this guy I'm not a psychopath, before he takes me away for a full-cavity search.

But *can* I do that? Can I assure him?

Once upon a time I would have handled this situation magnificently. The old Joel Sinclair would have had no problems smoothing things over with a complete stranger.

But now?

After what's happened in my life recently?

'I'm so sorry!' I tell him in a panicked voice, as he beckons me out of the scanner. 'I just remembered I think I've left my Hoover on at home!'

'Pardon me?'

Shit! I meant to say *oven*! Nobody leaves their bloody *Hoover* on at home!

Oven! I meant oven!

'Ah aha ha,' I laugh in a tight, high pitch. 'I . . . er . . . I . . .'

Think of something, you bloody idiot, otherwise this guy is going to be knuckle deep in you in the next twenty minutes!

'I . . . have a . . . have a *Roomba*! It's a Roomba that I have!'

He eyes me suspiciously. 'A Roomba?'

'Yeah! You know . . .' For some reason I stick my elbows out and start to twist back and forth like a right Cockney geezer. 'Roomba, Roomba, stick it up your jumpa.'

Look, I'm panicking, okay?

This is a tense, *awful* situation, and I'm trying to break the tension with a little light comedy relief.

The security guard looks at me like I've just vomited all over the floor. 'Are you alright, sir?' he repeats.

I deflate instantly. 'Not really. I've been overworked and stressed for months in a job I'm getting worse at every day, am in desperate need of a holiday, and I've just seen my ex-wife for the first time in two years.'

This garners me a look of actual pity. 'Ah, I see. Been there, done that. Well, you have a nice holiday, sir,' he says, and waves me on.

I'm slightly stunned, but I don't need telling twice.

I hurry over to where my rucksack and its contents are still confined in trays at the end of the conveyor belt, and start to gather up my things.

'What on Earth were you doing?' Cara asks as she comes to stand next to me, having already secured all of her stuff.

I look at her for a second. 'I have absolutely no idea,' I reply, with extreme honesty. The kind of honesty I should have exhibited earlier when I spotted Amy. 'Shall we go and find that coffee?' I suggest, zipping up the rucksack.

'That's a great idea.' Cara beams and holds out her hand. I take it in mine, and we trot off into the environs of Terminal 5 like a couple of excited teenagers on their first date.

And I *am* excited. I absolutely still am.

The thought of this holiday in the Maldives has basically kept me going for the past few weeks, and I'm incredibly grateful to Cara's grandfather for helping me pay for it. As bosses go, he's not such a bad one. I just wish I was doing a better job in return for his generosity.

Come on, man. Stop thinking about all of that. Just enjoy the time you've got away from the place!

I swallow down my feelings of inadequacy for about the thousandth time, and return my attention to matters at hand – namely the acquisition of coffee and the avoidance of the woman who was instrumental in my slide into the very same inadequacy that plagues my life.

And now that I remember who her partner is, I want to avoid him just as much. I can't help but think he might have had something to do with—

No. Just stop, Joel. What the hell's the point? It's been two years. Just let it go.

I give myself an internal slap across the face, and take a deep breath.

We head over to Costa and pick up a couple of flat whites. I'm grateful for the caffeine on this chilly spring morning, as I didn't sleep all that well last night. I never do when I'm travelling. The coffee's probably not going to help my skittish mood, but it'll at least keep me awake.

I try my very hardest not to scan everyone as they pass by while I sip the flat white at the table Cara managed to grab for us right next to the main concourse.

'Are you people-watching?' Cara asks, with a wry smile on her face.

Obviously, I wasn't trying hard enough . . .

'Yeah,' I admit, thinking that it's better to be partially honest about what I'm up to. 'You always get a right mix at the airport, don't you?'

Which is no word of a lie. The eclectic bunch of holidaymakers rushing by us is a sight to see and no mistake. People from all walks of life and ethnicities are crowded in here, offering a melting pot of humanity that I'm not normally used to seeing – living as I do in the rather dull south-east of the country.

And as long as I don't see a certain blond-haired woman and her sodding boyfriend Ray, I'll be absolutely fine.

Cara and I finish our coffees and she suggests a little light browsing around the myriad shops that fill the terminal, giving bored people like us the chance to waste a few minutes while the clock ticks down to the gate opening.

I'd obviously like to just stay in one place to maximise the chances of Amy avoidance, but the airport is awfully busy – thick with travellers on this particular Monday morning – so I guess I won't be taking too much of a risk if I trail around after my girl-friend as she browses.

Besides, if she sees anything she likes, I might just buy it for her as a surprise. I'm feeling guilty about keeping the Amy-sighting to myself, and would like to make it up to Cara, even if she has no idea what I'm trying to make up for.

And so, for the next forty minutes, I follow Cara around as she flits from shop to shop, inspecting their wares carefully as she does so. I do this in a permanently heightened state of awareness, thanks to both the caffeine and the secure knowledge that my ex-wife is around here somewhere, with Mr Five Bedrooms In Sevenoaks.

Nothing takes Cara's interest in Prada, Gucci or Armani – which I'm mightily relieved about. Cara quite likes her fashion labels, but thankfully none of the brands she really loves are here at the airport.

When we hit WHSmith, though, I'm more than happy to buy the two books she takes a liking to, as well as the three magazines she picks out. The flight to the Maldives is eleven hours, so I don't blame her for wanting so much stuff to keep herself occupied. I loaded up my iPad with games and Kindle books last night for exactly the same reason.

'Can we go get something to eat? I'm ravenous,' Cara says, stifling a yawn, as we walk away from Smiths. I glance at my watch. It's nearly 11 a.m., and we still have a good hour to kill until we can go to our gate, so some brunch would be ideal. We've been on the go since six thirty this morning, so it's no wonder Cara's hungry. I could eat a horse myself.

And if we stuff ourselves now, we won't be that hungry when we get on the plane, and can safely avoid the first of the two in-flight meals that we'll be subjected to. Cara's grandfather Roland may have been kind enough to contribute to the cost of this holiday, but that sadly couldn't extend to anything above economy seating on the plane.

No complaints from me, though. We wouldn't be going on this trip at all if they hadn't had a flash sale on Expedia for this specific week – and the package only came with economy seats. I'd rather sit in cattle class than miss out completely on a bargain luxury holiday.

We make our way up to the Gordon Ramsay restaurant – which Cara had recommended to her by Barry Gasleak at the agency. His name is not actually Barry Gasleak, of course – it's Barry Cross, but he's had no less than three houses he's sold suffer gas leaks over the twenty years he's been in the estate-agency business, and that kind of thing leads to a nickname, whether you like it or not. It's still better than some of the nicknames I've been getting at work recently . . .

We plonk ourselves down in an open booth that we are lucky enough to find empty at the back of the restaurant, and order a couple of English breakfasts.

By the time I look towards the bar to see a waiter approaching our table with them both in his hands about fifteen minutes later, my stomach is gurgling away with extreme hunger – so it doesn't take me long to demolish a good half of my plate, once it's put in front of me.

'Easy there, big fella,' Cara says with a smile, as she tucks into her veggie English breakfast. 'You'll get indigestion.'

'Sorry,' I reply, swallowing a barely masticated bit of sausage, 'I didn't realise how famished I was.' I have to smile as I do this. Cara likes to mother me now and again, like a hen with her chick – which is hilarious given how much younger she is than me. But I can't pretend I don't like it.

'I told you, you should have eaten more than that instant porridge sachet this morning,' my girlfriend remarks, as she looks down and daintily carves off a bit of her poached egg.

'Yeah, you're right. I always tend to not eat much when I know I'm travelling,' I admit, popping the rest of the sausage into my mouth. 'I guess I'm a bit nervous that I might—'

There's a sudden silence from my side of the table.

'Never mind, at least you'll have eaten plenty now, so—' Cara looks back up from her poached egg to see that I have completely disappeared from view. 'Joel? Where the hell have you gone?'

Poor Cara. Here she is having brunch with her boyfriend, on the cusp of their all-inclusive bargain holiday to the tropics, and he's been abducted by aliens.

What other explanation can there be for his sudden and total disappearance?

Hideous creatures from beyond known existence must have created a portal in reality, and sucked Joel Sinclair through to their strange and mind-bending alien realm.

Either that, or he's just seen his ex-wife entering the same restaurant in which he's currently munching his way through an English breakfast, and has ducked underneath the table so fucking fast that there was an audible popping noise as the air rushed in to fill the void left by his immediate absence.

Cara leans to her left and looks down to find me scrunched up uncomfortably, with my head almost between my legs, and a large piece of half-chewed sausage in my gob.

'What are you doing?' she asks in confusion, glancing around at the diners seated next to us, who have noted my antics and are watching on with bemusement.

I think for a moment.

Is there any possible way I can lie myself out of this situation convincingly?

Probably not. Not unless I can somehow persuade my girl-friend that my entire head has suddenly become a hundred times heavier than normal.

I don't think that's a *thing*, though, is it? I've never heard of a medical condition that causes your head to rapidly increase in density for no apparent reason. Pretty sure that would have made it into *The Lancet* at some point.

No. I'm just going to have to come clean, and admit the real reason for my sudden impression of a meerkat who's just seen thirty lions come charging over the nearest hill.

'Amy,' I say, through my sausage.

'What?' Cara responds, barely able to understand me due to the amount of processed pork in my mouth.

'Amy here,' I tell her in a muffled voice. 'My eg-wige. She'd here in da gludy airgort.'

'What?' Cara repeats.

I should really swallow this stupid sausage, otherwise my communication abilities are not going to be up to snuff, at a time I really need them to be firing on all cylinders. I have a lot of explaining to do.

I take a moment to chew the sausage a little more, before swallowing it down in quite a painful fashion. My appetite has completely deserted me.

'I said . . . my ex-wife Amy is here!' I stage whisper at Cara – for some inexplicable reason. We're in the middle of one of the busiest airports in the world. Unless Amy has developed the hearing capabilities of Superman, I doubt she could hear what I'm saying from all the way over there, even if I was shouting at the top of my lungs.

Cara instantly goes wide eyed, and swivels her head around to look behind her.

'No! Don't!' I wail, not wanting to give our position away to Amy – who is standing with Ray Sevenoaks at the entrance to the restaurant, both of them looking at menus. It's a saving grace they're both staring intently at them, otherwise there's a very good chance she'd have seen me masticating my sausage. Cara and I are at the back of the restaurant, but in direct line of sight of the entrance. It wouldn't take much for Amy to glance up and see us. She always did have eyesight like a fucking hawk. She is to small crumbs left on a kitchen counter ten feet away what a kestrel is to an unsuspecting dormouse.

Cara turns back around again, and looks down at me. 'Bloody hell, Joel! What is she doing here?'

I choose not to answer this question as the answer is pretty damn obvious. I don't blame Cara for coming out with it, though. Seeing Amy is enough to frazzle anyone's nerves to the point where they start to not make much sense.

'Just . . . just keep staring this way, and with any luck she won't look over here. If we act normal, everything should be okay,' I tell her, not electing to elucidate any further on why I've suddenly decided that hiding under the table is something approaching normal behaviour.

'What am I supposed to look at?' Cara asks. For some reason she's also started to stage whisper.

'The wall!'

She glances up. 'But there's nothing on it!'

'Your plate then!'

She glances down. 'It's empty!'

'Just look in your lap then!'

So, now 'normal' appears to be me hiding under the table, and Cara jerking her head around like a chicken who's worried the kestrel is coming for it next.

Given that the other diners close to us are now watching our exploits with not a small degree of confusion and befuddlement, I'd say we're acting so far away from normal that I expect my friendly security guard to come and grab me at any moment for some cavity-searching fun out the back.

I raise my head to look over at where Amy and Ray are still studying the menus. As I do, I glance at Cara, who is staring down into her lap, and flicking her eyes back and forth.

Even from here I can see that Amy has got her Frown Face on. The Frown Face of Amy Caddick (I'm assuming she goes by her maiden name these days) is a thing that will be scored across my brain until the day I die.

Many times I have seen it. Many, *many* times – especially in the last two years of our marriage when everything was breaking down like a French car from the nineties.

I'd be on the receiving end of the mildest version of the Frown Face when I left crumbs on the kitchen counter, or forgot to fill the dishwasher. My – shall we say – *relaxed* attitude to household chores never sat well with her constant desire for permanent tidiness. The most severe version of the Frown Face was the one that greeted me when we had to sign the divorce papers, closely followed by the one I got aimed at me the day Amy left her job.

The Frown Face might be my saving grace today, though – if you'll pardon the unintentional poetry. The Frown Face indicates that Amy is not happy with the contents of the menu put in front of her. Ray Sevenoaks and his disgusting orange Hawaiian shirt are obviously happier with the choices on offer, as I can see him pointing a few things out to her.

Good luck with that, boyo. Once the Frown Face of Amy Caddick has appeared, the chances of you getting rid of it without total capitulation are slim to none.

Just don't look over here. Please *don't look over here.*

Finally, Amy shakes her head and says something to Ray that for a moment makes him look a little deflated, but he almost instantly perks up again, and smiles at her.

Yes. That's right. Turn around and bugger off, the pair of you. Let me continue with my sausage in peace.

'Joel?' Cara asks, still looking down into her lap like she's a six-year-old being told off for eating the last biscuits in the tin.

'Hang on, sweetheart,' I say, like I'm watching a particularly rare and dangerous gorilla, half hidden in the forest. 'They might be leaving.'

And . . . sure enough, the menus go back down on the table just off to one side of the entrance, and both my ex-wife and her five-bedroomed partner turn on their heels and walk away.

My heart, which has been pounding like a big bass drum this entire time, starts to slow its rhythm, and I sit back upright with a tight grin of relief on my face.

'They've gone,' I tell Cara, as I feel the muscles in my back start to unwind a little.

'Thank God for that,' she replies, looking up again. 'Of all the bad luck. Where do you think they're going?'

I shake my head. 'No idea. I couldn't see what the luggage tags on their suitcases said.'

Bollocks.

Bollocks, bollocks, bollocks.

'Suitcases?' Cara replies suspiciously. 'How could you have seen their suitcases in here?'

'Ah . . .'

You silly bastard. You silly, silly *bastard.*

'I may . . . I may have seen them out there, while we were checking in,' I confess, not making eye contact.

'You did?' Cara's eyes flash. It's not nice when Cara's eyes flash. It rarely happens, but when it does, she can look quite scary.

'Yeah. I couldn't be sure it was her, though. I really couldn't.'

Oh, Joel. That's not *true*, is it? You'd know that ponytail and purposeful stride anywhere. You were right next to them for six years of your life.

Cara's eyes narrow. 'You should have *said something*, Joel! Given me a warning!'

'Yes, yes . . . you're right!' I say in a desperate tone. The last thing I want is for Cara to be mad at me. This is supposed to be an exciting, fun trip away for us both. It can't start off on the wrong foot like this. 'I should have told you . . . but I really wasn't sure it was her, and I didn't want to trouble you with it.'

This seems to mollify Cara. The scary eye flash has definitely gone. Though she still looks pretty unhappy, to be honest.

I can't say I blame her. Being sat here with the curious eyes of the nearby patrons on us can't be a fun experience for her. It's not for me, either.

I look over at the entrance to the restaurant again to see that there is absolutely no sign of the two of them now. They've been swallowed back up in the heaving mass of the Heathrow holiday crowd.

'Of all the bad bloody luck,' Cara says in a low voice.

'That's just what I thought,' I tell her with a lop-sided smile. Taking a chance the gesture won't be rejected, I lean across the table and take her other hand in mine. Luckily for me (and the rest of this holiday) Cara doesn't pull her hand away. I give it a little squeeze. 'Look, it doesn't matter. It's just a stupid coincidence, and we're only going to be here for another half an hour or so, until we go to the gate. Why don't we just stay in here until then, order a coffee, and bugger about on our phones? I'm sure we won't see them again. This place is just too big.'

Cara continues to look downcast for a moment as my words sink in.

I probably shouldn't say this, but she always looks quite adorable when she's being a little pouty. She has the most beautiful set of lips, even when they are in the pout position, and her lovely brown eyes are only made all the more glorious when they're a bit glossy.

I really have struck it so incredibly *lucky* with Cara. And seeing my ex-wife here today will do nothing to stop me being happy about going on holiday with this fantastic woman.

Cara nods once to herself, sits back and runs both hands slowly through her shoulder-length chestnut hair. This is always what she does when she's relaxing, so I think it must be a good sign. 'Yeah, I'm sure you're right,' she eventually says with a smile. 'I just don't want to see Amy ever again. Not after everything that happened.' Her hand reaches out and takes mine again. 'Not after what she did to you.'

I nod and return the smile – though it's one laced with regret. 'I know. It's okay, though. In a couple of hours we'll be thirty thousand feet in the air, and she'll be long gone.'

Cara smiles even more broadly at this, before giving me a comically disparaging look. 'Alright . . . but if you see your mother here as well before we get the chance to get on the plane, please bloody tell me, eh?'

I chuckle. While Cara actively dislikes Amy, she does everything she can to get on with Mum. It's a bit of a pity Mum is always a bit *cold* around her – for reasons I've never been able to establish, beyond the fact that she always got along with Amy very well.

'I promise I will,' I tell her, though I don't think we're in any danger of seeing either my mother or father here. They've both become avid staycationers in recent years. Airports might well be a thing of the past for them.

One of the waiters comes back over to our table to clean away our plates, and I ask him to bring Cara and I both a cup of coffee.

Yes. That's a great plan, Joel.

We'll just sit here for another thirty minutes, enjoy another cup of coffee and then make our way down to the gate. With any luck Amy and Ray the Hawaiian Shirt King will have already buggered off to wherever it is they're going, and we won't run the risk of bumping into them again.

Either that or Amy would have browbeaten the bloke into visiting whatever restaurant took her fancy, and they'll be in there. Amy was always something of a sushi fiend, so they might be in Itsu – which I'm pretty sure is in the opposite direction of where Cara and I will have to go to get to Gate 14 and our flight on a British Airways A380.

Yep. Everything is going to be absolutely *fine*.

Once we're in the air I can relax in the safe and secure knowledge that I am flying away from all the stresses and strains of my life – especially my bloody job, with its dwindling client list and unpleasant work colleagues.

It's an added bonus to know that I'll also be flying far away from the person that made my job such a bloody nightmare in the first place.

Marrying Amy Caddick was the worst mistake I ever made.

Somebody very intelligent and clever once said that you should never mix business with pleasure . . . and I wish I'd listened to them. If I hadn't fallen for Amy when we started selling houses together, then I wouldn't have got myself into the mess that I did. I should have kept it strictly professional. I should have maintained some distance.

But then, without Amy, would I ever have been as good at my job as I was? Would I ever have been as successful? Would I ever—

No!

No more, Joel!

Do *not* rehash all of that *again*!

I take a couple of deep breaths and attempt to centre myself.

It doesn't matter. None of it does. It's all in the past – especially Amy. And very soon I will be flying away from all of it.

Cara and I will be off to the Maldives to have fun and make new memories. Very soon, *her* face will be the one I think of when I picture those gorgeous white sands and sunny skies in my mind – not Amy Caddick's!

She can just bugger off to whatever destination it is she's going to with her bloke – hopefully across the other side of the world from me.

It never occurs to me for a second to think that Amy could be going to the *same place as us.*

Why would it, though, eh?

That would just be *crazy* unlucky, wouldn't it?

What kind of cosmic joke would have to be played on me for that to happen?

Monday

AMY – A COSMIC JOKE

I wasn't too sure about the Hawaiian shirt to start with, but it's grown on me.

When Ray appeared in the bedroom doorway this morning in it, posing for all he was worth like some kind of catalogue model, I couldn't help but laugh.

'You're not actually going to *wear* that are you?' I asked him.

'I am indeed!' he replied, starting to manfully flex his muscles in an utterly ridiculous way. 'I think it makes me look rather *sexy*.'

This sent me off into fits of giggles, which were only stifled when Ray came over to the bed and started to give me a lot of sublime morning kisses.

It was a lovely way to start a day; a day that's likely to be very tiring.

Long-distance travel and I have never really got on with each other, but it's been so long since I've been on holiday that I'm quite happy to bear with it on this occasion. *More* than happy.

Because Wimbufushi awaits at the other end, and a week of sun, sea – and hopefully slightly less garish clothing on my fiancé.

He insists on wearing it to travel in, though, which I just have to shake my head about and laugh. Ray's usually such a well-dressed, well-thought-out and somewhat straight-laced individual. To see him loosen up a bit is something that I have to confess I very much enjoy seeing.

I just wish the damn thing wasn't quite so *orange*.

I don't think I've ever seen anything quite that orange in my life, to be honest. It's quite disconcerting. And when you marry it with the brand new white jeans Ray is wearing, it's like I'm walking around with an ambulatory traffic cone. It's testament to Ray's self confidence that he just about manages to keep the whole thing below the level of complete farce. You could almost believe from his body language that looking like a separated yoghurt is a perfectly sensible clothing choice.

No. Not a separated yoghurt – a salmon sashimi. A six-foot-two piece of salmon sashimi, just like the one that I'm about to devour.

'How's the sushi?' Ray asks, picking out a bit of chicken from his teriyaki soba and popping it in his mouth.

'Great,' I reply, chopsticking the salmon sashimi as best as I am able with my limited skills. 'Thanks for letting me come here instead of that Gordon Ramsay place.'

'Not a problem, sweetheart. I'm happy if you're happy.'

. . . which in many ways, could be Ray's mantra, God bless him. I'm a very spoiled woman, and I know how lucky I am.

Hence why I'm sat here in Heathrow, making my way through several bits of sushi, before getting on a plane to the most beautiful place I've ever been in my life. A place I've longed to revisit ever since I went there with . . . *that other bloke.*

Ray didn't even bat an eyelid when I saw the deal come up on Expedia, and confessed that I wanted to go back to the same island I spent my honeymoon on. He absolutely and completely believed me when I told him it was all about my memories of Wimbufushi itself, and not the man I was with at the time.

And then he went and booked the week on the island in the time it took me to have a shower.

'Oh Ray!' I exclaimed, when he told me what he'd done. 'Can we take that much time off work, though? With the business expanding the way it is?'

He shrugged. 'It's my company. I can go on holiday whenever I want. And this deal is too good to pass up. Simon can handle things while we're gone. It'll be fine.'

Ray has slightly more faith in his second in command than I do – Simon can be a lazy bugger if he gets half a chance – but I can't pretend that leaving work behind for a week won't be a much-needed rest. The Boat Show in Birmingham really took it out of me last month, and with both Belgium and Helsinki on the horizon, I might collapse if I don't get a chance to get away from it all for a while.

'We'll have to leave fairly soon,' Ray says, looking at his watch. 'The gate's opening shortly.'

I nod, munching my last piece of sushi. I feel the usual butter-flies I get whenever I fly start to flutter around in my belly, making that last mouthful of salmon a difficult one. I've managed to keep them at bay all the way here in the car, through check-in and pass-port control, but now we're just about to get on the plane, they are making their presence felt, as they always do.

'Don't worry, sweetheart, it'll be fine,' Ray says, instantly read-ing the expression on my face correctly. *The other bloke* never man-aged to do that. He always used to think I was angry at him. Even if I was just feeling a little bloated or tired, *the other bloke* thought it was because he had done something wrong. It was one of his worst character traits.

Not Ray, though. Ray reads my emotions *far* better.

'Thank you,' I tell him, after swallowing the remnants of the sushi. 'I know it'll be okay, but you know how I get.'

'I do . . . but just think about the island and that water bungalow you've been telling me all about. Picture it in your head, if you feel nervous.'

'I will,' I tell him, and I do indeed briefly visualise the view from the bungalow's veranda – which comprises of nothing but the bluest sea you've ever seen, gently lapping up against the wooden stilts the bungalow sits upon. Along with a sky that, if anything, is ever bluer – punctuated only by the occasional wispy bit of white cloud.

Ah, yes. That's the stuff.

I feel the butterflies start to settle a little, as I wash the sushi down with the last of my Sprite. 'Shall we go then?' I suggest to Ray, feeling up to the task now that my hunger and thirst have been taken care of.

'Absolutely,' he replies, rising from his seat and pulling the handle out of both my travel suitcase and his. He hands me mine and leans forward to give me a kiss.

If you'd have told me two years ago that the best feeling in the world would be getting a kiss from a man in white jeans and an obnoxious orange Hawaiian shirt, I would have laughed in your face.

Ray guides us towards the correct gate for our flight, and I'm honestly happy to let him take the lead for once. At work, he always lets me take control of client sales as much as I am able, and has no problem tasking me with difficult jobs. I don't receive any favouritism whatsoever from him – and thank God for that.

Holland Yachts only has a relatively small staff of twelve at the moment, and if I was treated any differently to anyone else, I'd be hated in seconds. If anything, I think Ray gives me more of the hard tasks to accomplish to compensate for the fact that we're in a relationship. And I have no problem with this at all. While it increases my workload and stress levels more than I'd like, it's totally worth it, as I'm not seen to be getting any favouritism from the boss just because I lie in the same bed as him.

Today, though, I'm more than happy for Ray to be the one to shoulder the responsibility of organising our travel plans. My brain is very much enjoying the rest, and intends to wallow in it as much as possible.

We arrive at the departure lounge to find it already chock-a-block with people. This is not a surprise. The Maldives has always been a very popular destination – now more than ever, given that climate change seems to be threatening their very existence. Everyone wants to experience the islands now, because you might go there in a few years and find yourself wading around in a permanent foot of salty water.

That's probably another reason why I suggested the holiday when I saw the flash deal come up. I loved Wimbufushi so much – despite the presence of *the other bloke* – and want to experience it again, while I still can.

As Ray and I join the crowd gathered around the gate desk, I'm pleased to hear I don't detect much in the way of crying babies.

My ears are always hyper alert for them whenever I fly. There's nothing worse than arriving at your gate and hearing the sound of a screaming baby – who you know will end up being seated right next to you. Ray managed to secure us the bulkhead seats I asked for, with the extra leg room, for the eleven hours it takes to get to the Maldives. This is *wonderful*, but does come with the high chance of a baby sat next to me in a bassinet the whole way.

The fact I can't hear or see any small babies in the crowd gives me hope for a quiet flight. I always go for the bulkhead seats if I can, figuring that the risks of getting a baby next to me are quite worth it if it means I can stretch my legs out properly, instead of getting arthritis of the knees from several hours of having them all bent up because of the seat in front of me.

Ray wheels his flight case towards the last two empty seats and I follow him over, still listening out for the tell-tale sound of a crying child. I still don't hear one, but by concentrating on the sounds coming from our fellow passengers so much, I do hear the following, coming from somewhere to my left.

'Oh God in heaven, *no!*' a man's voice cries out. There's something very *familiar* about it.

I swivel my head around to find out who is making such a ruckus, but all I see is a large pot plant next to one of the square columns that support Heathrow's upper floors. The potted monstrosity – which I believe is some sort of cheese plant – is shaking.

I'm assuming it wasn't the cheese plant that just blasphemed across the departure lounge. I think more people would be looking at it, if it had been. Pot plants achieving sentience is the type of thing that would draw people's attention, I would have thought. It would be a trifle hard to ignore.

As it is, a few people are looking up at something or someone *behind* the cheese plant and the column, but none of them are sketching the sign of the cross or backing away in terror, so I can safely assume that it's probably nothing to worry about.

I park my butt down on the seat next to Ray and pull my phone out of my pocket. As I do, one of the ground staff talks over the tannoy to tell us that the flight will begin seating in five minutes. *Excellent.* Ray timed things to perfection, as always. He's always so solidly dependable.

I spend a little time tending to my farm in Stardew Valley while we wait to be called up to board the flight. Those with disabilities and parents with small children are called first. There are three of the former and only two of the latter, and all of the kids are at least toddler age.

Phew.

Then first class is called as I'm watering a small patch of cauliflowers on my farm, and by the time I've collected a few corals and shells from the tide pools on the beach, the back rows of the plane have also been called up.

When the tannoy asks for people seated in rows sixty to eighty to come forward, both Ray and I stand, as we're in seats 67D and 67E. As we begin to walk forward, towards the boarding desks, I hear a strangled cry – from my right-hand side this time.

I look over to see that the pot plant is once again shaking for all it's worth, as if someone has brushed hard up against it. What is going on over there?

Walking between two rows of departure lounge seats, I have to resist the urge to look back over my shoulder as a commotion begins behind me. Someone is obviously playing silly buggers back there – but it's really nothing to do with me, so I'm not going to trouble myself with it. I'm sure it's probably just someone who's afraid of flying – even more than I am.

That reminds me of what I'm about to do, so I start to take some long, deep breaths, concentrating on being mindful as I approach the desk with my ticket and passport out for inspection.

I don't care what's happening behind me. I just care about centring myself and keeping my nerves at bay.

This starts to do the trick as the smiling BA flight attendant scans my ticket and hands it back. By the time I'm walking down the ramp to the tunnel that leads to the plane's open doors, I am feeling a little better.

'Okay, sweetheart?' Ray asks me, noticing that I'm concentrating on my breathing.

I offer him a weak smile. 'Yeah. Just keeping myself calm. I'm sure I'll be fine once we've got into our seats.'

And indeed, even as I board the plane and start down the right-hand side towards my seat, I do feel a sense of calm wash over me. The breathing techniques I looked up on YouTube really are having an effect. When we have to pause in the aisle, as a woman struggles to get her luggage into the overhead compartment, I continue my breathing exercises, ignoring everything else going on around me.

I'm only jerked out of my centred concentration when I hear a kerfuffle going on behind me again. This time I do look over, to see a man with thinning hair on top of his head, and wearing a pink shirt and black jeans, walking down the aisle opposite me . . . backwards. This is possibly the strangest thing I've ever seen.

There's something *familiar* about his awkward gait and the way his shoulders look tighter than a snare drum, but I can't quite put my finger on why. I certainly don't know any tall, skinny men with thinning hair who'd wear a pink shirt like that. None at all.

The man is scuttling along backwards, performing the world's most clumsy moonwalk, with his head down and his shoulders hunched, like a crab who's just been caught stealing the last bread stick.

Ahead of me, I hear a loud thump as the woman finally gets her luggage into the overhead compartment, and my side of the aisle starts to move again.

I proceed forward, now trying to ignore the strange man. Whatever issues he might be having are nothing to do with me. I have my own problems. I don't intend to start this flight in a state of panic, so it's very important for me to stay in my calm, centred place as we go through the worst part of the flight – take off.

I make my way past the emergency exit, and turn to my left as I get to the next bulkhead. My seat is 67 E, the second one along, and I'm happy to see that the overhead compartment is empty. My carry-on suitcase is considerably lighter than that poor woman's, so I have no trouble getting it secured, before moving forward to my seat.

I pick up the little bag that contains my eye mask, toothbrush and toothpaste, along with the small pillow that I will pop behind my back later, to make sure I'm as comfortable as possible. As I do this I look up to see the man in the pink shirt emerge from behind the other side of the bulkhead.

He looks absolutely terrified.

As I lock eyes with him, it's my turn to let out a strangled cry.

JOEL.

It's fucking JOEL.

The strength starts to drain out of my legs. I blink rapidly several times in a row. Whatever success I may have had calming my nerves is immediately and comprehensively undone. I could spend the rest of my natural life searching the never-ending backwaters of YouTube's content looking for stress-relieving exercises, and I would still never find one that could help me with the situation I find myself in now.

You could also inject me with a combination of Valium, Prozac, valerian root, chamomile and lavender essential oil, and it still wouldn't slow my heartbeat, or stop my legs from shaking one fucking jot.

In my absolute panic, my body completely overrides my brain and does the best thing it can to counteract the horror that's just been placed in front of me. In a desperate act of self-preservation, it lobs my small pillow at Joel's head. This will accomplish nothing, of course. In no way will a ballistic British Airways pillow remove me from this horrifying situation. If only it could.

The pillow bounces off Joel's stunned forehead, and pinwheels across the cabin, to fall in the lap of an elderly woman, who is taking a sip from a bottle of water. Remarkably, she manages to spill not a drop as she squawks in surprise at the sudden arrival of the squishy oblong.

'Oi! What did you do that for?!' Joel exclaims, hand going to his forehead.

'WHAT?!' I bellow. No more words will form in my mouth. I'm just so incredibly poleaxed by this turn of events that proper language has deserted me.

'WHAT?!' Joel bellows back at me.

'WHAT?!' I repeat.

'HOW?!' Joel cries, deciding to mix up the vocabulary of our conversation a bit. With any luck we might proceed to sentences of more than one word at some point, before the flight attendants arrive to arrest me for using a British Airways pillow as an offensive weapon.

'What are you doing here, Joel?!' I eventually force out. 'It is *you*, isn't it?'

You'd think that I'd have no problem recognising my husband of four years, but in the two years it's been since I saw him last, he's changed quite a lot. He looks a lot *older*, for starters. There are wrinkles on his face that I've never seen before, and his skin has a sallow complexion to it that ages him even further. The hairline's receded a fair bit as well.

He also looks *tired*. That's the biggest difference. Joel always had a boyish charm about him, but with the extra two years of what I can only assume must have been a stressful life, he looks more like a man now than he ever did when we were married.

Then there's the pink shirt.

There's nothing wrong with it. It looks like an expensive, well-made shirt – and that's kind of the problem. Joel is the type of man who is no stranger to wearing a crumpled t-shirt and a pair of old blue jeans that are probably at least a week past the date when they should have gone into the wash.

He's still wearing the jeans (sort of – these are clearly more expensive than the ones he used to wear), but the crisp pink shirt is the type of apparel I'd never have imagined seeing him in when we were together. I can't quite consolidate it with the face that sits atop it. The two are just far too incongruous.

On top of all of that, I'm still in complete disbelief that Joel is on the same plane as I am, so you'll forgive me for questioning whether he's actually here or not.

'Yes, of course it's *me*!' he snaps back, his brow lowering rapidly to convey his displeasure at this horrific turn of events. I'm sure my brow is equally as low. They could probably start a limbo competition with one another. 'Are you going to the Maldives?' he asks me.

What a crushingly *stupid* question. It's perfectly okay for me to doubt the evidence of my own eyes, but for him to actually come out and ask me whether I'm going to the same destination as the plane I'm on is idiotic.

The two things are *completely* different, I'm sure you'd agree.

'Of course I bloody am!' I snap back.

Behind Joel, the other passengers are starting to get understandably tetchy that he's holding them up. 'Could we get by, please?' a middle-aged man in a sky blue hat says, indicating to Joel that he'd like to move around him.

'Yes, Joel,' I say to him, 'you should probably go and find your own seat, so this poor man can get by.'

Joel gives me a look that could sink a thousand ships. And then he does something that makes my toes curl. He steps backwards, so he's in front of the bulkhead seats next to the window. Joel is sitting in the *same bloody row of the plane as we are.*

'Oh, you have got to be fucking kidding me,' I say in a hoarse, horrified whisper.

Joel points at my seat as the old boy in his sky-blue hat moves past us. 'Are you . . . are you sat there?'

This is another blindingly stupid question from my ex-husband. One that I don't have time to answer, because at this point Joel's travelling companion emerges from behind Sky Blue Hat Man's wife, as she hurries to keep up with her husband.

Good grief.

It's bloody *Cara Rowntree.*

Joel is going on holiday with my *old boss's granddaughter.*

You couldn't make it up. You honestly couldn't.

Are they *dating?*

Is Joel actually with a woman who's well over a decade younger than him? The one who used to parade around the office like she owned the place, and was indulged so thoroughly by Roland Rowntree that it made the rest of us all want to throw up – *especially* Joel?

'Hello, Amy,' Cara says in a flat voice. She's not surprised to see me, evidently. I wish I could say the same thing.

Cara and I never really spoke that much. Her boobs never impressed me the way they did most of the men in the offices of Rowntree Land & Home. Even if I wanted to talk to her more, I wouldn't have been able to get past the small throng of estate agents hovering around them like bees around a pair of particularly scrumptious sunflowers. She knew how to manipulate more or less every man at the agency, up to and including her grandfather.

Joel was never one of them, I should add. Not that I ever noticed. Which makes it all the more remarkable that they appear to be going on holiday together.

'Cara,' I reply, my voice, if anything, even flatter.

'Shall we, er, sit down, Amy?' Ray says in a worried tone from behind me. I look around to see that his eyes are out on stalks, and his face has gone very red.

Looking back, I see that Joel has retreated to the seat by the window, and is now attempting to look everywhere but at me.

He's gripping a black rucksack for what looks like dear life, and is holding it in such a way that suggests he's ready to parry away any more ballistic pillows I choose to chuck at him. Lucky for him, I'm fresh out.

As Cara Rowntree joins him, two muscular young men with blond hair, blue eyes and wide, open smiles interrupt my view of my ex-husband and his (hah!) girlfriend by claiming the two seats next to the ones Ray and I are sat in.

They are Australian.

Neither have said a word yet but they are most definitely *Australian*. Only that country breeds enormous, tanned and good-natured kids like this.

Now my confrontation with Joel has been interrupted, I slowly take my seat, my brain afire with disbelief and horror. I have to resist the urge to crane my head past Sydney's finest, just to check that Joel and Cara are still there, and that I haven't imagined the whole thing.

Ray parks himself in the seat next to me and rests a hand on my leg. 'Is that . . . Is that—'

'Yes,' I snap at him, and immediately curse myself. It isn't Ray's fault this turn of events has taken place. I shouldn't take my frustration out on him. 'Sorry, Ray,' I add quickly, 'I just wasn't expecting to see him here, that's all.'

'No, I bet,' he replies. 'What are the odds, eh?'

'I wouldn't like to imagine.'

'Quite incredible, really.'

'Yes, it is.'

Please don't say it's a small world, Ray. I don't think I could take that.

'Will you be okay?'

I attempt to unclench my fists. I'm only partially successful. 'Yes. I think so. At least they're not sitting right next to us. I won't have to look at him the whole flight.'

To confirm this, I look back across the plane to where Joel is sat, and am pleased to discover that his seat, along with Cara Rowntree's, are set a little back from mine, and my view of them is indeed obscured by both of the strapping young men.

'How ya going?' the one closest to me says, as he notices that I'm looking in his direction.

'Fine, thanks,' I lie, affecting a smile that doesn't reach my eyes.

'Oh right . . . That's, er, that's good then,' he replies in a thick New South Wales accent, looking slightly perturbed as he does so.

You think you're perturbed, my antipodean friend? You haven't just come face to face – for the first time in years – with the man who ruined your life and got you fired from the job you loved.

My new Australian friend then makes a concerted effort to turn away from me and talk to his associate, which suits me fine, as I'm not really in the mood to chat right now.

'Do you want to swap seats with me?' Ray then asks. For a moment I am extremely tempted to take him up on his offer, but if I do it'll be obvious to Joel what I'm doing, won't it?

And I won't give him the satisfaction of seeing me move just so I can get further away from him. I *won't*.

The wall of Australians between me and his seat should be more than enough of a psychological barrier. I don't need Ray to join it.

'No, it's okay,' I tell him. 'I'll be fine here.' As I say this, I subconsciously sink down into my seat a little. It is something I will find myself doing an awful lot over the next eleven hours.

As the rest of the passengers get themselves settled into their seats, I sit in mine, staring at the bulkhead in front of me, trying to properly process the unlikely turn of the events that have occurred.

My fears over flying have completely evaporated in light of what's just transpired, but that hasn't slowed my heart rate down, or relieved my feelings of anxiety one little bit. It's just that instead of feeling anxious about plummeting to my death from thirty thousand feet, I'm now stressed out by the prospect of travelling *along* at thirty thousand feet with my least favourite person in the world, who is going to the same place as me.

I honestly couldn't tell you for certain which prospect is *worse*.

The next several hours of my life are spent in a permanent state of tension. I have never really given the qualities of my peripheral vision that much thought, but now I realise that I must have the best peripheral vision in human history, because Joel can't make one single move out of his seat without me seeing it.

Every time he shifts himself, stands up, goes to the toilet, leans forward to tap on the TV screen affixed to the bulkhead in front of him, or opens up the overhead compartment to get something out, I can see his every move – despite my concerted attempts not to.

And the horrible thing is I know damn well he's doing the exact same thing with me.

Do you have any idea how hard it is to make sure you don't get out of your seat at the same time as another passenger who's close by?

You'd think that over the course of eleven hours, it would be quite easy to move about the plane cabin without them also doing the same thing at the same time as you. It turns out, though, that it's completely impossible.

If I need to get up for a pee, Joel apparently feels the need to go rummaging around in his rucksack for something. If I sit forward to turn the volume up on my TV screen, he gets up to go to the loo himself. If I call the air steward over to ask for a glass of water, he is standing up to stretch his legs.

It's *interminable*.

Hour after hour of trying your damned hardest to avoid another human being, and failing over and over again, leaves you with a headache, a backache and suffering from the kind of insomnia that people are committed to asylums over.

I usually manage to get a few hours' sleep on a plane when I'm on a long-haul flight. I remember that the last time I took this trip, I got a good six hours. This time, though, sleep is about as likely as Superman flying past and giving me a thumbs up.

I just can't forget about the arsehole sat four seats away from me. I'm not keen on the rest of him, either.

I'm not one to drop into maudlin thought, given that it generally accomplishes nothing, but with little else to do other than watch movies I've already seen or listen to music I've heard a thousand times, I can't help but sit and dwell on the sheer bad luck I've been presented with.

What exactly are the odds of getting on the same plane as the ex-husband you haven't seen in two years?

A thousand to one? A million to one?

Of all the planes, in all the airports, in all the world he has to get on to mine . . .

Casablanca isn't in the selection of movies available to me unfortunately, so instead of watching that I'm just going to have to get drunk.

It's the only way I can think to get some bloody sleep.

My eyes feel sandy and sore, I can't stop yawning and I'm getting that horrible *sicky* feeling you always do when you haven't had any sleep.

I call the passing air steward over to ask him to get me a glass of wine. At virtually the same time I do this, Joel also gestures towards him.

There's a horrible moment where both Joel and I have our hands up like eager school children, both attempting to grab the steward's attention. We're also desperately trying not to look at each other, which is especially hard when we're also trying to catch the steward's eye.

I end up jerking my eyeballs about like someone's just squirted raw amphetamines into both of them, while simultaneously trying to keep my head low and away enough not to look at Joel, but also high and forward enough to hold the steward's attention. Joel is pretty much doing the exact same thing, so we now both look like *bobbleheads* of eager school children with their hands up. Bobbleheads that are attached to the dashboard of a car driving across large sheets of corrugated iron.

The poor steward looks at both of us for a moment before deciding to do the traditionally polite thing and serve the lady first.

I'd like to say I didn't feel a small sense of victory about this, but I'd be lying.

The first glass of wine is downed in about five seconds, with the second and third being consumed slightly slower, at one minute and ten minutes respectively.

So, now I'm drunk . . . and still fucking *wide awake*.

This is the most miserable flight I can ever remember being on.

All because of one bloody person.

I sit and watch the minutes to our destination tick down on the flight display. The little graphic of the plane we're on slowly shifts towards the Indian Ocean at a snail's pace. And all the time I do this, I can see him: right there in my peripheral vision, every time he so much as moves slightly out of his seat. The two Australian oak trees next to me have both fallen fast asleep, slumped in their seats, so don't offer me the barrier they did earlier in the flight.

Oh God in heaven, this is absolute *hell*.

Sheer, thirty-thousand-feet-in-the-air hell. I think I'd welcome a vast and destructive blow out of one of the engines right now.

Mind you, the way my luck is going, I'd end up surviving the crash . . . along with only one other person.

Joel and I would be set adrift together in an inflatable raft, and there's no way I'd be able to avoid him then, is there?

I could probably eat him, if I had to, though. I wouldn't have a problem with that.

The plane shifts another inch towards the Maldives on the screen in front of me, and I have to stop myself from biting down hard on my own lip.

Beside me, Ray is snoring softly. He went out like a light hours ago. I could wake him up and have a chat with him to break up the monotony, but he drove us all the way to the airport this morning, in awful traffic. He deserves the rest.

So instead I just sit there and stare at the screen, as the pixelated plane edges closer to the Maldives at the speed of shifting continental plates.

After ten minutes or so of this, I feel an uncomfortable fullness in my bladder. Time to get up for another pee. That should keep me occupied for a good three or four minutes. I'm pretty sure I don't need a poo, but I might sit there for a bit anyway, just to see if anything happens. That'll waste another five minutes, if I'm very lucky.

No sooner am I out of my seat though than Joel is also unbuckling his seat belt.

It's like the bastard is doing it *deliberately*.

This time we can't help but lock eyes. I can see that he looks as tired and haggard as I must. I don't think he's managed a wink of sleep either. Joel was never a good sleeper while travelling, though. I remember that about him.

Part of me wants to sit right back down again and ignore him. I can hold my bladder for a few more minutes. But then, another part of me – the bit that's just downed three small plastic glasses' worth of cheap white wine – is feeling a lot more defiant.

I am *not* going to sit back down again. Not this time. Joel can be the one to cringe back into his seat. I am going to the toilet! I am going to have a pee – and possibly a small, time-wasting poo – and nobody and nothing is going to stop me!

I will just fucking stand here like this until Joel sits back down again!

He doesn't do this.

Instead, he also stands there, in a clearly obstinate fashion, waiting for *me* to be the one to slink back into my seat.

Therefore we now enter a Mexican stand-off. One apparently conducted by two zombies. The nine hours we've been on this plane have not been kind.

'I'm going to the toilet,' Joel says to me in an ice-cold tone.

I lift my chin. 'So am I,' I reply, my voice nearly a sibilant rasp thanks to the lack of sleep – and probable dehydration from only consuming white wine for the past few hours.

Neither of us move.

Quite why, I have no idea.

There are four toilets just past the bulkhead. All of which are empty right now. There's literally no reason for my ex-husband and I to be locked in this stare-down.

And yet, it continues.

Perhaps it's the alcohol, perhaps it's the lack of sleep, perhaps it's the mutual loathing.

Whatever it is, it's apparently going to go on until one of us breaks the stare.

Everyone else is pretty much asleep in the darkened cabin, so there's no audience for this bizarre, silent exchange.

The air fairly crackles between us. You can almost feel the wall of resentment. If I reached out my hand right now, I'm half convinced it would meet a solid object.

The stare goes on . . . and on.

It's probably only been about ten seconds in reality, but in my frazzled state of mind it feels like a lifetime.

And I can't stop it. I can't break out of it.

He must be the one to break. Joel must be the one to look away!

And so it goes on.

Nothing will end it.

We will be stood here when they tell us to buckle up because the plane has to land – and I'm not even sure that'll move me.

Nothing can bring this stand-off to a conclusion!

Other than a long, sonorous fart emanating from one of the two Australians, the one closest to Joel, who is fast asleep with his head tipped back on the seat.

No stare-down between hated enemies can survive a long, sonorous fart, especially when its stench starts to be circulated by the plane's air conditioning.

'I am going to the toilet again,' I declare to Joel, trying my hardest to shut off my olfactory senses by sheer will alone.

'As am I,' Joel replies.

It's as if the Australian fart was a toilet-based clarion call. A trumpet of permission to end this stand-off and proceed forthwith to the convenience.

I manage to break the stare with Joel, and climb over Ray's legs to get out into the aisle. I don't see what Joel is up to. I no longer care.

I spend a good ten minutes in the loo, just to make sure that I won't have to enter into a second stare-down, and leave hoping against hope that Joel has already taken his seat.

Thank God in heaven . . . he has. And looks to have fallen fast asleep.

I know he hasn't, though. Joel was never a man who could get to sleep quickly. I know he's faking it just to avoid looking at me.

That's fine. Fine and dandy. I don't want to look at him, either.

I climb back into my seat, noting that the flight has less than two hours remaining.

That's good.

That's *excellent*.

Only two more hours of having to be in that man's enforced company.

Then we will be off this plane, and Joel can disappear off to whatever Maldivian island he may be visiting, and Ray and I can get on the speedboat to Wimbufushi, and I can forget all about this horrible bloody flight and my run-in with my least favourite person.

There's no chance Joel and Cara Rowntree can also be going to Wimbufushi. None at all. That would be patently *ridiculous*. There are hundreds of Maldivian islands. *Hundreds* of them.

No. They'll be off to whatever island they're holidaying on, and I'll never have to see him again. I breathe a sigh of relief at this prospect.

Only two more hours and this holiday can get back on track. And then I can forget all about Joel Sinclair, safe in the knowledge that he's nowhere near me anymore.

It was a massive coincidence that they were booked on the same plane, and a bigger one that they were sat right next to us. But that'll be the end of it.

This is the real world, and coincidences don't just keep piling up on top of one another.

Yes indeed. This will be the end of the coincidences.

No doubt about it!

Tuesday

JOEL – ARRIVAL

'Are you fucking *kidding me*?' I blurt out.

Everyone waiting on the dock for the speedboat turns to look at me.

This can't be happening. It just *can't*.

Maybe I'm hallucinating.

Maybe the fact I've had no sleep in almost twenty-four hours has led my brain to create monstrous visions as punishment for keeping it going so long without rest.

I've heard of this type of thing before.

I seem to remember reading a news story about a guy who hallucinated carrots.

Just that.

Nothing else.

Carrots.

Over and over and over. Every day of his life. There were carrots everywhere. Nobody could get to the root cause of the problem. He'd never suffered any kind of carrot-related trauma in his life. But for some bizarre reason he just kept seeing non-existent carrots wherever he went. Big ones. Small ones. Carrots of all shapes and sizes.

The article ended with him moving to the country to grow carrots. He figured if he was going to see carrots everywhere for the rest of his life, he might as well make a bob or two out of it.

Very sensible thinking there.

I half thought about tracking him down to seek his wisdom. Anybody who can think like that is probably worth listening to.

Maybe that's what I'm cursed with as well. Only instead of seeing carrots, I am plagued by five-foot-four blond women. One in particular.

'Oh bloody hell,' Cara says, as she sees what I'm staring at.

Well, that settles it then. I'm obviously *not* hallucinating. Judging from the fact Cara's face has gone very white, I can tell that she's seeing exactly the same thing as me.

I suppose this is a good thing. Hallucinations probably aren't a sign that your brain is functioning all that well. I'm glad my brain remains healthy and hallucination free.

Or at least, it would be healthy, were it not being battered by the horror of what it's directing my eyes to witness.

Amy is here.

Standing on the same dock, waiting for the *same* speedboat.

Standing right there with Ray Holland – who has changed into another Hawaiian shirt. This one is bright blue with surfboards on it.

This can't be happening.

'This can't be happening!' Amy says out loud.

Oh Christ, I think, *she can read my mind!*

She's going to suck out my thoughts! She's going to feed off my lifeforce, like a five-four blond psychic leech!

Aaaaarggh!

Get a fucking grip, man. That is just the sleep deprivation talking.

Well, you might think so, brain, but you also made me remember the story about the carrot-hallucination bloke, so I'm not entirely sure you're the best source of advice right now!

'Are you guys going to Wimbufushi too?' Cara asks Amy and Ray in a stunned voice, as we walk on to the crowded, narrow wooden dock.

Other than my ex-wife and her partner, there are another ten people waiting for the speedboat as well.

'Yes. We are!' Ray replies, trying to sound positive about the whole thing – as if it were four long-lost friends who coincidentally turned up on the same dock, waiting for the same speedboat to take them to the same island. I'm sure that would be a *lovely* experience for all concerned.

This is *far* from that.

'It's a small world, isn't it?' he adds, maintaining the chipper tone of voice. From beside him Amy is trying her hardest not to rip off one of his arms and beat him to death with the wet end. I know that expression very well.

'Yes, it is!' Cara replies, also now talking like this is a perfectly happy little scene, enjoyed by all.

I don't speak.

Neither does Amy.

We both know what's going on here. We've both realised what's bloody happened.

She's decided to go back to Wimbufushi for another holiday, because it was such a lovely place, and I've done the same. All in the same week because of that bloody Expedia deal.

It's not actually much of a coincidence that we're both standing on this dock, waiting for the exact same speedboat that transported us there six years ago. *Of course* we'd both want to go back to the island again. It was such a wonderful place. It has Tarkan's cocktails, wall to wall sunshine, and an atmosphere slightly more laid back than a drunk horizon.

Why would either of us want to go to any other of the *thousand* or so islands in the Maldivian archipelago?

No, the only real coincidence here is that we both decided to travel on the exact same fucking *day*. Everything after that was almost inevitable.

'We must stop bumping into one another like this!' Ray says, ending with a brittle laugh. He's obviously been with Amy long enough to know the danger signs. He knows what the Frown Face of Amy Caddick entails.

I would feel sorry for him, but then I have to remember that I don't know *how long* he and Amy have been together. They could have been carrying on behind my back, for all I know.

Mercifully, the resort's speedboat then arrives, driven by what looks like a fourteen-year-old. I can see him smiling broadly at us all through the window of the boat's enclosed cabin. The speedboat is pristine white, with a long sweeping blue line running down one side. The blue is the same glorious aquamarine colour as the sea under our feet.

I have to put my hand up to cover my eyes as the hot Maldivian sun glints off the window, while the speedboat turns itself around to moor.

It's a glorious day weather-wise, and I should be relaxing into the holiday very nicely right about now.

Instead, I'm tense, knackered and cursing my luck.

. . . so, pretty much the way I feel at home every day, then. I could have stayed there and saved myself all the bother.

Good grief.

Another fourteen-year-old puts out a metal gangway from the side of the speedboat to the dock, and walks over to join us. I'm all for giving the young a chance to earn a daily crust, but are we entirely sure it's a good idea to put them in full control of a forty-foot-long speedboat?

I remember being greeted by two very similar young men six years ago.

They'd both be in their twenties by now, and judging by the early age they start working hard here in the Maldives, I surmise one of them is probably the president of the country by now.

The second fourteen-year-old (who is probably a lot older than that in reality, if I actually think about it sensibly for a moment. It's just that the Maldives obviously has a habit of breeding people of a youthful disposition) bids us on to the speedboat with a warm smile that neatly echoes the ambient temperature. It may be early on Tuesday morning, but the tropical heat is already making itself very apparent. I can't wait to get out of these clothes. The combination of plane dirt and sweat is getting a bit unbearable. Maybe I should have bought a blue surfboard shirt to change into.

There's an unspoken agreement between Cara and me to hang back a bit to allow Amy and Ray to get on the boat ahead of us.

We're literally the last to board, and therefore get the worst seats possible. The ones right next to the two kids – who both inexplicably have bare feet. Controlling a large speedboat full of sweaty tourists shouldn't be a thing you can do with bare feet, but these two seem to manage it with no problems whatsoever. That's the confidence of youth, that is. About the only thing I can do in bare feet these days with any confidence is sleep. And even then I have to put socks on in the winter.

The boat pulls away from the dock and putters slowly out of the large harbour that sits alongside Male airport. They certainly do have this transport to the islands business set up very well. It took no time to get off the plane, through customs, and on to the boat – with several cool towels and refreshing cold drinks to be had while doing so. They've streamlined the process even more since I was here last.

As we move out into deeper water, the boat picks up speed and the teen driver points it to what I think is south, and revs the engine.

Off we go then. Off out into paradise.

If paradise can be had with your ex-wife in tow, that is.

For the next forty minutes, we are all jostled and jolted by the Maldivian waves. No sooner have we crested one then we're hitting another, sending pain up through my backside, as it bounces off the hard plastic chair I'm sat on.

I can't help but look at where Amy and Ray Surfboards are sitting back and enjoying the sun, while Cara and I are huddled under the cabin's roof, trying not to look at the toe jam on the driver's feet.

Amy always likes to be sat at the back. It's a thing of hers. She did it last time, and nothing has changed for this trip.

Ugh. And I can't believe I'm here to see how smug she is about it.

I feel Cara squeeze my leg and look around to see her giving me her best unspoken sympathy. Bless her. She can see how difficult this is.

I offer a weak smile in response, and try to avoid looking past her at where Amy and Ray are now giggling with another couple of people they've got talking to – a portly bloke (not German) covered in tattoos, and his dolled-up wife.

I remember Amy and I did that together six years ago, with two people from Leicester. Maureen and Roger, if I recall. Or was it Morag and Reginald? One of the two.

Oh *God.*

Is this what this holiday is going to be like now, because Amy is here? Am I going to spend the entire trip recalling my *previous* visit, just because my ex-wife is so close at bloody hand?

I expected a few things to throw up old memories, but it will surely be worse with her on the island with me, no matter how much I try to stay away from her.

My eyes go wide as a further thought occurs: I never actually told Cara that this is the exact same island I came to on honeymoon.

Why the hell would I need to?! She didn't need to know something like that!

After all, it doesn't matter, does it?

Or rather, it *didn't* matter, right up to the point I stepped on to that dock and saw Amy and Ray Surfboards.

Oh *Christ*.

It's bound to come up at some point, isn't it?

Do I confess all to Cara at the first opportunity? Or do I hope I can get away with it for a while, until we've settled in?

Congratulations, Sinclair, you've kept important information about your ex-wife from your new girlfriend, not once, but twice now. Cracking job.

Shut up, brain. Go back to thinking about carrots, will you?

Cara leans right into me to be heard over the sound of the speedboat's engine and speaks into my ear. 'Smile, baby. It's all going to be fine. Don't let her ruin this for you. I'm not going to.'

I don't know whether it's the fatigue, the lack of sleep, or the discombobulated state of my brain, but her words make me well up. She's so lovely to me.

And she's absolutely *right* too.

I can't let Amy ruin this holiday.

I *won't* let Amy ruin this holiday.

Amy Caddick's days of ruining my life ended two years ago, after we lost that stupid mansion house, and our marriage fell apart. What happened with Goblin Central was the worst thing that's ever happened to me in my career as a real estate agent, and Amy tried to pin the blame on me for all of it! Even when I did everything *right*!

She didn't believe me, though! *Oh no.* As far as she was concerned I screwed everything up, and she wouldn't believe a word of what I had to say! Joel was the bad guy *again* . . . no matter how hard I tried to convince her that I fucking wasn't!

Then she takes me to the cleaners in the divorce. As if Goblin Central was just the big excuse she'd been waiting for to screw me into the ground completely!

And now she dares to be sat at the back of this speedboat, laughing and giggling with her newest victims? She dares to think she can ruin my holiday, two years later . . . after all of that?!

No!

No, I say!

There will be no holidays ruined by Amy Caddick! Not today! Not this week!

In my mind, I start to see an image of Mel Gibson in his blue *Braveheart* face paint shouting directly into my face.

'*We will not allow it!*' Mel screams, turning his horse. '*We will not give her the satisfaction! We will love every second of this holiday, whether she likes it or not!*'

Damn right, Mel! You tell me!

'*She will not stop us from having fun! She will not stop us from loving life! She will not stop us from relaxing, forgetting about how awful work is for a while, and recharging our batteries!*'

Yes! Yes!

'*Now! Sit back in your seat, breathe in that salty air, and enjoy your fucking holiday!*'

'Joel, are you okay?' Cara asks, looking at the clenched fist I'm holding out in front of me. I don't quite know when I subconsciously raised it. Probably around the time Mel was screaming about batteries.

I quickly drop it, and smile at Cara. 'I'm fine, baby! I really am!'

And to show her how fine I really am, I give her the biggest kiss imaginable, not even breaking away when we thump into another cresting wave.

I don't look past her face to see if Amy Caddick is watching what I'm doing, because I frankly don't care. Mel Braveheart has told me I am going to enjoy myself and ignore her presence, and that is exactly what I plan on doing. Come hell or high water!

As I sit back from the kiss that has left Cara with a stunned-but-happy look on her face, the speedboat slows down, and I get my first view of Wimbufushi island in six years.

It looks *incredible*.

A shining cay of sand and tropical palms, small enough to walk right around in less than half an hour, and replete with some of the best accommodation and catering you could hope to come across in all your years on the planet.

Down here at the bottom end of the Southern Ari Atoll, the islands are spread out enough that you can't see another one on the horizon. There's literally nothing out here, other than the Wimbufushi resort, and about a million manta rays, coral reef sharks and the occasional dugong.

It's paradise.

And I'm here for a whole week again.

. . . *with the same fucking person.*

No! Be quiet, brain! Listen to what Mel told us! We are here with *Cara* . . . and nothing else matters!

That seems to shut him up.

This is probably for the best, as Wimbufushi is the type of place where you're supposed to shut your brain off completely. It's good that he's getting some practice in early.

The speedboat powers its way closer to the island, and eventually comes alongside another pier. This one is long, entirely on its own, and jutting out from the beach into the kind of azure blue ocean that the summer sky is insanely jealous of.

Once we're docked, our friendly fourteen-year-old once again lays the gangway down to allow us to step off the boat and on to the pier – where we are greeted by a smiling Maldivian man in the most pristine white uniform I have ever seen, flanked by four petite Maldivian ladies in red dresses with thick gold trim. They are all holding trays, on which stand some exotic and extremely attractive looking drinks in tall glasses. I don't remember being greeted with complimentary drinks first time I was here. They must have upped their hospitality game.

This suits me fine. The more changes they've made on the island for the better, the less time I'll spend wallowing in memories of Amy I don't want to have.

If Cara and I had to wait to board the boat last, then at least we get to climb off it first. This also means I get first pick of the lovely drinks on offer. There are two colours available: one an orangey yellow, and one a light green. I wait for Cara to choose hers, and then pick the orangey one – because you would, wouldn't you?

As I take a sip of what turns out to be an extremely refreshing fruit cocktail of some description, the man in the white suit beams at us all happily.

'Good morning, everybody!' he says with a smooth, warm Indian accent. 'Welcome to Wimbufushi Island Resort and Spa! My name is Azim, and I will be your chief host while you are on the island. If you would all like to refresh yourselves with a drink, I will escort you to our reception area, and we can show you to your rooms.'

Our two young escorts to the island are now joined by several men in white shirts and blue striped skirts (there's probably a proper name for these, but I am an absolute philistine, so have no idea what it is) who busy themselves taking our suitcases from the back of the speedboat, and trundling them off down the pier. They are headed for a large, squat building made entirely of wood with a thatched roof that sits a good twenty or thirty yards back from the beach, just in front of the thick green foliage that lies in the centre of the island. Inside is a big desk that looks like it was hewn from a piece of very large driftwood. I vaguely remember this being the Wimbufushi resort reception.

The rest of the guests on the speedboat have now filed away, and are taking their choice of drinks. I am delighted to see that Amy and Ray are the last ones off, and so have to settle for two of the green drinks. Neither looks happy about it.

Super-duper.

You know, if you're going to spend this entire holiday scoring cheap points against Amy, I'm just going to think about carrots all day long, my brain informs me.

I wonder if there's carrot in this drink?

You see what I mean?

Yes, alright. Point taken.

'So, please do all follow me now,' Azim bids us. 'Our staff will be pleased to take your luggage straight to your accommodation.'

I look over at the reception again to see the men – in what must be traditional Maldivian clothes – taking instruction from a short and rather squat woman dressed in a white suit like Azim's. Each one takes a ticket, and starts to head off towards the left or the right.

On the right, as you look down the island's length, past the lush tropical greenery and a long golden beach, you can see a walkway jutting out into the water that leads to a series of dark-wood water bungalows on stilts. There is a similar arrangement on the other end of the island, but they are hidden from my view at the moment. If you looked down on it from above, Wimbufushi would resemble a crab, with the island itself as the shell, and the two long lines of water bungalows acting as the pincers.

To the left of where I'm standing, there is a long row of beachside bungalows, nestled in the island's foliage enough to make them quite hard to see. These ring the outskirts of the whole island, giving my metaphorical crab a residential crown.

I spot my suitcase, along with Cara's, as they are being moved towards the water bungalows, and immediately feel a small thrill of excitement wash over me.

I get to live here for the next week.

Ex-wives be damned – that's a fucking *great* thing.

Azim starts to walk down the dock and we dutifully all follow. I maintain a quick pace to keep right up with him, making sure we're well ahead of Amy and Ray Surfboards.

I finish off my cocktail as I do this, and immediately wish I had another one. It was extremely refreshing, and I need that right now, given that I'm still dressed in my travelling clothes. The pink shirt Cara bought me for my birthday last month is a little too thick for thirty degrees, as are the black jeans she bought me for Christmas.

I need to get into my board shorts and singlet as soon as is humanly possible.

Cara is looking a little overheated too, given that she's in a pair of blue skinny jeans and a silver blouse. I bet she can't wait to get into her holiday gear, either.

. . . and neither can I. I saw the clothes she packed in her suitcase last night. They were all *tiny*.

I blink a couple of times as the wooden pier gives way to warm Maldivian sand. It wasn't last night though, was it? It was *two* nights ago. I've been on the go for so long now, I've forgotten what day it is.

It only takes a few moments to reach the reception area.

It's the sandiest reception I've ever been in, that's for sure. They simply haven't bothered flooring the area. What would be the point in a place like this? It's all open to the warm, tropical air, and doesn't have walls on three sides, just thick columns of rich mahogany wood holding up the roof.

Azim stands in front of the enormous driftwood desk, on which is perched an incongruous desktop PC. Those two things really don't belong together, unless you're on a luxury tropical resort in the middle of the Indian Ocean.

The short woman joins Azim, a broad smile on her face. It's in stark contrast to the serious, business-like expression she was wearing while she was dealing with the porters taking the luggage to our rooms. She holds a small box and a clipboard. Behind her on the reception desk are several gleaming white folders with the resort's logo embossed on the front.

'Well, everybody, thank you once again for choosing Wimbufushi Island Resort and Spa for your holiday,' Azim says. 'May I introduce you to Anju, who will be giving you your room key cards.' Azim indicates the lady to his left, who broadens her smile and bows her head slightly. 'She will call out your names, and if you would come forward to collect your keys and welcome pack from her, that would be most appreciated. We will begin with those of you staying in our water bungalows.'

My heart skips a beat. That's us.

Oh my God . . . very soon I'll be ensconced in a luxury water bungalow overlooking the most beautiful place on earth. I wonder if I can order a Tarkanian Sin City from room service?

Anju steps forward a little and calls the first name. A middle-aged, rather nondescript couple move forward to collect their welcome packs and keys. If he doesn't play golf at least three times a week, and if she doesn't drink a little too much prosecco with her girlfriends on a Thursday afternoon, I'd be amazed.

Anju hands them both key card and welcome pack. As she does, one of the porters instantly appears at her side. They have this all down to a very fine art, it's plain to see. Again, I don't remember this level of service from my first time here, but I concede I may have been just as tired and out of sorts when we arrived on our honeymoon, and I've forgotten.

This train of thought makes me look over at where Amy and Ray are standing off to our right, slightly closer to Anju. I've tried my best to ignore them and concentrate on everything else around me, but my stupid brain has wandered over to them again.

I snap my eyes away from Amy, and concentrate hard on Anju, hoping to hear our names called out.

This doesn't happen straight away. After the middle-aged couple are led away by one of the smiling porters, Anju then reads the names of another pair standing in the shade of the reception area. These are two young people, who really have no business being here. He looks about twenty-five, and if she's more than twenty I'd be surprised.

This is *awful*. People of that age should not have access to this kind of holiday. It's something you should have to strive towards for a good decade or two before you can afford it – and then only barely with Expedia concessions. But these two don't look like they've done a day's work in their lives. They must have rich parents. Or be YouTubers. That's how young people get rich these days, isn't it? They change their hairstyles, or throw themselves at plate glass windows on YouTube.

The young couple – of whom I am sickeningly *jealous*, if we're being completely honest about it – move forward to collect their welcome packs, and are also led away by another one of the porters.

'Mr Holland and Ms Caddick,' Anju then reads out.

So they're not married then.

And she's definitely gone back to her maiden name.

This shouldn't bother or surprise me in the slightest, but it *does*. It really does.

The gruesome twosome step forward and collect the welcome pack from Anju. As they do I take great interest in the sand beneath my feet. Look how lovely and white it is, would you? I'm led to believe that at least some of it is made from fish poo.

I don't know why this fact has squirrelled itself away in my brain, or even if it's accurate, but it's something I heard once and it has always stayed with me, just because it must take a mighty amount of fish to make enough poo to help create an island like this.

And are they small fish? Or big fish? Because big fish would be better, wouldn't it? I'd imagine they poo a lot more than the little ones. But why doesn't the poo float away before it gets the chance to become part of the island? Or is there a species of fish that has developed the ability to breathe air, and flops its way up on to the island for a crap?

They've gone, idiot. You can stop thinking about fish poo now.

I look up to see that my cantankerous brain tells the truth. Amy and Ray are now a good thirty feet away, being led across the white (possibly fish-poo laden) sand to the long walkway that extends out from the beach and towards the water bungalows.

'Mr Sinclair and Miss Rowntree,' Anju says, and Cara and I move forward.

'Here you are, Mr Sinclair,' Anju says, handing me the welcome pack and small envelope containing our key card. 'Everything you need to know about the island is contained within our pack, but if you have any questions at all, I am here at reception, and you are welcome to call by pressing zero on your room phone, or visit any time you wish. Please follow Edward, who will take you to your bungalow.'

Edward is a slight young man with an infectious smile, and insists on taking my rucksack, along with Cara's. We say thank you and goodbye to Anju, and follow Edward as he starts to make in the same direction as where Amy and Ray have gone.

And boy is Edward keen to get us to our water bungalow as quickly as he can. He takes off so fast across the sand that it kicks up under his Maldivian skirt as his flip flops struggle for purchase on the powdery surface.

Divested of our heavy rucksacks, Cara and I are just about able to keep up with him, even though it's starting to make me sweat quite profusely, as we march past several thatched beach umbrellas, under which sit a few lounging sunbathers. Wimbufushi is the kind of resort that never feels or looks overcrowded, simply because it only caters for a small number of guests.

Something occurs to me at this point that makes my blood run cold. Edward is motoring along the beach so fast that he's catching up to the porter escorting Amy and Ray – who is much slower, fatter and older than our sprightly guide.

What was a thirty-foot gap has rapidly shrunk to below twenty. If Edward keeps this pace up, we'll catch them before we reach the bungalows.

'Er, Edward?' I ask, in as light and friendly a tone possible. 'We don't need to go so fast!'

Edward looks around at me with that beaming smile of his. 'Go fast, sir? Okay!'

Oh fuck. He's obviously misinterpreted what I said. Possibly a language-barrier thing, or maybe the fact he's got our rucksacks hoiked so far up around his ears that he didn't hear me properly.

Either way, he's now battering along the beach at such a rate of knots, we're guaranteed to come alongside Amy and Ray before we get to the bungalows.

I try to tell him to slow down again, but he's so intent on fulfilling what he thinks are my wishes to go faster that he doesn't appear to hear me at all this time. So to keep up, Cara and I are now stumbling across the white powdery sand like a couple of new-born foals, all awkward legs and audible grunting.

Oh God. He's getting *nearer*!

Amy's porter is a few feet before the wooden walkway now, and still proceeding at a much slower rate than we are.

Amy's going to think I'm doing this *deliberately*! She's going to think I've told Edward to move as fast as possible, to beat them to the bungalows!

I don't want that! I want to amble slowly along, feeling the warm sun caress my face – not race along at the fastest pace imaginable, with the sand filling up my shoes!

Sure enough, just as Amy's porter is just about to step on to the walkway, Edward comes barrelling past him like the outside chance at Aintree, and launches himself on to the wooden jetty. This only gives him an extra burst of speed now he's on a more solid surface.

I come stumbling past the three of them with my head down, staring at the sand for all I'm worth. What the hell else can I do? Wave as I go past? Offer my heartfelt apologies? Give them the finger?

None of those seem like appropriate options, so I just motor past, trying not to make eye contact. Poor old Cara follows on behind, huffing and puffing for all she's worth.

I'm not a hundred per cent sure, but I think I hear Amy tut as my feet hit the walkway.

Amy likes to tut. She can express more with a tut than some people can with an entire litany of swearwords.

Well, there's bloody nothing I can do about it! It's not my fault Edward is in training for the bloody Maldivian Olympic team, is it?

Is the hundred metres across sand carrying two North Face rucksacks an Olympic event? Because Edward here would be a fucking shoo-in.

We continue to hammer along the wooden jetty for a good fifty or so yards, until Edward banks towards the entrance of one of the water bungalows. Such has been his turn of speed that we've left Amy and Ray in the dust – or rather, sand.

The bungalows are arranged so that only two of them are accessible from the smaller walkways that break off from the main one – which has widened considerably since we got to the start of the two rows of bungalows on either side of it.

Edward powers his way to the water bungalow on the left-hand side of this specific walkway, and turns towards me expectantly, holding out his hand.

Oh fuck. Does he want a tip? I literally don't have any spare change on me, and even if I did, it'd probably be a couple of pound coins – which would be about as much use to Edward as a chocolate teapot, unless he was planning a trip to see the glorious touristical wonders of England's green and pleasant land.

'Give him the key card, Joel,' Cara says rather breathlessly from beside me. 'He wants to let us into the bungalow.'

'Oh, I see,' I reply, feeling instantly stupid. I hand over the cardboard envelope and stand there politely as Edward takes out the key card and runs it over the entry scanner next to the solid wood door carved with rather lovely flowers.

The door clicks from somewhere in its internal workings, and Edward pushes it open.

I let Cara walk in before me, and then follow her. 'Wow,' I breathe, as I cross the threshold and see what's inside.

'Yeah,' Cara agrees, taking in the rather lovely surroundings that will be our home for the next week.

The last time I came to Wimbufushi, I was accommodated in one of the beach bungalows – which was lovely enough. But this place is a whole order of magnitude more luxurious.

To the front of the bungalow is a wide-open room, with a massive super-king-sized bed against the wall, and a colossal comfy-looking couch in front of it. An equally large cream chaise longue sits along the left-hand wall, and there's an enormous television on a wall bracket in the right-hand corner.

Beyond all of this is a set of windowed sliding doors that lead out into heaven.

A decked veranda has two gigantic loungers sat on it – and, yes, I am well aware of how many adjectives I'm using to define this water bungalow that all basically repeat the same description: everything in here is *huge*. Including that view.

Beyond the veranda is the horizon, an ocean of cool blue water and a blue sky only interrupted by a few scudding high-altitude clouds.

Cara and I walk over to it like a pair of zombies, while Edward quietly puts our rucksacks on the chaise longue. He's probably seen this reaction from guests a thousand times before, and is well used to waiting while they dribble about the view in stunned amazement.

The beach bungalow had a lovely view of the ocean too, but it really didn't have the same impact as standing on a water-bungalow veranda like we are now.

It feels like you're floating in the view itself, with nothing between you and it. It's an *incredible* sensation.

Cara takes my hand in hers as we both just stand there for a moment, gazing out into gorgeous infinity. I look around at her. 'I'm really glad I'm here with you,' I say to her.

'Me too,' she replies, and gives me a soft kiss on the cheek.

Cara and I then drift back into the bungalow, barely able to stop ourselves from turning to look at the horizon again as we do so. Edward starts to tell us about the amenities we have in the bungalow, including the free mini bar, multi-channel satellite TV, and tea- and coffee-making facilities, but I only hear half of what he has to say.

61

My attention is only really brought away from the view when Edward indicates down at our feet.

'There's a glass floor,' I point out, going over to stand on it.

Slap bang in the middle of the lounge area, in front of the couch, is a square patch of floor that is see-through glass, instead of hardwood. Through it, I can gaze at colourful coral, and some equally colourful tiny fish. It's quite hypnotic to watch them swimming about, as the sea level gently rises and falls with the waves.

I look back up at the transcendent view, then back down at the hypnotic floor glass. Back up, back down. Back up, back down.

There's every chance I'm just going to spend this entire holiday switching between these two glorious views, unable to take my eyes off either of them.

Edward smiles, and says we should now follow him to the rear of the bungalow where he can show us the bathroom. I manage to pull myself away from the two visions of natural beauty laid out in front of me, and do as he says.

Edward takes us around the back of the wall the bed is up against to show us the bathroom and dressing area. On the other side of the wall is a long set of ornate, dark wooden wardrobes.

To the right of us is a closed-off toilet, and behind gorgeous wooden walls – also carved with flowers – is a beautiful freestanding bath and rain shower. There's also a large double sink vanity against the back of the bungalow behind yet another wall, above which hangs an ornate mirror. The whole bungalow has a definite open-air feel to it, while still retaining the right amount of necessary privacy. It's incredibly well laid out, and quite something.

'Bloody hell,' Cara says under her breath, as the tour concludes back at the open front door to the bungalow. 'Thank you, Edward.'

He beams at her. 'My pleasure, madam.'

No, Edward, this is entirely *our* pleasure . . . You've let us into heaven – and there will be a place in my will for you.

This water bungalow is incredible.

Completely *perfect*.

Absolutely—

'Are you fucking *kidding* me?' I hear Amy's voice stab into my ears, breaking my happy little train of thought completely.

I turn and look out – to see Amy, Ray and their porter all stood at the threshold to the bungalow next door . . .

Tuesday

Amy – The Horror Next Door

Accidentally eating an entire tarantula.

Finding out your parents were war criminals.

Winning a lifetime supply of dog shit.

Contracting a disease that makes all of your teeth fall out, and renders you incapable of saying any word other than 'bosom'.

All of these things – and many more besides – are both more likely to happen and infinitely *preferable* to what's going on in my life right now.

The same flight. The same week. The same island. The bungalow next door . . .

It's as if some malign entity is controlling my life for its own hideous amusement. A malevolent puppet master, sitting over me and Ray, pushing us around like pawns on a chess board, laughing itself into insensibility at our reactions to all of the gross, inexplicable 'coincidences' it's forcing upon us. Maybe it's doing it just for its own amusement – or maybe it has an *audience*. A collection of ethereal, otherworldly psychopaths, who live to take delight in the misery of others.

If I ever chance to come face to face with this entity – which is about as likely as finding yourself in the *fucking water bungalow next door to Joel* – I will kick it right in the testicles.

You hear me, you smug bastard?

There will be a reckoning!

Oh yes, there *will be* a reckoning, or my name is not Amy Caddick! And you and all of your friends will rue the day! You will rue, I tell you! *Rue!*

'Are you okay, sweetheart?' Ray says, coming to stand next to where I'm gripping the edge of the sink and staring into the mirror. I'm not sure how long I've been stood here thinking up impossible things that still feel more likely than my current circumstance, but it's probably been quite a while. Long enough for Ray to have had a shower, certainly.

'Yes, yes, I'm fine,' I reply in a brittle voice. 'Just very jet-lagged.' I can't let him see how angry I am about my ex-husband being next door.

'Why don't you go relax on the veranda for a bit?' he suggests. 'I'll make us a couple of drinks from the mini bar. They have a nice white wine in there.'

White wine.

That sounds like a good idea to me.

White wine will help me to relax.

That should piss off the malevolent entity somewhat. I bet it doesn't want to see me *relax*. That's not funny for it in the *slightest*.

'Yeah, okay,' I say, snaking an arm around his naked torso to give him a kiss. Ray's naked torso is usually enough to make me want to do more than just kiss him, but I am extremely jet-lagged right now, so I'm not quite in the mood for any of those kinds of shenanigans just yet.

I try to ignore the fact that I'm probably also not in the mood because Joel is only a few feet away from me. I walk through the bungalow and go out on to the veranda.

Aah . . .

That's better.

There's that view again.

It's the one I remember well from my honeymoon six years ago, and one that is even better this time around thanks to the upgrade to the water bungalow.

I cannot *wait* for the sunset this evening.

Even if I fall asleep this afternoon, I will set an alarm to make sure I am awake to see it. I've been dreaming about that sunset for weeks now, and intend to drink in every single second of it, lying here on that comfy sun lounger with a glass of wine in my hand. I had Ray ask the resort for a bungalow that faced west, and they were happy to oblige (for an extra fee, of course; I wanted to pay for it, but Ray had none of it).

Actually, come to think of it, I don't know whether that sun lounger is comfy or not. It certainly looks it, but I think I'd better give it a try just to make sure.

Yep, it's more comfortable than our bed back at home.

I sink down on to it, feeling some of the tension drain out of me as I do so. There's every possibility I'll fall asleep right here and now, if I'm not careful.

But that would be absolutely *fine*, as I'm on holiday, and sleeping during the day is a thing you can do on holiday without worrying that you're getting old. I have a feeling it's secretly the reason why most people take a holiday in the first place. The sun, sea and shenanigans are lovely and everything, but having an excuse to just conk out at three o'clock in the afternoon is worth all the money and hassle it takes to get here all by itself.

I manage to stay awake long enough for Ray to bring me a white wine, but by the time I'm halfway through it, I can feel myself sliding into unconsciousness.

Fabulous.

Maybe I'll just have a half an hour snooze to charge my batteries a bit – and then I'll suggest to Ray that we go for a walk around the island to get better acquainted. It's obvious a few things have changed since I was here last, and I'd like to see what's different.

But first . . . forty winks.

Yes.

That's the stuff.

A gentle afternoon snooze . . .

'Where's the sun cream?' Joel cries out to me from the back of the bungalow.

'It's in the zipped compartment of my suitcase,' I tell him in a slightly sluggish voice. Why can't he find these things for himself? I don't know how many times I have to tell him to—

I sit bolt upright on the lounger, instantly awake.

I'm not here with Joel!

'Sorry, sweetheart?' Ray asks from the doorway into the bungalow. 'Did you say something?'

'No! No, nothing!' I tell him.

But I did say something, didn't I? I said something to my bloody *ex-husband* – as if we were still together!

But why? Did I dream it?

'It's definitely not out here!' I hear Joel shout again.

Oh God. He's on his bloody veranda too!

The bungalows are thankfully completely obscured from one another visually by tall fences made from what looks like thick

67

bamboo, but that doesn't do much to stop sound from travelling over.

'Oh, I've found it, Cara! It was under the lounger! Do you want me to come and do your back?'

I grip the edges of the sun lounger harder than I did the edges of the sink.

Every word that falls out of his mouth makes me *cringe*. There's an obsequious tone to the way he speaks that makes my teeth tingle. There's a reedy quality to his voice that I just – can't – *stand*.

And it's a mere few feet away from me.

For the whole of the next week.

I swing my legs off the lounger and get up, striding over to the bamboo fence and opening my mouth to shout over at Joel to shut the hell up.

But I manage to bring myself up short before I actually do, thank God.

I'd sound like a crazy woman.

So instead, I punch the bamboo fence, making it ripple slightly. This does nothing, other than to hurt my hand, so I turn on one heel and march back into the bungalow, pulling the glass sliding doors closed as I do so.

Ray looks up from where he's sat at the small desk that sits under the TV, with a quizzical expression on his face. 'What are you doing?' he asks me.

I point out at the veranda. 'I can't do it, Ray!'

'Can't do what?' He rises from the seat, his face a picture of concern.

'I can't . . . *I can't listen to him!*'

'Who? Joel?'

'Yes! He's out there next to me! I can hear his voice floating over, and it puts my teeth on edge!'

Ray's brow knits in what I hope is worry, and not anger at me feeling this way. 'Oh no. That's no good. Maybe we should go for a little stroll around the island? That'll get you away from him, and by the time we get back maybe you'll be a little . . . a little calmer?'

Bless him, Ray is trying to understand, but I can tell he's having difficulty with it. I'm sure to him having his fiancée's ex-husband next door is awkward – but nothing really more than that. He probably doesn't get why I'm so much more riled up about the whole thing. But then, I never really went into the details of what happened with the breakdown of my marriage, and the house that Joel christened Goblin Central. I didn't want to put Ray through it.

Maybe it's time I laid things out a little clearer, though . . .

I need Ray to understand why I'm so unable to just ignore Joel's presence here on the island. I need him to know that it's not because I care about Joel anymore – it's because of what happened with that stupid house!

'Yes, maybe a walk would be a good idea,' I tell him. 'It'll help clear my head a bit, and we can have a chat about why Joel being here has made me this upset.'

Ray's face is a picture of hurt confusion. He *does* think it's because I care about Joel still, I can tell. I must nip that idea in the bud as soon as possible.

'Okay, come on then,' I tell him, walking over to pop my flip flops on. 'Let's go see what's what.'

Ray nods his head and puts his Birkenstock sandals on. Now we're actually at the resort, and he's in his chino shorts, the Hawaiian shirt doesn't look quite so incongruous anymore. In fact, he looks just the part.

I probably do too, now I'm in my cotton summer shorts and vest top.

Ray opens the front door for me, and for a second my heart jumps into my throat as I look across the wooden walkway to the front door of Joel's bungalow.

If I see their door swing open right now, I'm likely to scream at the top of my lungs.

Thankfully, it doesn't, so I hurry out of our door as quickly as possible, and scurry to the start of the main, wide deck area between the rows of bungalows.

This is *intolerable*.

I cannot spend this whole holiday scurrying around like a frightened mouse!

Ray joins me and laces his hand in mine.

Good. That's a good sign. He's obviously not angry with me, but he still has that vaguely worried look on his face.

I have to set his mind at rest.

It takes me a good fifteen or so minutes to work up to it, though. I spend those minutes, as we slowly circumnavigate the tiny island of Wimbufushi, trying to marshal my thoughts into a sensible order, which will enable me to get my point across as quickly and as succinctly as possible.

This isn't easy, as I keep getting distracted by the bloody scenery, which is, of course, flippin' gorgeous. On my left is a wall of waving palm trees and other tropical plants and trees, and on my right is the most beautiful ocean on Earth. It's a little hard to formulate the contents of a serious conversation with stuff like that hanging about.

But then that's the point of a place like this, isn't it? You're not *supposed* to have serious thoughts here. You're supposed to forget all about serious stuff like that, and just drift along in a serene holiday fug, lulled by all that beauty around you.

But I have to talk to Ray – aesthetically perfect island environs be damned!

'Ray, can I say something?' I eventually blurt out, just as we round the tip of the island, to begin the walk back towards the other end.

'Of course,' he replies. 'Shall we go and sit down by the pool? Maybe dip our toes in?' Ray points over to where a long, low building is situated in a raised position slightly above the beach. In front of it is an infinity pool that I remember frolicking in quite happily six years ago.

At first the memory of Joel doing the same thing makes me want to run away and go nowhere near the pool, but I take a deep breath, come to my senses and nod. 'That sounds nice,' I reply, and we make our way over to it.

There are about six or seven guests lounging around the pool, but none are actually in it. It's a lovely swimming pool, but entirely surplus to requirements, given how inviting the sea is.

Ray and I kick off our shoes and sit at the pool's edge. When I dip my toes in, I shudder with pleasure as the cool water caresses them.

I look out at the horizon, and take another deep breath. 'Ray, I don't want you to think I'm mad about Joel being here because I care about him anymore.'

'Okay.' There's a note of caution in Ray's voice I'm not happy to hear at all.

'Nothing could be further from the truth. I've had no problems forgetting about him completely in the past two years – which makes his presence here all the worse.'

'Right.'

'You've probably noticed I'm . . . quite angry.'

'Yes, I might have.' Ray tries not to smile ruefully as he says this.

'Well, there's a good reason for that. I never really went into the details of how my marriage to that idiot actually broke down, did I?'

'No. You told me you had a lot of arguments at work, and that the marriage just fell apart because of it. I didn't want to pry, because it was obviously hard for you to talk about.'

I nod. 'That's right. But I owe you a better explanation, so you understand why I'm so mad he's here now.' One last deep breath. 'I lost everything thanks to Joel's slapdash attitude towards everything, and because of a house called Goblin Central.'

Ray's brow furrows as I say this.

Sigh.

Time to explain . . .

Joel and I were business partners before we were in a relationship. We both came to work at Rowntree Land & Home within six months of each other. He was a slightly more experienced agent when he started, but I had more enthusiasm for the job, I think. RL&H only dealt with high-end properties, dotted across the whole of the UK. Nothing was under a million, and quite often the prices soared into the tens of millions.

There was an obvious attraction between Joel and I, but we tried to resist it at first – because mixing business with pleasure rarely works out for the best. That attraction created great chemistry between us as agents though, and sparked off a working relationship that was of huge benefit to us both. Joel always used to refer to me as 'his muse'. He used to say my presence alongside him always boosted his confidence and his chemistry with the clients, which helped us sell the houses. The fact he had complete trust in me to handle all the important stuff did as much for my own sense of self-worth.

We started dating after only a few months of knowing each other, and within a year we were the agency's 'power couple'. Joel was very good at his job, but I think I may have been even better.

I came into work every day with a spring in my step, eager to go to the next enormous, grandiose property. Joel always tended to be the more ostentatious of the two of us. He definitely was the one to charm the clients. But I was the brains of the operation – at least I like to think so. I handled the details. Clients came to rely on me for both my accuracy and my discretion. We were often dealing with famous or rich people, given the size of the properties we were selling, and it was Joel's job to wine and dine them, while it was mine to make sure everything was properly taken care of.

I loved my job and, for my sins, I also loved Joel.

Marriage was rather inevitable. Not least because us having the same surname would solidify our power-couple reputation even more at RL&H.

And after the marriage, the next two or so years were very exciting – and very profitable. Okay, Joel and I could rub each other up the wrong way from time to time, but that's the hallmark of any creative, ambitious relationship, isn't it? The disagreements and arguments we had were down to a combined passion for the job we were doing.

We just worked together so damn well. We complimented each other in a way that was almost spooky.

And we kept the money rolling in, much to the delight of Roland Rowntree, the aging owner of the agency. It was a barely concealed secret that he was thinking of handing off the responsibility of running the whole operation to Joel and me when he retired. We would be set for life.

But after two years of this, things started to . . . deteriorate.

You see, Joel and I are very different personalities. He was never a *details* person – whereas I have always been someone careful about that kind of thing. His attitude towards things like paperwork and due diligence absolutely *stank*, and I frankly started to resent him for that.

I didn't like having to haul him up on things that he should have taken care of that he found boring, and he hated it when I did.

Our passion for each other, and our jobs, kept this resentment under wraps for a long time, but eventually the cracks started to show. You just can't hide differences like that forever.

Our success at RL&H meant that the pressure on us to continue to sell even bigger and better properties grew almost exponentially. And we all know what happens to cracks when you apply pressure to them, don't we?

We started to argue all the time. Began to pick at one another's character flaws. Where once our differences were the fuel that fired our partnership, now that fuel was the catalyst for an almost constant supply of disagreement, resentment and conflict.

It was horrible.

But I still loved Joel, and he still loved me. So we kept going with it, papering over those cracks as best we could. Both of us were probably terrified that if we couldn't make our marriage work, we'd lose our working partnership as well. And we were *so close* to taking over. So close to running Rowntree Land & Home ourselves. That prize was just too huge a thing to sacrifice.

Then Goblin Central came along . . .

The house was a huge twelve-bedroom mansion, about five miles off the M3 corridor in Hampshire. It had everything. So much so that if I tried to list it all now, I'd still be talking by the time Doomsday arrived.

It certainly ended up being my own personal Doomsday, both for my job and my marriage.

Joel nicknamed it Goblin Central because it had gargoyles on the roof above the enormous double doors. Eight of them in total. Ugly buggers they were, each and every one.

I think he even named them individually, but I can't recall all of them. They all began with B though. Boris, Burt, Barrington and Boglinchops. I remember those four at least.

Joel gave nicknames to everything and everyone. It was one of his worst traits. Although some of them could be very funny, for the first few years of our marriage I probably thought it was a charming quirk of his personality.

Goblin Central was a much-coveted property by all high-end real estate agents in the country, given its size and price. Whoever got to sell it for the vendor would earn a gigantic amount of kudos within our relatively small field. And big contracts always lead to *more* big contracts. Roland Rowntree was desperate for RL&H to land the deal.

So were Joel and I. It would pretty much guarantee our ascendency to the top of the company.

It all came down to a meeting with the owner – a pompous and unpleasant fellow by the name of Viscount Alastair De Ponsonby Long.

Yes, that was indeed his full name.

He insisted on being called Viscount Long – though Joel secretly called him Lord Ponsonbollocks. In fact, I think the full nickname might have been Lord Ponsonbollocks of Twatingly Gardens, but I can't quite remember. I know Joel only ever used that name when he was talking to me about him. The same goes for all the nicknames Joel used to make up. They were a private joke between me and him, nobody else.

Apparently, Lord Ponsonbollocks – sorry, Viscount Long – was in line to the throne in some capacity, but I never found out how close. Not that close, I would surmise. The whole royal family and its offshoots would probably have to die in a nuclear war before good old Alastair got the chance to sling on the ermine and crown.

If we had attended the meeting, I'm sure Joel and I would have secured the contract to sell the house (which was actually called De Ponsonby Manor). We'd already met with Viscount Long's people, and had spoken to him on the phone. This was to be the big sales pitch meeting that would guarantee him as a client.

The meeting never happened.

Because Joel is a fucking idiot.

A *disorganised* idiot, who got the time of the meeting completely *wrong*. We were supposed to be there at 1 p.m., and we didn't turn up until 6 p.m. – a whole five hours late for the meeting, and two hours after Viscount Long had agreed to let Bishop & Rose arrange the sale. The Bishop & Rose Estate Agency were our chief competition at the time, and were a constant source of annoyance to Roland. He wanted to beat them, and beat them hard. You can imagine how delighted he was to find out we'd fucked up our opportunity to put one over on them – or rather that *Joel* had fucked up our opportunity to get one over on them.

It was my fault, though. My own stupid, stupid fault.

A couple of weeks before the Goblin Central meeting, Joel and I had a huge argument (again) about his lax approach to our combined admin work, after I discovered that he forgot to put *another* expenses claim in on time. This was a small, petty thing that should have been a minor source of irritation, but those cracks we talked about magnified everything out of all proportion.

Biblical proportions to be more accurate. That's how big the argument was.

At the end of it, Joel *promised* me he'd do better. He'd be more careful with the details. And I stupidly believed him – to the point that I allowed him to be the one to arrange our incredibly important meeting with Viscount Long. As a test of his commitment, if you will.

What a fucking idiot I was to do that.

Because – of course – Joel screwed up the appointment time. I couldn't even rely on him to get that fucking right!

He denied it. Repeatedly. Until the spit was flying out of his mouth. He was adamant he'd put the right time down after his phone call with the viscount.

But I'm not an idiot. And I know what kind of man he is. The kind of man who will do a slapdash job of anything that bores him, and make stupid mistakes, even when the stakes are so high. Five-hour stupid mistakes that cost us the biggest sale of our lives.

Can you believe he even tried to say that I must have gone into our work calendar and accidentally changed the time of the meeting? As if I'm the one who doesn't know what she's doing? I kept that bloody appointment calendar one hundred per cent right for *four bloody years*. The one time I let Joel have a go at it, he fucks it up completely!

The next few weeks of my life were *hell*. Any trust left between us was gone. The faith in our working partnership was gone, as it was with our personal relationship. What love there was left between us was drained in that instant.

Losing Goblin Central was a catalyst for some very nasty things to come out – now the cracks had turned into *canyons*. Things I won't talk about now. It's all too horrible to recall.

But Goblin Central was definitely the straw that broke the camel's back.

We filed for divorce within three months.

You can only imagine what it was like to go to work together.

An absolute *nightmare*.

The power couple had fallen apart completely, and were barely able to be in the same room as one another, let alone sell houses together.

Everything, and everyone, suffered.

And then, a mere two months after the divorce, with Joel on one side of our office and me on the other, the biggest injustice of the whole thing occurred: I was told to pack my bags and leave. I was essentially fired from the job I loved, simply because I'd fallen out with my husband.

Oh, Roland Rowntree gave the excuse that my work standards had slipped dramatically since we lost Goblin Central, and he was right about that – but can you blame me? I was going through a bloody divorce! And he didn't pin much of the blame on Joel, if any! No . . . it was all dumped on *my* shoulders.

I have no actual proof, but I'm willing to bet Joel had a large part in getting me sacked. I can just picture him in my mind's eye, sat at Roland's desk, dripping poison about me into the old man's ear for all those months . . .

So that was that. I was done. Strung up like a fucking kipper. Thrown out with yesterday's rubbish. Fired from a job I adored, all because my ex-husband was too stupid and feckless to book a damned appointment correctly!

'Thank God you were there for me, Ray,' I say to him, fighting back the tears of rage that threaten to overwhelm me every time I talk about what happened two years ago. 'If you hadn't been, I don't know . . .'

I trail off, looking down at my feet as they swirl around in the chilly pool water.

'Well, I'm very glad I was,' Ray replies. 'I may not have stayed in the place in Sevenoaks for long in the end, but coming to your old agency to look for a new house was entirely worth it. Best decision I ever made.'

'And the best decision I ever made was letting you talk me into coming and working for you,' I tell him. 'I could have easily just gone to another estate agency, but it wouldn't have been the same. I needed a change, and you gave me it.'

Ray then takes my hand in his. 'My pleasure, sweetheart. And thank you for telling me everything now. It means a great deal. I can totally understand why having Joel here this week is making you so mad.' Ray's face darkens. 'I quite fancy giving him a smack across the chops myself.'

I feel a thrill run down my back. It's incredibly regressive of me to say this, but I can't pretend it doesn't give me a feeling of pure pleasure at the prospect of this wonderful man going and giving Joel a clout. Ray loves me in ways Joel never did or could.

'You don't have to do that,' I tell him. 'Just . . . just understand it if I can't let it all go and just enjoy myself. Especially with him and Cara Rowntree next door.'

'Cara *Rowntree*?'

'Oh yes. I forgot to mention that bit. Joel's new girlfriend is Roland Rowntree's *granddaughter*. I believe she went to work at the company sometime after I left. She obviously got her hooks into my ex-husband at some point. From the look of the way he fawns over her, I'd guess it's a new relationship, though.'

'Bloody hell.'

'Yeah.' I give him a bitter smile. 'It's just *delightful* to have them both a few feet away from me.'

Ray's eyes squint for a moment in thought. Then his jaw clenches. 'There's something we can do about that, I think.' He pulls his legs out of the pool, climbs to his feet, and holds out a hand. 'Come on, let's go have a word with that Azim chap.'

I take his hand and get to my feet as well. 'What are you going to do?'

'I'm going to get us another water bungalow. One far away from the two of them. I'll not have your holiday ruined because they are here.'

Oh my. I think I've gone a bit *gooey*.

I'm so very, very sorry about that.

Going gooey is not a thing that I do.

I didn't even do it when Joel and I were looking for a house for Gareth Gates. And this was a person I had a serious crush on when I was a teenager. The lisp was adorable. But I was all business the entire time we had dealings with him. If anything, Joel was weirder around Gareth than I ever was, and he was a Metallica fan. Joel never did do well around celebrities. We bumped into Kelly Brook at a party once, and he insisted on calling her Melanie, for some reason. Even after she told him her name was Kelly, he still did it. About three or four more times. The poor girl eventually walked away in disgust. That was a potential client we lost that day as well.

Anyway . . . regardless of celebrity encounters that happened firmly in the past (I don't like to think about my old job too much these days) I am definitely feeling pretty gooey right now, at Ray's insistence we change water bungalows. He's such a *take charge* kind of man, and I love that.

Even though I'm betraying the sisterhood by admitting it, it's still true.

I love it, I love it, I *love it*.

We head off to reception, where we are greeted once again by Anju, who is more than happy to call for Azim when Ray explains the situation. He doesn't go into that much detail with Anju, but definitely gets it across that we'd very much like to change bungalows, due to being next to unwanted travel companions.

Azim then appears from out of the jungle.

I know that sounds ridiculous, but that's what happens. Somewhere back there, hidden from the sight of all the guests by that luxurious foliage, are the buildings where the island's staff live, and where all the actual work gets done around here. Everything is artfully hidden away from us, though. All I can see at tree height are a few glimpses of buildings, coloured in a drab greyish brown that makes them disappear into the background.

I recall that the last time I was here, I felt a little uncomfortable at the idea of all those Maldivians being trapped in the centre of the island like that, while we sun ourselves out here – and that feeling has now returned as we watch Azim come forward, out of *the places we do not go*. His disarming smile makes me feel a little bit better, but then I suppose the smile is designed to do just that, isn't it?

Ray then explains the situation in slightly more detail to Azim. He doesn't mention my history with Joel, but makes it very clear to Azim that we would like to move away, in no uncertain terms.

I'm afraid this makes me gooey again. It's the firm tone of voice, you see. The only reaction you can possibly have to a tone of voice like that is to go a bit gooey. If you're me, that is. Azim doesn't look gooey, and neither does Anju. In fact, both look highly concerned, such is the effective job Ray is doing of laying out our grievance.

'Let me see what I can do,' Azim says. 'Please head over to the Reef Bar and enjoy a refreshing cocktail from our bartender Tarkan while I see to this matter.'

That's a dismissal.

It's an incredibly polite one – including the promise of cocktails, but it's a dismissal none the less. Azim obviously wants to get to work, and doesn't want us to see how he operates. This is fine by me. I've never been one to want to know how the sausage is made.

Anju escorts us across the island to where the Reef Bar sits slightly back in the waving palm trees, and not that far away from the infinity pool.

Ray orders us both a Bellini while we wait. It still tastes quite *fantastic*.

Some fifteen minutes pass before Azim arrives to tell us the good news. 'Mr Holland, Ms Caddick, I'm pleased to say we have secured you our only free bungalow, on the other side of the island, over there.' Azim points past us to the second set of water bungalows that poke out into the ocean on the western side of Wimbufushi.

I feel a wave of relief wash over me. 'Oh, thank you!' I tell Azim, nearly spilling my drink.

'It is my pleasure,' he replies, that disarming smile being used to full effect. 'If you would like to go back and pack your things, I will have our staff transport all of them to the new bungalow as soon as possible.'

I want to hug him, I truly do. But as that would probably be a little over the top, I wait until he has left and give Ray a massive hug instead. 'Thank you so much for this. I can enjoy our holiday again now, I think.'

Ray smiles and kisses me. 'Good. That's exactly what I wanted. We'll finish up our drinks, and head back. We'll be in our new room within the hour – as far away from Joel and Cara as possible.'

This deserves another hug, don't you think? I may have gone a bit gooey, but that doesn't mean I can't hug the life out of this wonderful man for what he's done for me.

Luckily, I see no sign of Joel or Little Miss Rowntree as we go back to gather our things. I don't hear anything of them either as I repack my suitcase. They must have gone out themselves, or are engaged in something inside their bungalow that I can't hear and *now I'm picturing things I don't want to, so I'd better just go get my toothbrush and do my absolute level best to remove the image I now have in my head that will haunt my dreams for some time to come.*

Twenty minutes later, Ray and I are being let into our new accommodation, which looks exactly the same as the old one, except it's half a mile away, jutting out into a completely different part of the coral-filled Indian Ocean.

Sighs of relief all round.

I might not be able to get away from my ex-husband completely, but at least I can sleep soundly on my veranda now, not having to hear his whiny little voice asking for the sun cream.

We unpack all over again, which is made slightly more pleasant by the calming music Ray plays on the TV surround sound system as we do so. He's doing all he can to improve my mood and get me to relax, and I love him for that about as much as I do for getting us this much needed move in the first place.

His reaction to my story of woe was about as positive as I could have hoped for, and I have to wonder why I didn't lay it all out for him in detail sooner. We've been together now for a year, and engaged for three months. I shouldn't feel the need to keep anything from him.

But was that it? Maybe not.

I don't think I've been able to tell the whole sorry story to him previously just because it's too damn painful to talk about.

Ironically, even though the cause of my pain is only half a mile away, it's still easier to divulge everything when you're thousands of miles away from where it all actually happened. There's a strange feeling of *disconnection* from the world when you get out here in the middle of the Indian Ocean, and I suppose that makes it easier to confront and deal with the sins of the past.

I gaze over at the clock on the bedside cabinet to see that it's not long until our first all-inclusive meal of the holiday. Excellent. I can hear my tummy rumbling like a mad thing. I can't wait to gorge myself on the enormous buffet they provide here on Wimbufushi – all of it cooked by extremely talented people locked away in one of those grey buildings at the interior.

But first, before we go to dinner, I think I'll go and sit out on the veranda again to enjoy some late afternoon sun. My last attempt at doing this was rudely interrupted by Joel Sinclair and his search for sun cream – but there will be none of that this time around. Ray has taken care of that for me.

I slide open the door to the veranda, and take my place on the sun lounger.

When I look out on to the ocean, I am vaguely disappointed to see that the thing the lounger is built for is nowhere to be seen.

'Where's the sun?' I say to myself out loud, looking out at a clear blue sky, just starting to darken at the edges as the day moves into evening.

My mouth drops open as I realise why I can't see the sun from my vantage point.

We've *moved*.

We've changed water bungalows.

And that means our view has *shifted*.

And it's shifted so much that the sun is now going to set *behind* the bungalow. If I want to watch it go down, I'll have to either stand at the front door, or go and invade the bungalow opposite. And I'm not sure the inhabitants will take too kindly to that.

Don't seethe, Amy. It'll do you no good whatsoever.

But I *want* to seethe.

I want to seethe so much that it becomes a superpower with which I can fight crime on my return to the UK. Seethe Woman they will call me, and my costume will be bright red with a set of gritted teeth as my insignia.

I've lost my *sunset*.

My beautiful sunset.

The thing I've dreamed about for weeks.

All. Because. Of. Joel. Sinclair.

Damn him!

I'm well aware of how entitled and brattish this might make me sound – I'm in the Maldives, in a water bungalow, and it's thirty degrees in the shade – but I've dreamed about that sunset for six years now. At times of great stress I've used it as a visualisation to calm me down. Me, lying on a sun lounger just like this, with a drink in my hand, watching the sun gently set on the horizon . . .

I even have it as my screensaver on my computer at work. A professionally taken version of it at least. I don't use one of the cack-handed shots Joel took; I found a much better picture on the internet.

And it's been taken away from me.

If I want to watch the sun go down now, I'll have to go and sit on the end of the walkway our bungalow is on. That will be fine, I guess. But it won't be private. It won't be *just for me*.

And I won't be able to do it with my boobs out. Which, if I haven't mentioned yet, is part of my little sunset fantasy. For what reason I know not – but I just liked the idea of doing it with my boobs on display to the slowly sinking orb of burning hydrogen. Let's just call it a sub-conscious predilection I have no control over, and move on.

No. There will be no half-naked sunset-watching for me. Joel Sinclair has seen to that.

Damn him!

'Everything okay, sweetheart?' Ray says, as he comes out to join me on the veranda.

'Yes! Of course!' I reply in as bright a voice as I can manage.

I can't let him see I'm still upset about Joel's actions – not after all he's done to make this holiday as comfortable as possible for me.

I'll just have to suck up my disappointment about the lack of sunset and move on.

Just like I had to move on from losing the job I loved two years ago.

Ooh.

You're not going to get away with it, Joel.

I'm going to make sure you bloody don't . . .

Wednesday

JOEL – EXCRUCIATING

'She's definitely gone,' Cara remarks, as I come out of the shower, rubbing my head with a towel.

'Really?'

'Yep. I heard a bit of a commotion, so I looked through the spyglass in the front door, and I could see a Chinese couple going in with their son. Amy and Ray have definitely moved away.'

I smile with relief. 'Fabulous. She must have made the poor bugger go and change bungalows. Amy can be a right harridan when she doesn't get her own way.'

'I still can't believe they're on the same island as us,' Cara says, getting up from the bed and stretching her arms out wide. 'Of all the bad luck.'

'Yeah. Bad luck,' I reply in a non-committal tone, before going back to the important business of drying my hair – which is already bone dry, if we're being honest about it.

I'm doing this because, of course, I'm still *not* being honest about why it's not such an astounding coincidence that Amy and Ray have chosen this island.

'I'll get dressed and we'll go over for breakfast,' I tell Cara, as I head back to the wardrobes, so she's out of sight.

Coward.

When I emerge back into the main room, Cara is standing, looking out of the glass double doors at the horizon. She looks absolutely adorable in her jean shorts and flip flops. Her long chestnut hair is tied up in a ponytail, and I have to once again wonder how I managed to find myself in a relationship with someone like her.

You're far too old for her, I tell myself for the millionth time. And for the millionth time I ignore myself.

'You look lovely,' I tell Cara, as I move over to hug her from behind.

'Thank you,' she replies and turns her head to give me a kiss. Her face then turns a little quizzical. 'You look . . . *different.*'

'Really? How?'

She tilts her head. 'I don't know. Maybe a little less . . . *tight?* Around the eyes?'

I look out on to the horizon. 'It's probably that,' I venture. 'Views like that have a habit of making your eyeballs relax a bit.'

Cara laughs. 'Maybe, but maybe it's just because we're away from work.'

I nod. 'Quite possibly. It's nice to be free and clear from somewhere you've been crashing and burning for so long.'

Cara shakes her head and frowns. 'Stop that. You're brilliant at your job. I wouldn't be half the saleswoman I am without everything you've shown me over the past eighteen months. It's one of the main reasons why I'm with you.' She grins. 'That, and that cute smile of yours. You can't help it if some people at work are arseholes, and things are . . . a bit dry for you at the moment.'

'More than a bit,' I say ruefully.

Cara kisses me again. 'Forget about it. We're here now, and work doesn't matter.'

'Okay,' I say, really trying my hardest to agree with her.

'Good. Now, let's go to breakfast, shall we? I'm famished,' Cara says, patting her belly.

'Yep. Me too. Let's go.'

Which we do, holding hands, and delighted to be out and about on such a beautiful day.

There's nothing quite like the first full morning of a holiday. You've had a decent wash and a good night's sleep, and feel ready to take on the day.

And by 'take on the day' I mean eat as much as is humanly possible and fart about for the rest of the day, doing nothing much at all. Day one of a holiday should always be spent this way. There's plenty of time for all of those excursions and that entertainment business later. Day one should be all about indulging your inner sloth.

Two things put a massive smile on my face when we reach the restaurant area, and the breakfast buffet. The first is that they are serving waffles. I adore waffles more than is healthy for a man in his late thirties. Especially when you add bacon and maple syrup into the equation.

The second is that there is no sign of Amy or Ray. And because they're not here, it means I'll probably avoid them completely this morning. Amy is always an early riser on the first day of a holiday. I have no idea why, but it's just the way she is. If they're not in here now, then they'll have been and gone already, given that it's nearly ten o'clock.

They turned up after Cara and me at dinner last night. I caught sight of them over by the seafood buffet, while I was sipping my second Sin City of the night. Luckily, they didn't sit anywhere near us, so I was able to just about digest my pad thai noodles okay and drink my cocktail, but I can't pretend that the joy of my favourite Wimbufushi drink wasn't somewhat marred by the knowledge that they were quite close by.

My breakfast this morning is *fantastic*, and by the time half eleven rolls around, I am ready to roll out of this restaurant, and go for a nice bimble around the island. There's a hammock slung between two palm trees on the western end I want to give a very close inspection.

'Don't forget we're booked into the spa at midday,' Cara says, sipping her coffee.

I try my hardest not to grimace.

I'd forgotten about that.

Forgotten that Cara spent a good couple of hours last week booking us in on a lot of the island's activities – which includes a visit to the luxury day spa.

Spas conjure up images of mud and cucumbers in my head. Two things that have no business being thought of at the same time. Mud is something you encounter when at a music festival, or on a long hike. Cucumbers are strictly the province of afternoon tea and clumsy innuendo. They should never be put together, under any acceptable circumstances.

I'm not sure I want to visit the Wimbufushi Spa, but I fear I may have no choice in the matter. Cara has made the bookings, you see, and has already paid the extra. I just want to work on my convincing impression of a stunned sloth for the rest of the day, but instead I will have to go to a building where people will come at me with mud and cucumbers.

'What did you say I could have done?' I ask Cara.

What I mean is: what is the easiest spa treatment I can have? But I can't say that, as I don't want to sound unenthusiastic about the whole thing. This holiday has not got off to the best start with the whole Amy business, so I'm keen to make sure Cara gets what she wants today, with me along for the ride.

'A relaxing massage, Joel. You need one. I don't expect you to have the stones treatment like I'm having, but a massage will be really good for you. Help you relax a little.'

She's right about that. The last few years at RL&H have left me tighter than a snare drum. Struggling to find and maintain a client list when you've lost your mojo completely will do that to you.

'Okay, that sounds fine to me.' It doesn't really, but I want to make Cara happy.

'Great. Shall we head over there then? Make sure we're on time?'

'Absolutely.'

We both rise from our seats, and head off in the direction of the spa, which is housed within several small huts on stilts over the water, on the southern edge of Wimbufushi.

This requires us to walk around the island, as there is no way to cut through the middle – that's where all the staff live, and is strictly off limits to us gormless tourists.

I'm thoroughly enjoying the stroll along the white sandy beach until . . .

. . . yes, you've guessed it. Look who's coming the other way, from out of the luxury spa we're about to enter?

'Oh shit,' I say, slightly under my breath, as I watch them walk down on to the sand, and in our direction.

'No. Don't do that, Joel,' Cara replies. 'We're here to enjoy ourselves, and we're not going to let those two ruin that, are we?'

I see the determination on her face, and it puts steel resolve in my spine. 'No. You're right. We're not.'

I take her hand and plaster on what I hope is a happy and relaxed expression.

As we get closer to Amy and Ray, I can see that they too are doing their best to not seem bothered about running into us.

Therefore, please enjoy four people who all look like they've just been told by the serial killer that he likes to keep people alive who look happy all the time.

'Morning!' Ray says in a cheery voice, as we all come within chatting distance. There isn't a crackle of dark energy in the air, but you'd be forgiven for expecting one.

'Hello!' Cara replies, equally enthusiastically. I can feel the grip on my hand tighten.

'Lovely, isn't it!' I crow, sounding ecstatic about the mere fact I'm alive.

'Absolutely,' Amy says, in what anyone else would assume is a calm and relaxed manner, but I know is the potential prelude to the serial killer getting a taste of his own medicine. 'Are you . . . are you headed for the spa?'

Translation: *Die in the pits of hell, Joel.*

'Yes, that's the plan!' I reply.

Translation: *You first.*

'It's a great way to relax.'

Translation: *Oh no. Please. After you. I can kick you in the arse-hole, to get you moving.*

'Yes. So I've heard. Very much looking forward to it.'

Translation: *Yes, I'd better go before you, just to warn them all that something far worse than them is about to appear.*

It may be thirty-two degrees today, but in this little patch of Maldivian beach it's about twenty below.

'Well, we'll be off for our treatment, then. Don't want to be late,' Cara says, sensing that if she doesn't get me away from this little conflab soon, my hastily constructed façade of holiday happiness will completely fall apart.

'Yes. We're off to do a bit of sunbathing,' Ray tells her.

'Well, enjoy that then.'

I feel Cara pull at my hand, and I'm happy to be led away. There's a final moment where Amy and I lock eyes again. Somewhere – far away, deep below us, and in a place even hotter than this beach – I hear a shrill scream of terror.

'Bloody hell,' I say explosively, as we continue our way down the beach and on to the boardwalk leading to the spa's eight huts – the first of which is the small reception for the facility, being manned by two slight Maldivian women in identical white spa outfits, which have a touch of pyjamas about them, and more than a little medical scrubs.

'Well done, you did very well,' Cara tells me as we approach them. And I'm inclined to agree with her. Amy will not have the satisfaction of seeing me unhappy today.

It's a bloody good job she's not standing next to me now then, as I am told what treatment I'm going to have to endure in this spa – a full body massage.

I *do not* want a full body massage.

'Full body' implies that there will be attention paid to the bottom. And the bottom is a man's own private kingdom. I do not want it assailed by a small Maldivian woman.

But . . . I promised I would do everything I could to keep Cara happy, so I continue to affect my holiday-happy expression as I am led away into a nearby hut by one of the girls, who identifies herself as Suha – a pretty little woman who can't be more than five feet tall.

Suha bids me enter the small changing area in one corner of the hut – which is decorated exactly like our water bungalow, only with the addition of a large massage table and a variety of big glass pots full of some kind of oil. No idea what the oil is, but there's an awful lot of it about. The massage room is open to the ocean, of course. Just like every other building here on the island.

My masseuse tells me that she's just going to pop out while I get myself comfortable, and will return very soon. She suggests I strip down to my underwear and lie on the massage table, covering myself with the towel that she's placed on it.

This is fine, as I don't particularly want to get undressed with her in the room.

After I've divested myself of my clothes, I nervously settle on to the table, and await Suha's return.

I really should try to relax and look forward to this. Cara is right – a nice massage *will* do me the world of good.

But it's very hard to get my muscles to unbunch, not least because I've just had another run-in with my ex-wife.

And when I hear what I think is her voice again, coming from somewhere outside, they tighten even more. I prop myself up, breathless on the table, waiting to hear if I'm right – that the witch queen has returned to haunt me – but when I hear nothing more, I take a few deep breaths and lie flat again. I must have been mistaken. She's probably long gone with Ray, off to torment the local sea creatures with her looks of disapproval, no doubt.

A couple of minutes later Suha returns, carrying a basket of massage oils, seeming a tad out of sorts. There's a slight look of confusion on her face for a few moments, but by the time she's chosen which oil to use, and clipped it to her belt, the composed look has reappeared.

'Okay, Mr Sinclair. Please just relax and let me get to work. Would you like some music on?'

'Why not?' I reply.

'Alexa,' Suha says, over to the white Echo on the table in one corner, 'play album one.'

The massage room is instantly filled with calm, plinky plonky music. I'm sure it has a proper name, but I always like to think of it as plinky plonky music. Okay, there's some *wumm*ing going on as well, and not a little *blang*ing here and there, but it's mostly plinky plonky.

Suha does indeed get to work, by rubbing massage oil into my back, and starting to run her fingers over my muscles in a way that I find both disconcerting and quite pleasurable. It feels like she's lightly probing me for signs of tension and pain, which she has no problem finding, given that I am basically one giant ball of tension these days.

But what she's doing feels quite marvellous, so I relax a little more on to the table, enjoying both the plinky plonky music and her probey wobey fingers.

Boy, Cara was on to a winner here. I don't know why I ever doubted her. A man could get used to this kind of treatm—

Meeaaaargh!

What the hell is she doing?

I can feel Suha's thumb digging into what is clearly a large knot just below my right shoulder blade. This sends a bolt of pain through me.

'Just relax and take a nice deep breath,' she says, continuing to apply pressure.

Jesus Christ. Relax? With her thumb digging right in and—

. . . *oh.*

Actually, I do feel the pain going away. And a weird sense of 'loosening' around the area the knot is in.

After a moment, Suha relaxes and takes her thumb away, leaving me with an ache in the area she prodded that is not altogether unpleasant.

Let's hope that's the only knot like that she finds, because I—

Uuuurrrgggh!

Nope, there's another one! This time on the left side, close to my neck. The pain from this is worse than the first. It's like somebody has decided to stick a ball point pen in me. But again, Suha

95

commands me take a deep breath. And I do so, feeling that odd loosening sensation once more.

This is obviously what her ministrations are meant to accomplish, but I'm not so sure the benefit is worth all the pai—

Bleeerrghhh!

This one's on the lower left of my back, right where my kidney is. Or, should I say, where my kidney was, because I'm sure the hideous pressure she's applying must have dislodged it.

I can't stand this. It's just too much. I thought I was getting a nice, gentle massage, but instead I'm being stabbed repeatedly by thumbs that must be constructed of titanium. I should just get up and leave before she's allowed to do any more damage.

But then Cara's face swims into view, and I know I have to endure this massage until it's over. She's paid for me to have this, to help me with my tension problems, so I should see it through. And what Suha's doing is relieving tension, even if that comes with a large degree of agon—

Vluuurrrggh!

Suha thumbs me in the neck on the right-hand side this time, so at least the resultant dull aches will feel more balanced up.

How is she doing this?

Suha is barely tall enough to go on rides at Chessington, and is skinnier than the latte I have to drink these days to keep my cholesterol levels low. How is she able to summon up such force?

I take another couple of deep breaths as she continues to work on me, willing this massage to end, but knowing it has really only just begun.

I have to trust Cara though. I have to trust that she knows what's best for me. This will *help me*. It may feel like I'm being ramrodded by a sentient jackhammer, but the results must be worth it.

Listen to the plinky plonky, Joel.

Concentrate on the plinky plonky.

Feel the warm Maldivian sea breeze caress your skin, and lose yourself in the plinky plonky. That's the only way you're going to get through this.

Yes.

The plinky plonky.

Ignore the stabby wabby, and the agony wagony, and just listen to the plinky plonky.

. . .

This does help.

Marginally.

With it, I am able to endure the next ten minutes of Suha continuing to target every knot and cramp in both my back and my legs.

And then, she moves on to my bottom.

We have already discussed how a man's bottom is his own private kingdom, and should be respected as such, but the invading force of little Suha is not taking any prisoners. The Kingdom of the Sinclair Rear is getting the blitzkrieg treatment, and there's nothing I can do about it, if I don't want to upset Cara.

Remember the plinky plonky.

It will save you.

But all the relaxing spa music in the world cannot possibly hope to take your mind off having a small Maldivian woman thumbing your arse. I doubt there is anything in the world that could do that – save for maybe having another small Maldivian woman thumbing your balls.

Suha isn't actually getting into any places she shouldn't – her thumb is working at the outside of my buttocks, close to my hip – but I still feel violated, nonetheless. Even if every time she relaxes her thumb, I feel that intense sense of loosening going on in the muscles she's working at.

I can safely say that I haven't felt the tension leave my body like this in months. It's just a crying shame that it has to be replaced by a kind of horrific sweet ache that now suffuses my entire being. I feel like I've been trampled by a cow that's simultaneously force fed me a pound of cannabis. I'm completely exhausted by it all.

'Are you okay, Mr Sinclair?' Suha asks, as she relieves the pressure on my left buttock.

'Blrrrrrmmm,' I reply, unable to give her any more than that.

'Okay, that's good,' she replies with a pleased tone to her voice.

She must be fluent in the language of The Massaged. Able to discern what people are saying to her through slack, squashed lips with practised ease.

I'm not one hundred per cent sure she's translated my mutterings all that accurately, though. I'm not sure 'blrrrrrmmm' means 'Why yes, Suha. I am having a most satisfactory and relaxing time. Pray continue to dig your thumb into my bodily person while I enjoy the plinky plonky.'

Maybe I should elucidate further on my ambivalence towards the treatment she's currently administering. Possibly it might be a good idea to ask her to stop, before every single part of the back of my body is crying out.

'Mrrrrrrrble,' I say, as Suha thumbs me right up both sides of my spine, running all over the bits she's being poking and prodding. This wakes them all up again, and the ache returns to full on pain.

I can't take any more. I must say something.

'Hrrrrrrgle.'

No. Something a little more lucid than that, you pillock!

And then Suha says something that's guaranteed to keep me up at nights. 'Now please flip on to your front.'

I shouldn't do it. I should just thank her very much for everything she's done, and get the hell out of here – but again my thoughts return to Cara. She wanted me to go through this massage, and I must trust her. Trust her that being meticulously thumbed by a psychopathic five-foot Maldivian woman is just the ticket. Just the thing to make Joel Sinclair a happier, calmer individual.

And so, I do as I am told, and Suha gets going on the front of my thighs and arms.

Now I'm on my back, and my face isn't quite so smushed into the massage table, my speaking in the language of The Massaged has changed accent.

'Heeeeeeee,' I say to Suha, like a moped in the distance.

I realise that the plinky plonky has ended, and has turned into more of a ting tang tong. This is a slightly rarer form of calming spa music, employing the doubtful tones of what sounds like a small metal cup being whacked rhythmically with a spoon. It's not as 'relaxing' as the plinky plonky, if I'm being honest, but it still does the job of taking my mind off where Suha's thumbs are going.

The massage (or torture, depending on your point of view and pain-tolerance threshold) goes on for another ten minutes, all while the ting tang tong echoes around the room.

Suha eventually finishes up with having a good old poke around my neck. She cradles my head in both hands, and starts to work at the back of my skull with all of her fingers.

'Haaaaaaaa,' I say, indicating that the moped has acquired a couple of extra strokes to its engine.

So, now I am one giant ache from head to toe. It doesn't feel like there's a spot left on my body that doesn't hurt.

This means that Suha is done for the day. And I should be grateful, but now I very probably have to move off this table, and I'm not convinced that's going to be possible for me.

'Please feel free to lie here for a while before dressing,' Suha tells me. 'I will return to the reception area and await you.'

'Than' you,' I manage to say. Not sure what I'm thanking her for, mind you. Probably for stopping.

Suha departs, leaving me once again alone in the massage room. This time, though, I am one of The Massaged, as opposed to an ordinary, functioning human being – irrevocably altered by the experience I have just undergone.

I can't move for a good five minutes – the prospect is just too horrifying to contemplate.

But eventually, as with all things, my time here must come to an end. I have to leave, before Suha returns and decides she hasn't thumbed me enough for one day, and wants to have a go at my internal workings. I can only imagine what having my pancreas poked by Suha would feel like.

Taking what I hope is a deep enough breath, I lift my head and shoulders, marvelling at two things as I do. One is the fact that my entire back feels a lot more languid than it did half an hour ago, and two is because it feels like the fucking cow we spoke of earlier has trampled over me again, this time wearing hobnail boots and listening to The Sex Pistols.

'Oh fuck a duck,' I say breathlessly, as I sit upright and try to move my legs over the side of the table to get off. Every movement is agony. Loose, flowing agony.

I manage to stand with the assistance of holding on to the table, and begin the complicated and long process of getting over to the changing area to put my board shorts and t-shirt back on again.

Picture, if you will, someone doing an impression of C3PO from *Star Wars* while comprehensively drunk.

That's about right, I think.

I can't help but let out a moan of pain as I step back into my shorts, followed by a wail of absolute distress as I put the t-shirt back on over my head.

I then shuffle my way over to the door to the massage room, and pause. I can't go outside like this. I'll look like I've aged sixty years in the space of thirty minutes. What will Cara think? I don't want her to see that the massage she recommended for me has left me in this state. It would upset her greatly.

I have to shake it off a bit and pretend I'm extremely pleased about the treatment I've just undergone.

And it's one thing to pretend you're in a good mood to your ex-wife while strolling down the beach, but it's quite another to pretend you are to your girlfriend, after Pat the Cow has moshed her way through 'God Save The Queen' across your entire body.

I spend a few moments arranging my face into one of relaxed contentment. I think I do a pretty good job, excepting maybe for the twitch coming from my left eye.

With this done, I open the door and step out on to the broad walkway that all of the spa's huts are accessible from, and make my way gingerly back to the reception.

No! Not *gingerly*! Stride like you've just had the greatest experience of your life!

I attempt this, but it's very hard to stride when you're a ball of agony. It comes off looking more like I'm being puppeted along by someone with a healthy dose of Parkinson's.

I spot Cara at the reception desk, chatting to the other Maldivian girl, who must have administered her hot stone treatment.

I have no idea what a hot stone treatment is, but if it's anything on the level of what I've had done, it must have involved the insertion of said hot stones into many bodily orifices.

Cara doesn't appear to look like she's had a boiling pebble shoved up her bum, though, so I guess I'm the only one who's been through torture this afternoon.

'Joel! How did it go?'

'Super! Lovely! Enjoyed every minute of it!'

Cara looks aghast. 'Why are you talking like that?'

'Talking like what?'

'In that weird high-pitched voice?'

'Am I?'

'Yes! Didn't the massage go well?'

Bloody hell, I'd better lower my voice an octave or two, or I'll really give the game away.

'Oh yes!' I tell her, compensating for all I'm worth. 'It was super! Smashing! Lovely! Great!'

'Why are you talking like the *Bullseye* man?'

'Pardon me?'

'You're talking like the *Bullseye* man. The guy who used to host that show Grandad always loved to watch when I was little.'

'Jim Bowen?'

'That's the one. Why are you talking like Jim Bowen, the *Bullseye* man?'

I don't know, Cara. Why does anyone do anything these days?

'The massage wasn't good, was it?' Cara says, looking anxious.

Oh, fuck it. I've messed up royally here. I haven't convinced her at all.

Time to come clean, I think.

So you're going to tell her that this island is where you came with Amy, then?

Fuck off, brain! You're not helping! Go back to day dreaming about the plinky plonky music, or I'll get Suha to give you the thumbing of your squishy life!

'Joel? What happened?'

My face scrunches up. 'It was the *thumbs*, Cara!'

'You what?'

'She *thumbed* me. She thumbed me all over!'

'She thumbed you?'

'Yes! The whole time! The levels of thumbage were completely off the charts!'

Cara's brow furrows. 'That's not right, though. I just booked you in for a nice full body massage. It was supposed to be relaxing and gentle.'

I shake my head. 'No, no. Not gentle. Not relaxing.' I hold up both thumbs in front of her. 'Thumbs, Cara. It was all thumbs.' I wiggle them about a bit to underline my point.

Cara turns and sees Suha at the back of the reception, arranging bottles of massage oil. 'Excuse me?' she says.

Suha turns and walks over with a practised smile on her face. 'Yes? What can I do for you, Miss Rowntree?'

'The massage you just gave my boyfriend . . . He says you . . . thumbed him a lot. That's not usually part of a full body massage, is it?'

Suha looks confused. 'No, madam. I gave Mr Sinclair the full acupressure remedial sports massage.'

Cara looks dumbfounded. 'Why did you do that?'

Suha continues to look very confused. 'Because your friend asked me to change it to that. She paid the extra money for it.'

'What friend?' Cara and I say in unison.

Now Suha looks a little terrified, as if coming to some sort of horrible realisation. 'Your . . . your friend came up to me before the treatment, and told me you'd be happier with the remedial treatment.' Suha looks at me. 'She told me your name, your date of birth, and what bungalow you were in. She said you really wanted to have a proper remedial massage, but was afraid you couldn't afford it, so she paid the extra.' Suha smiles, trying to extricate herself from a situation that's clearly getting away from her. 'I thought it was a very nice gift for her to give you.'

My jaw – so recently loosened by Suha's administrations – tightens enormously. 'This . . . *friend*. Was she about this high, with blond hair and wearing white shorts?' I say to her, hovering my hand at about Amy's height.

Suha nods. 'Why, yes.' She looks scared to death. 'Is she not your friend? Should I not have changed the massage?'

I can't speak. My mouth has stopped working. The sheer, unbridled fucking *cheek* of my ex-wife has rendered me mute.

'No, no. It's not your fault,' Cara tells the girl. 'You've done nothing wrong. Thank you very much.'

'Grrrrrrd,' I say. This is not the language of The Massaged. This is the language of The Enraged. I doubt it's a language poor Suha speaks. Her job is to make sure people don't feel that way.

I turn towards the beach, not uttering another word, and begin to walk towards it, still wincing like a mad thing at all the pain in my body – which I now know has been caused by Amy Caddick and her never-ending supply of pure evil.

I should have *known*. I should have known that she'd do something like this. After all, this is the person who did all she could to ruin my reputation at Rowntree Land & Home after what happened with Goblin Central. She blamed me for the loss of that contract then (even though I did everything bloody *right*!), and now she has the *barefaced* cheek to deliberately change my massage from a nice, relaxing one, into something that will ensure I'll be having nightmares about giant Maldivian thumbs coming at me for the rest of my life.

I hit the beach, staggering angrily away from the spa. All I want to do now is get back to the bungalow and soak in a nice hot bath, which will hopefully do something to take this hideous all-body ache away.

Any relaxation that my muscles may have undergone has been completely wiped away by my ex-wife's audacity. They are as tense as they have ever been.

'Fucking bloody fucking woman, and her fucking bloody fucking bloody cheek . . .' I grumble to myself as I lurch along the beach.

'Joel! Hang on!' Cara says, trying to catch up with me. When she does, she puts an arm in mine and slows me down. 'Are you okay?'

'Okay?! No, Cara, I'm not okay!'

I instantly regret this outburst. None of this is my girlfriend's fault. She's not the one I should be mad at.

'I'm so *sorry*, Cara,' I say to her, trying to get my rage under control. 'None of this is your fault.'

'No. It's that *bitch's*.'

The venom in Cara's voice is quite something. She's usually such an upbeat person. This is a side of her I've never seen before, and I would be worried about it were it not for the fact that she's angry at Amy.

Amy could make Gandhi homicidal, so I'm more than happy to give this dark turn in Cara's demeanour a pass.

'Why would she *do* something like that?' Cara asks, eyes burning.

I shrug my shoulders. 'That's Amy for you. Vindictive, she is. You know what she was like after the marriage broke down, before she left the agency. Spent her entire time trying to convince everyone it was my fault we lost Goblin Central.'

'Yeah, I remember you saying.' Cara looks indignant. 'I can't believe she did that. You *did* put the right time in that calendar.'

'I did!'

'And there's *every* chance she could have accidentally altered it herself in the weeks leading up to the meeting.'

'Exactly!' I reply, nodding enthusiastically.

'And then to take so much from you in the divorce settlement. To be so vindictive about it all . . .'

'I know!'

'Anyone who'd do that . . . well, it's no surprise she'd play such a horrible trick on you.' Cara then hugs me in a manner full of both sympathy and understanding. It's rather lovely.

I am once again reminded of how great she's been in the last few months since we started dating, and how none of what's going on here now is her responsibility. She's just got caught up with a very nasty individual, who I was once stupid enough to marry.

What if Amy had changed Cara's treatment, and not mine?

The mere thought of this makes my blood boil even more.

Oh . . . you're not going to get away with this, Amy. I don't know how I'm going to get you back for this, but I will. I promise you that.

Revenge is coming, Amy Caddick. And there will come a time when it will be served on you for the things you've done today. You mark my words!

Big, serious, long words!

Not plinky plonky! Not ting tang tong!

No!

Revenge!

It will be mine, and it will be *sweet*!

Wednesday

AMY – REVENGE IS SAVOURY

Okay.

I probably shouldn't have done it.

I should have just walked away from the spa, let Joel have his massage, and got on with my holiday.

But . . .

It was such a *perfect* opportunity, wasn't it?

And it was only a practical joke. Nothing too nasty. Just a little dig in Joel's ribs, to help make me feel better about losing my sunset.

I told Ray I needed to pop back to the spa because I'd forgotten my sunglasses (which I had, by the way! I'd left them on the counter at the reception) and when I got back there, I saw Joel's name on a ledger in front of Fareeda, the lovely girl who'd done my shiatsu.

And then . . . I don't know. The devil got into me, I guess. A devil created by the past few days of having Joel Sinclair close to me again, and all the bad memories that his presence has dredged up.

It was simplicity itself to tell Fareeda and the girl working on Joel that he really wanted the remedial massage instead. They took me at my word, once I'd convinced them I knew Joel well.

And I *do* know him well!

. . . well enough to know that getting such a hardcore massage would be the last thing he'd want.

But the devil spoke in my ear, and I did what I did – and then I ran away giggling to myself.

Actually, properly *giggling*. Like a bloody schoolgirl.

It all seemed like such a jolly jape at the time. But now – as I sit here on the edge of the bed, chewing a fingernail and staring out past the veranda at the sun not setting – I'm forced to conclude that it probably wasn't such a good idea after all.

And I know this because I haven't told Ray about it. Which means I'm feeling guilt and shame about my actions, and don't want him to look at me with disappointment. Because that's what he would do, I just *know it*. He wouldn't approve of me stooping to such a childish act – and I'm pretty sure I actually agree with him on that one.

There's nothing I can do about it now, though. What's done is done.

I'm sure Joel didn't mind a harder massage than he was expecting, anyway. It probably did him some *good*. He looked incredibly tense this morning as we passed them both on the beach.

Yes.

Yes, that's right. I didn't do anything wrong, *really*.

It's not like I cocked up an appointment and pushed my ex-wife out of a job, is it?

That steels my resolve again.

No.

Everything is fine. There's nothing to worry about.

'Are you ready to go?' Ray asks me, as he comes out from behind the wall our bed is against, dressed in a rather fetching set of white linen trousers and shirt.

'Yes, I think so,' I reply, getting up from the bed. This is made a little awkward by the fact I'm wearing my brand-new yellow Boden dress, which I probably should have bought in a size larger, if I'm being honest with myself. It's fine when I'm upright, but a little tight when I'm seated.

But it flatters my bottom to such a degree that I'm happy to put up with a little discomfort. It's only for one evening . . . and this is a special evening, after all.

Wimbufushi's Twilight Meal and Movie event has become something of a legend on TripAdvisor. I've read countless reviews of how wonderful it is over the past few months, and am incredibly eager to experience it for myself. It wasn't something they did when I was here six years ago, and is one of the highlights of this holiday that I've been anticipating the most.

The set-up is simple: the island's guests eat a prepared meal on the sands, under a beautiful twilight sky, before moving over to a lot of comfy beanbags when it gets completely dark, to plop themselves down in front of a temporarily erected movie screen for the main feature.

The film tonight is *An Affair To Remember*, which is a lovely old romance that I remember watching when I was an impressionable teenager. It may have just been the rampant hormones, but I recall it having quite an emotional effect on me, and I'm looking forward to seeing if it has a similar impact as an adult.

I'm *not* looking forward to Joel and Miss Rowntree being there – which they are bound to be, because of how popular the Twilight Meal and Movie is. Nobody comes to Wimbufushi these days without attending the event, and I know Joel is a bit of a sucker for old movies. Their presence is virtually guaranteed.

Unless he can't move properly because of that massage you made him have.

'I'm really looking forward to this,' I say to Ray, ignoring my annoying conscience. It's not going to do me any good to dwell further on my mistake from earlier.

'Me too,' he replies, and slips a hand into mine. 'Shall we?'

'Yes!' I say, and give him a huge smile.

The prospect of snuggling up to Ray on a big beanbag, while a classic romance plays out in front of me, is one that makes my heart flutter with pleasure.

As does the sight that greets us, as we arrive at the long, broad expanse of sand that makes up almost the entire western side of Wimbufushi island.

The usual thatched wooden umbrellas that we lie under to stay out of the hot tropical sun have been removed to make way for about two dozen tables, each lit with their own bamboo torch. Further along from these are an equal number of beanbags, set out in four staggered lines in front of a large white screen and digital projector.

Above my head the sky is a fiery orange colour, as the sun disappears below the horizon. Very soon, the inky blues and blacks of the early night will replace the diminishing influence of the sun, and the stars will start to come out – tiny pinpricks of incandescent light in an ocean of silky darkness.

Yes . . . I have been fantasising about this moment for a long time now. So much so that I am able to describe it in such a lyrical fashion. I'm normally a very straightforward kind of woman, not prone to such flights of fancy, but give me half a chance and a decent run up, and I can be poetic. Even if it is done is a somewhat clichéd fashion.

From the pocket of his linen trousers, Ray produces a card, which was hand delivered in an envelope to us by one of the island's staff earlier this afternoon. On it is our invitation to the Twilight Meal and Movie. Needless to say there's a lot of gold embossing going on with the invitation. It wouldn't be right without it.

'We're on table twenty-two,' Ray says. He looks up and surveys the layout in front of us. 'They've all got the numbers on those little bamboo signs. Let's go find ours.'

I nod in agreement, and we make our way between the carefully laid-out tables and find ours quite close to the beanbags. As we sit down, I make a point of not looking for Joel Sinclair. A lot of the other guests are starting to sit down at their own tables, but I have no interest in seeing if any of them are my ex-husband and his young girlfriend. This is going to be a happy, fun evening for me. For me and Ray.

A waiter comes over to our table and pours us both water. He asks us what drinks we'd like, and I chose a margarita while Ray opts for a whiskey sour.

After the waiter has returned with them, Ray and I spend the next few minutes chatting and sipping our cocktails, as we wait for every guest to take their seat.

I don't even let the smile falter on my face when I do see Joel arrive just over Ray's left shoulder. He's walking a bit awkwardly. Actually, he looks like he's in a fair amount of pain. My grip on the margarita glass tightens ever so slightly, as I try to concentrate on what Ray is telling me – something about orders for the new Sunseeker yacht when it gets released next month. But I'm having trouble paying attention, as my heart has risen into my throat because I've realised that my little practical joke has definitely not been treated as such. Joel looks genuinely distressed.

And then, after he's sat down gingerly in his seat, he scans the tables around him, and his eyes momentarily lock with mine.

I instantly look down at my drink, feeling a flush of shame suffuse my face.

Don't! Don't do that. You made a silly mistake, but Joel doesn't deserve to see you looking upset!

Ray is finishing his story about how the Sunseeker rep lost his shoe over the side of the catamaran last week, and when he stops talking and smiles, I look right at him and laugh, as if I'd heard even half of what he had to say.

Ray looks a little taken aback at the strength of my reaction. A man losing a shoe over the side of a moored catamaran is somewhat amusing, but hardly warrants the level of laughter I'm responding with.

Never mind. If Joel is still looking over, he'll see me having a *whale* of a time. To back this up, I reach forward and take Ray's hand in mine.

Look how romantic I'm being!

Look how in love I am!

Look how everything is right in *my* world!

I don't look past Ray's shoulder again to see if Joel is taking in my little pantomime, even though every fibre of my being wants me to.

The waiter returns and asks us what we want for our meal.

I glance at him with a fixed smile on my face and pick up the menu. I have no idea what I want to eat. I haven't thought about it *at all*. Not when I've been concentrating so hard on not paying my ex-husband any attention, and looking like I'm having the time of my life.

I flip open the menu and scan down the page.

'I'll have the dover sole, please,' Ray tells the waiter, closing his menu and handing it to him.

Shit. I really should have paid closer attention to what I wanted to eat.

'I'll have . . . I'll have the . . . I'll have the Bolognaise, thank you.' It's a boring choice, but it's the only Italian thing on the menu, and I'm a sucker for Italian food. Always have been.

'Of course, madam,' the waiter replies with a smile.

'Only, do you do a vegetarian option? Beef gives me digestive problems.'

Oh God!

Why did I tell him *that*?! He doesn't have to know that!

My face flames red again, this time with embarrassment, but then I remember I'm trying to look like this is the best night of my life, so I grin at the waiter like he's just told me I've won the lottery.

'Of course, madam. We always have a vegetarian option.'

'Thank you!'

Grin a bit wider, woman. We might not look convincing enough at the moment.

Now I'm gurning at the poor bloke like I'm about to jump up and fork his eyeballs out. No wonder he hurries away from the table as fast as his legs can carry him.

'Are you okay, sweetheart?' Ray asks, taking in my over-the-top performance.

'Yes! Yes, I'm fine! Just happy to be here. Here with you. It's lovely.'

And boy do I look *happy*. So very, very bloody HAPPY.

Yes, yes. Happy, happy, happy, happy.

I'm having the time of my *bastard* life, right here, right now.

My eyes flick up over Ray's shoulder, and I can see that Joel is no longer sat in his seat. I'm acting like this for nothing.

I pick up my margarita and sling the rest of it down my neck.

'Whoa! Go easy, Amy!' Ray says with a chuckle. 'You might want to wait for your food.'

He's probably right, but the half glass of margarita is already working its magic as it warms by entire being. I give up trying to pretend I'm having the best time of my life, and instead try my hardest to just have a nice time. My audience has buggered off somewhere anyway, so no point in carrying on with this silly charade.

Over the next ten minutes, while we wait for our meals, I make a concerted effort not to pay Joel any attention whatsoever once he comes back to his seat – and I'm pleased to say I'm quite successful. It's not the easiest thing in the world to ignore how much fun your ex appears to be having with his new girlfriend over a glass of wine, but I give it my best of British, and whip my brain until it disregards everything he's doing.

I actually do such a good job of this that I've almost forgotten he's even here by the time the waiter pops a large bowl of spaghetti Bolognaise under my nose.

It smells absolutely divine.

I'm sure it *looks* fantastic as well, only it's a bit hard to tell because the sun has gone completely down now, and our only illumination is the bamboo torch next to the table. This does not give off much light though, so it's tremendously hard to actually see what my meal looks like.

Never mind. I guess you have to make some concessions when you're eating under the starlight on a gorgeous beach. I don't think I'd trade the glorious light show going on above my head for a better look at my spaghetti. The dark night sky is absolutely studded with stars. I can even pick out the banding of the Milky Way galaxy. *Amazing*.

What's also amazing is the Bolognaise.

'Bloody hell,' I remark, after swallowing. 'This is *incredible*.'

Ray picks up another piece of fish with his fork. 'I can't disagree. This is the best fish I've ever eaten.'

The quality of the food has reminded me how hungry I am, and I'm afraid to say I do not go about eating my meal in the most ladylike of fashions, though I am careful not to get sauce all down my dress.

Whatever soy or plant-based product they use as a replacement for the beef is extremely tasty. It's almost impossible to tell the difference.

The Bolognaise – along with the three pieces of soft, fluffy garlic bread that accompanied it – are gone in less than fifteen minutes. I have to sit there sipping my second margarita while Ray finishes off his dover sole. I do this with more of an intense level of concentration than is entirely necessary, fearing that if I don't, I might be tempted to look up and see what Joel is up to.

Aaargh.

Why can't I just *ignore* him? Why does he sit in the forefront my mind like a fat, ugly frog that won't just hop off somewhere else?

Having him constantly in my eyeline, laughing and joking with Cara, doesn't help matters.

I shift a little in my seat as I continue to not look over Ray's shoulder at all. My dress – which felt a little tight before I left the water bungalow – now starts to feel quite uncomfortable, given that I'm now full of vegetarian Bolognaise.

I can't wait to get out of this upright chair and into a big, relaxing beanbag.

Also, the two margaritas are making my head swim a bit, so lying down on something big and squishy will be a godsend.

However, a further forty-five minutes elapse before our hosts bid us go over to the beanbags, if we have finished our meals. It's taken them that long to get the projector set up for the film.

I grunt in relief as we're told this.

I never knew how hard to it was to not look at something for forty-five minutes.

Try it sometime. Sit yourself in a room with a painting on the wall right in front of you, and look at everything other than it for three quarters of an hour. It's a lot more difficult than you'd imagine.

I've been looking at Ray's face, looking at his plate, looking at my plate, looking at the stars overhead, looking at the guys setting up the projector . . . in fact, looking at everything and anything except the thing that the stupid part of my brain actually wants to look at.

I'm very tired. And knee deep into the third margarita of the evening.

Oh, leave me alone. It gave me something else to look at.

With some considerable relief, I rise from the table and walk over to the beanbags. I want to get in position near the front as quickly as possible, before Joel gets there as well. If I get the front row locked down, he'll sit further back, I just know it. Then I won't have to play Don't Look At Joel anymore tonight. It's not a game I enjoy, and certainly one I don't think I'm all that good at.

'Wait up!' Ray says, trying to keep up with me as I stumble over the silky sand, my head thrust forward in a determined manner.

Soz, Ray, but I want that front-row beanbag. The big orange one in the middle that looks the comfiest of the lot. Nothing will stop me getting it. We might be about to watch *An Affair To Remember*, but I'm more concerned right now with getting a beanbag to remember.

I snort a little laughter as I close in on my quarry.

The three margaritas have clearly gone to my head. I don't normally find beanbags that funny.

There's a tricky moment when a senior couple nearly gets to the orange beanbag ahead of me, but I've got a good thirty years on the pair of old codgers, so manage to nip in there just before they do.

Now.

If you recall, I'm wearing a tight Boden dress that makes my bottom look lovely.

What it doesn't do is accommodate settling down into a beanbag very well.

If I was sober, I'd probably spend a good few moments awkwardly lowering myself down into it. But as I'm three margaritas deep, I instead spin around to face the movie screen, fling my arms out wide, and fall back into the big soft bag with a squeal of delight.

Ray arrives to find me spread-eagled, and can't help but laugh. 'You're drunk,' he accuses.

'I am not!' I insist. 'I'm just . . . just happy to be here.' Which is the God's honest truth. I think this is the happiest I've been since we arrived on the island, thanks to the alcohol and food.

Fuck Joel and his pre-pubescent girlfriend. I'm having a good time, and I'm about to watch a lovely romantic movie, with a lovely romantic man.

Super-duper.

Ray takes his place next to me and I immediately wrap myself around his left arm. Ray has *marvellous* biceps. I enjoy them at every opportunity that's presented to me.

I stay in this position, talking with Ray about nothing in particular, while the rest of the island's guests finish their meals and join us on the beanbags.

I am delighted to note that I have no idea where Joel and Cara have sat down. They're certainly not in the front row.

Lovely stuff.

Azim – Wimbufushi's main host, and wearer of all things white and pristine – stands in front of the screen, and introduces tonight's film. We all give him a polite clap as he then exits stage left, and the screen goes from plain white to a very old school Twentieth Century Fox logo. The picture quality is much better than I expected it to be – we're getting the full letterbox, widescreen experience here.

That ever-so-famous Fox fanfare plays, giving way to a snowy credits sequence and the film's theme song, sung by a man who must have taken a thousand lessons in how to croon that effectively.

I snuggle down into the beanbag even more as the credits roll, losing myself in both the nostalgia unfolding on the screen in front of me, and the warm, comforting glow of alcohol.

I stay that way for the first part of the movie, watching Cary Grant and Deborah Kerr begin a friendship that will eventually blossom into love aboard the *SS Constitution*.

By the time they make their promises to one another to meet again atop the Empire State Building, I am struggling a little to keep my eyes open. This beanbag is comfy, the air is warm, and the gentle sea breeze is wonderful.

Only Deborah Kerr's car accident shakes me out of my reverie a bit, but that only lasts for another few minutes or so before I'm back feeling snoozy again.

I'm trying my hardest to concentrate on the movie, but it's just so hard when you're—

Prrrp.

Oh God.

I just *farted*.

I throw a glance at Ray to see if he noticed.

No . . .

Thank God. He's wrapped up in what's going on with poor old Deborah Kerr and her injuries.

I have never farted in front of Ray. Not audibly, anyway. And I don't intend to start now.

Prrrrp.

Aaaargh! What the hell?!

Two unintended farts in a row?

That *never* happens to me.

Unintended farts that creep out whether you like it or not are supposed to only happen after you've passed the age of retirement. I'm far too young to be experiencing them!

Then I feel my stomach roll.

Any drowsiness I might have been feeling due to the comfortable beanbag and alcohol haze has instantly disappeared.

Grrrngle.

That was my stomach – or more accurately, my *bowels*.

I shift in the beanbag a little, so that I'm sat more or less upright. I can feel pain and discomfort starting to blossom in my bowelular area, and it is disconcerting to say the least.

Frrrrrrrrr.

Another fart – this one longer and more . . . er . . . *generous.* But it's happily captured by the beanbag, and rendered silent by it.

I look at Ray again, who is still engrossed in the movie. That accident must have really had an effect on him.

I think I'm going to have an accident that will have a bloody effect on me too, if I'm not careful. Okay, it won't be as bad as losing the use of my legs, like poor Deborah, but losing control of my bowels all over this beanbag won't exactly be a fucking walk in the park either.

I need to get up and get back to the bungalow, for what is fast becoming the need for an urgent poo.

To begin this process, I sit up a little straighter in the beanbag, and shift my upper body forward.

This results in another bottom burp. One that would have ended with a prize, if I hadn't immediately sat back down again and clenched my butt cheeks together.

Oh *fuck.*

Oh fuck, oh fuck, oh fuck.

I'm going to shit myself in front of Cary Grant.

'Are you okay, Amy?' Ray asks, having finally pulled away from the romantic drama unfolding before his eyes, thanks to me moving around so much.

'Yes. I think so. Just . . . just a little uncomfortable, thanks to my dress.'

That seems like a decent excuse. It's a half-truth, anyway. This dress is not the type of thing you want to be wearing in a beanbag. It's also not the type of thing you want to be wearing when your bowels are becoming more and more distressed by the minute. Distressed bowels require loose, flowing clothes. If I move too fast in this damn thing, I'll end up squeezing my stomach area, and forcing out another fart.

I really do need to get up.

'I think . . . I think I'm going to go and get changed,' I tell Ray.

'Aw . . . but you'll miss the movie.'

'That's okay. This is a boring part anyway.' It's not a boring part at all. We're just getting to the bit where Cary Grant bumps into Deborah Kerr again at the ballet. It's a vital scene to the movie's plot.

I'm afraid all considerations for their love affair have gone out of the window, though. I'd like to see how they overcome the odds stacked against them, but the odds are fast stacking up for me as to whether I'm going to get out of here with my dignity intact.

'Well, hurry back, then,' Ray says, a little disappointed, and goes back to watching the film.

God damn it, why has this happened to me?

I *never* need a poo in the evening. Especially not one this immediate. In fact, the only time I ever remember having digestive issues like this is when I've—

Oh, *Christ*. They must have cocked my meal order up and given me the *beef*!

That explains it!

I can't tolerate beef. I've never been able to. It always gives me this kind of trouble.

And I just ate a massive bowl of it, didn't I? Under dim lighting that didn't allow me to examine it too closely. No wonder it tasted so authentic. It *bloody* was authentic!

I can't believe the expert chefs of Wimbufushi could have got it so wrong, but they *must* have. That's the only explanation for my current horrific situation.

I have to get up. Right *now*.

I try to sit forward once again, and once again my bowels tell me that this is a very bad idea. The dress constricts around my waist, and I feel things rumbling down there that I really don't want to think about.

Okay, so sitting forward is out.

Maybe I can try gently rolling over, and pushing myself to my feet?

That should keep the dress as loose as possible, shouldn't it?

Frrrrrrgle.

Oh fuck me, that's the worst one yet! *An Affair To Remember* is going to become *A Follow-Through to Remember and Cringe about for the Rest of my Life*, if I don't get out of here!

Slowly, I start to roll myself over. Ray gives me a quizzical look.

'Beanbags, eh?' I say to him. 'Always hard to get out of!'

He nods, smiles and goes back to the film.

I manage to get fully turned around, so my belly is against the orange beanbag material. Then I shift my bottom backwards, and start to lift myself off with my arms.

My bowels roll again, and I immediately slam back on to the beanbag, because having my posterior raised is a sure-fire way of venting another accidental gaseous emission into the world.

'Having problems?' Ray asks. 'I can help if you like.'

'No, no. I'm fine! You just watch the movie!' I tell him, not wanting him any closer to me right now than is strictly necessary.

But now I am rather stuck, aren't I?

Whatever way I move, I am likely to fart once more. I can barely keep them in just lying here like a stranded turtle.

Fucking hell!

Why did they have to serve me beef?!

121

I thought this bloody resort was five star! Mistakes like this are supposed to happen at a motorway restaurant somewhere along the M25, not at a luxury Maldivian retreat!

When I do get out of this, I'm going to make a complaint. It really isn't good enough that I've been served beef by accident. It really isn't . . . good . . . enough . . . at . . . all . . .

I've spotted Joel.

He's a couple of rows back from me, lying in a beanbag with Cara next to him.

He has his hands laced behind his head and is staring right at me. There is a grin on his face. A smug, self-satisfied grin that instantly changes my entire perception of what's happened to me.

The chefs didn't make a mistake.

That bastard . . . that absolute hammering *bastard . . . changed my bloody order.*

Joel knows all about my problems with cow-based products. He was there that Boxing Day when I stupidly ate his mother's roast beef, so as not to appear rude. I spent most of that evening on the toilet.

And he knows how much I love Italian food. It wouldn't have taken a genius to figure out that I'd probably want to have the Bolognaise, but without the beef mince in it.

And he got up and left his table, didn't he? Right around the time the food orders were taken . . .

I go wide-eyed and slack jawed. The bastard has turned the tables on me! He did to me exactly what I did to him with the massage!

But I only did that to get back at him for ruining my sunset!

Aaaarggh!

Every facet of that smug smile he's aiming at me tells me that I have the absolute right of it.

This is all *Joel's* fault!

And now he gets to watch me struggle with bowels that want to empty themselves at the nearest given opportunity.

To hell with that! I won't give him the satisfaction!

In my anger, I act too hastily and jerk myself backwards off the beanbag. My butt goes into the air as I thrust out my arms, and my delicate grip on my bottom goes out of the window.

I fart directly into Cary Grant's face. And this one isn't slow, long and relatively quiet, either. It's a fucking *cheek smacker*. Big, propulsive and proud – it's the kind of fart that men working on docks will roar with laughter about, and probably award prizes.

Ray stares at my backside like he's just seen a rocket emerge from it. I stare at Ray like someone who's just had a rocket fly out of their arse.

'I'm so sorry,' I tell him. 'My dinner didn't agree with me.'

I'd say at this point it's less a disagreement and more like the prelude to all-out global warfare.

Ray does not speak.

What is there for him to say, honestly?

Nothing he could say would make this situation any better.

He could try, '*Oh no, my darling. Have you had an accident?*' This would be heartfelt, but also incredibly cringeworthy. That's the type of thing you say to a toddler, not your intended.

He could also try, '*Better out than in, eh?*' but that would mean the engagement would come to a swift end as soon as we returned to the UK.

Oh, what am I saying? Ray is probably not speaking because he's trying to work out how quickly he can pawn his engagement ring. I've just let rip into the face of one of Hollywood's golden stars. I wouldn't want to be engaged to anything attached to my bottom anymore either, would you?

Without trying to coax a response out of my soon-to-be-ex-fiancé, I get to my feet and turn in the direction of our water bungalow. My bowels roll once again in favour of this intent.

I hurry off, not looking at any of the other guests as I do so. I don't know if they heard (or felt) that fart, but I have no intention of finding out by looking at the expression on their faces.

And I most certainly do not look at Joel Sinclair as I rush away. God fucking forbid.

As I get past the last beanbag, though, I hear someone chuckle in the group behind me. *An Affair To Remember* is not a romantic comedy. It doesn't usually elicit that kind of response.

I know who's laughing and why . . .

But now is not the time to dwell on my ex-husband's machinations. Now is the time to hold my belly and hurry across the sand as fast as my little legs will carry me. I have to get back and get on to the toilet before disaster occurs.

It's only when I do reach the water bungalow that it occurs to me that I don't have the key card to get back in.

'Oh God in heaven,' I say in a quiet, terrified voice.

I gaze back over at the starlit cinema and contemplate hurrying back to ask Ray for the key. As I do, my bowels roll once more, this time with a sense of urgency that really should come with flashing blue lights and sirens.

I won't make it.

But I *have* to poo.

These two things are undeniable truths that I cannot avoid.

But what the hell am I going to do? I'll have to go back! I'll have to chance it! I'm either going to be able to hold it long enough to grab the key, or I'm going to unload all over Cary Grant. There are no more options available to me.

I start back down the walkway leading to our water bungalow, and step back on to the main one. To my right is Ray and *An Affair To Remember*, but on my left . . .

No.

There's *nothing* on my left.

Absolutely nothing that will help my situation.

That deserted, darkened pier at the end of the walkway, jutting out into the calm Indian Ocean, has *nothing* for me. There is simply not a damn thing about that secluded, empty pier, completely shrouded in the blanket of night, that can solve my current awful predicament in any way, shape or form.

I start in the direction of my fiancé and the key to our bungalow, before slowing to a stop, as my bowels continue their blue-light run to the scene of the accident.

Then I start to back up.

I pass by our bungalow, a grimace of fear and horror on my face about what I'm contemplating.

As I turn around, a small whimper escapes my lips.

I can't do this. I *shouldn't* do this.

This is the worst thing I will ever do in my life.

When it flashes before me as I lie on my death bed, this will be the thing that makes me cringe the most, if I do it.

And I went to a Steps concert once . . . and danced to *every single song*.

The end of the pier is now only a few feet away.

I start to pull my dress up over my thighs as I approach it.

The tears of shame that prick at the corners of my eyes would be flowing down my cheeks, but even they can't bring themselves to manifest on the body of a person that would do something like this.

I reach the edge of the wooden walkway, which widens out considerably to accommodate more beanbags (and I will never,

ever sit in one of them again after this, let me assure you of that) and turn around.

I then pull my knickers down and . . . oh God . . . *squat* – my bottom just about hanging over the precipice, with the cool ocean waters just below.

Look away.

I *beg* you.

Examine the cluster of stars in the sky. See how the graceful arc of the galaxy is easily visible? Look! You can pick out Mars, if you really look carefully, and concentrate *very* hard, blocking out everything else that may or may not be going on.

Please just look at all of those tiny pinpricks of incandescent light in the ocean of silky darkness.

And ignore the *sounds*. There are no sounds to be heard. None at all.

There is only the glory of the universe. Only the majesty of the heavens. Only the delight of the cosmos.

In this wonderous ballet, there is only room for the awe inspiring and incredible – such as the bloom of light from a far-off supernova. There is no room for the awful and horrible – such as the sight of a woman shitting on a fish.

Rather inevitably, as things . . . ugh . . . *come to a head*, I see Joel Sinclair's grinning face in my mind's eye.

. . . and to think, I actually felt *bad* about making him have that massage. I actually *regretted* my actions.

Well, I'm certainly getting my comeuppance now, aren't I?

But this is a thousand times *worse* than what I did to him. The level of escalation here is *intolerable*. Joel knows how badly I react to beef (and now, so does the Indian Ocean) and yet he deliberately had my order changed to ensure that this would happen.

Okay, I doubt he envisioned quite the scene I am making at this very moment, but he knew I would have severe problems.

This cannot go unpunished.

If Joel wants to escalate things, then *that's fine by me.*

He's been the architect of the absolute worst moments in my life and he's not going to get away with it.

I heave a heavy, heavy sigh as things start to conclude downstairs. My bowels are relaxing, having served their only purpose in life, and the feeling of severe discomfort has thankfully passed.

Oh God.

At least it can get no worse.

I have managed to avoid embarrassing myself any further in public. The only spectators to my downfall have been a few passing fish – who will probably regret the day they decided to have a nighttime swim around Wimbufushi for the rest of their fishy little lives.

But at least it's done. At least it is over, and no one has seen me.

Then, as if on cue, the lights go on in the water bungalow closest to me.

I hate you, Joel.

I hate you so very, very much.

Thursday

Joel – Escalation

I don't like kayaking.

Sorry, but I don't.

I once went on a scouting holiday when I was twelve, and was forced to kayak around Loch Lomond. It was mid-August – the height of summer – so the loch was of course freezing cold, and it rained constantly. I will never forget how uncomfortable it was to have cold loch water sloshing around my genitals, shrivelling them to a fifth of their normal size – which at the age of twelve was virtually invisible.

And it hurts your arms. I couldn't lift them the next day, after all that incessant paddling.

Don't even get me started on the *chafing*. There's so much of it. On all parts of your body. Constantly.

What made the whole thing even worse was that there were people on jet skis also using the loch at the same time as us. The comparison was not a happy one. They were propelled along by engines, and looked like they were having a blisteringly good time. I was propelled along by nothing other than my own upper body strength, and was covered in blisters.

Now, clearly kayaking in the Maldives is a vastly different experience to doing it in Scotland, but that doesn't mean I feel much keener about it. Yes, it's hot and sunny here, and I'm not wearing enough clothes to cause much in the way of chafing, but it's still the same thing when you get right down to it.

No.

I would much rather just carry on lying here on this sunbed, sipping my Sin City and reading my Kindle, with the gently lapping sea close by. It's been a slice of purest *heaven* for the past two hours, and the kind of thing I came on this holiday for. There's not a thing that makes me happier or more content than just lying with the sound of the ocean in my ears, a good book in my hand and my lovely girlfriend by my side.

Nothing would give me greater pleasure than to remain in this place for as long as is humanly possible. I am a man finally content with his (temporary) world, right here on this sun bed.

And that is precisely where I would have remained, were it not for the fact that I've just seen Ray and Amy out there in a bright yellow two-man kayak.

I shouldn't have looked up from my Tom Clancy. I should have just concentrated on the special forces men busting into the opium den, and ignored the outside world, but I stupidly looked up – and saw Ray manfully carrying the kayak down to the edge of the water while Amy followed him with the paddles.

And Ray – let's be brutally honest about this – is a very fine figure of a man. Those biceps are *enormous*, for starters. He seems to have no problem carting that kayak down to the shoreline at all.

And then there's the tiny white shorts.

Fully grown men should not be able to pull off tiny white shorts – and for the vast majority of us, this is indeed the case. If you tried to stick me in a pair, I'd look like the booby prize at a gay rodeo. People would point and take photos of me. Travelling freak shows wouldn't put me on their stage for fear of turning away the audience.

But Ray Holland somehow manages to carry off the tiny white shorts with huge amounts of aplomb. Maybe it's the tanned physique, maybe it's the natural self confidence that comes with being a massively successful yacht salesman (I looked up his company on Google and chewed on my own liver for half an hour). Whatever it is, Ray Holland has it.

And I'm insanely *jealous*.

I remember being envious of him when I met him at work, but I met a lot of rich, successful people back then, before Goblin Central and when Amy ruined everything. Ray was just one in a parade of clients I didn't measure up to.

Now though, he's got my ex-wife on his arm, and even though I wish I was nowhere near the evil harridan, I can't pretend I like to see her parading around with another man like that. She used to parade around with *me* – and even though I know I couldn't have pulled off the tiny white shorts when she was next to me, there was probably a part of me that thought I could have. Amy was a great confidence booster.

But now she's on Ray's arm and I don't like it one bit. He looks so much . . . *more* than I am.

In short, my alpha male switch has just turned itself on and demands satisfaction.

If Ray bloody Holland can take Amy out kayaking, then I can sure as hell do the same with Cara!

I turn my head to look at her. My brain freezes for a moment, as it always does when I look at her in a bikini. Cara Rowntree in a bikini is the best thing that's ever happened to me. It's also scary as hell, because it makes me realise and contemplate my own shortcomings. Someone with a body like that should really be with a body like Ray's. Cara could pull off tiny white shorts with ease.

'Cara? Do you fancy a bit of kayaking?'

She looks at me from under her large dark sunglasses, and appears to contemplate my suggestion for a moment. From the expression on what little I can see of her face, I'm not detecting much enthusiasm.

Can't say I blame her. This is the first period of peace and relaxation we've really had since arriving here. All the fun and games with Amy have kept things a lot more tense than they would have been otherwise. We've finally hit a nice, sweet spot, and moving away from it probably doesn't appeal in the slightest.

Cara would probably just like to lie here and sunbathe, the same as the sensible part of me. I should have kept my mouth shut.

But then she surprises me by saying, 'Yeah, okay. I wouldn't mind doing something a bit active after all that breakfast. You really shouldn't have let me eat that third pancake.'

Third pancakes are not something Cara has to worry about yet. Not at her age.

'You sure you want to?' she asks. 'I didn't think water sports were your cup of tea.'

'Oh, you know. We're on holiday. I like to try new things out.'

'Are you up to it after what happened with the massage?'

'Oh yes,' I reply, 'I'm perfectly alright.'

Which probably isn't all that honest – I still ache like mad, but my alpha male brain is overriding any pain centres around my body that might put up an objection.

'I'm fine to jump in a kayak, no worries.'

I make a massive point not to look over in Ray and Amy's direction at all as I'm saying this. The last I did see of them, Ray was manfully propelling them out into deeper water.

I need to manfully propel out into deeper water as well. The alpha male inside me demands it.

The alpha male inside me also demanded that I once drink the contents of a used ashtray full of water to win a fifty-pound bet, so it's clearly a complete fucking *idiot* – but Ray Holland's glistening muscles and tiny white shorts have woken it up, and it won't go back to sleep again until it has made my life immeasurably worse.

Cara nods and sits up, looking over at the rack of kayaks standing next to the small hut where the guy who monitors the water sports activities spends his day.

'There's plenty left. Can't be that many people out,' she remarks.

'No. Probably only one or two.' In tiny white shorts.

'Okay, then. Let's have a go. I feel up for it.' Cara then swings her legs over the side of the sun bed and stretches. Cara stretching in a bikini is something I'd have tattooed on my arse if I could get away with it.

She really should be with a guy who can wear tiny white shorts.

But, for the moment, she's with a guy in baggy black board shorts, and that'll just have to do.

After we've both applied a liberal amount of sun cream and thrown on t-shirts, we wander over to the hut and have a quick word with the water-sports guy – an ultra-cool dude in sunglasses called Jarvis – who is more than happy for us to take one of the remaining big yellow kayaks out on to the water. He doesn't give much of a safety briefing, beyond telling us to stay inside the white buoys that mark the circumference of the shallower water around the island. He also tells us to avoid the section of the sea where the island's boat plane makes semi-regular landings, which is demarked by the red buoys. All sounds simple enough.

Of course I attempt to manfully lift the kayak in the same way Ray did, and in doing so nearly put an end to this little jaunt before it's even begun, by putting my back out.

'Careful!' Cara says when I wince and stand upright with a disturbed look on my face. 'We'll pop the paddles inside it and carry it together.'

I try not to grate my teeth as we do this. Why can't I be as strong as Ray?

Because you don't like the gym – don't like hardcore exercise of any kind, for that matter – and would rather order a Dominos and watch Netflix.

Well, yes. This is true. But it doesn't mean I can't feel aggravated that I can't achieve what Ray Holland can, does it?

It kind of does, you bell end.

'Water looks lovely!' Cara remarks, as we approach it.

She's not wrong. I'm only doing this because of the alpha male idiot inside me, but to be honest, this seems like a great idea, anyway. The water looks more inviting than the gold embossed letters we received to last night's meal.

I lower my end of the kayak into the water and push it gently forward as Cara does the same. The ocean is warm, like a mild bath. So much so, that my testicles – so used to the temperatures of the waters around the UK – don't know what to do with themselves. Usually at this point they start retreating like what was left of the Light Brigade, but there doesn't appear to be any need to do that today.

Now to get into the kayak . . .

A task I must accomplish without falling into the water. If I don't manage that, any pretence of being able to copy the man in the tiny white shorts will vanish.

But I can't remember how to do it. Do I sit down on to it first and throw my legs over? Or step into it, and slide down?

At least I've got plenty of room to manoeuvre. The kayak has an open . . . what the hell do you call it? Cabin? Cockpit? Seaty bit? Well, whatever you call it, it's open and large, so I won't have to do any squeezing. This is just as well, as I really do like pizza and Netflix quite a lot.

Cara answers the question for me, by throwing one leg into the kayak, and gracefully pulling herself into it, sitting down as soon as her body weight has shifted on to it.

'Come on, then!' she says enthusiastically.

Should've stopped with the Tom Clancy, you goon.

I lick my lips with nerves, and try to copy what I just saw Cara do. This is only partially successful, as I have a lot more body weight to shift about than her, with a lot less co-ordination. There's a hairy moment when the kayak starts to wobble in a distressing fashion as I try to lift my other leg into it, but Cara prevents me from extreme embarrassment by using the paddles to keep it steady.

'Oof!' I exclaim as my butt hits the hard plastic seat.

A man who *oofs* like that when he does anything really should limit himself to reading Tom Clancy under a sun shade. Men in tiny white shorts do not *oof* like that in a kayak, unless they're having too much trouble shoving their large penises into them.

What are you doing, Sinclair?

Proving I'm worth it!

To who? Ray? Cara?

. . .

. . .

Amy?

Are you trying to let her know that you're still a confident, capable man, even without her?

Piss off.

'Chuck me a paddle and let's get going!' I say to Cara, holding out my hand behind me. She gives the paddle and sits back into her seat.

'Shall we go around the island?' she suggests.

'Yep! Sounds like a plan!'

And without waiting for a response, I start to power away from the shore, in a manner that almost feels like I know what I'm doing. It's all in the wrist, you see. You have to move them back and forth as you stroke, to make sure the paddle hits the water at the right angle.

Oh yes. I sound like I know what I'm talking about, don't I?

You would too, if the horrifying memory of your last kayaking holiday was seared into your brain. I'll never forget that week in Scottish wet hell. And nor will my inner thighs.

By stark contrast, kayaking around the Maldives is *exceptionally* pleasant. Not least because I have someone helping me propel the thing along.

We reach a point a good fifty or sixty yards out from the island, where the water starts to turn a deeper shade of blue, and slow our progress to a crawl.

'Beautiful,' Cara remarks, looking around her at the vast open ocean in one direction, and the gorgeous tropical island in the other.

'It is, isn't it?' I reply, feeling my shoulders relax and my face soften. The sound of the gentle waves lapping against the side of the kayak is a perfect counterpoint to the warm breeze caressing my face, and the fresh smell of salt water in the air. It's absolutely *glorious*.

For a moment, I forget all about the reason I wanted to go kayaking in the first place. Maybe it doesn't matter. Maybe I should just forget about Ray, his tiny white shorts, my ex-wife, and just enjoy this moment of peace and reflec—

There they fucking are!

Just heading around the edge of the island, past the water bungalows!

'Let's head that way!' I eagerly suggest to Cara, breaking her out of what was no doubt a moment of calm reflection for her.

'Oh. Okay,' she replies, a little shocked by my change of demeanour.

I don't have time to dwell on that, though, I need to get after Ray and Amy to prove that I'm as much of a man as he is.

Please bear in mind that this is the thought process of someone who once drank several mouthfuls of ashtray water just to prove the same thing.

I was sick for days afterwards.

This should give you some inkling of the trouble I'm going to cause myself today.

I begin to propel us towards where Ray and Amy are with great gusto.

Tomorrow morning, when I wake up in bed and reflect on what a horrific set of circumstances transpired the day before, I will do it with arms that I am barely able to lift.

Not to say that it feels all that great to be kayaking so manfully right at this moment. I'm still feeling the aftereffects of the thumbing I received yesterday, and my muscles are already sore.

I'll show her, though! I'll show her that her evil schemes haven't affected me in the slightest!

And I'll do that by kayaking the absolute *shit* out of this ocean.

'Bloody hell, Joel! Ease up a bit!' Cara exclaims from behind me. 'Why do we need to go so fas—' She grinds to a halt before she's finished speaking. Something has caught her eye, it seems. 'Is that . . . is that Ray and Amy over there?' Cara thrusts out a finger and points it at where Ray is propelling his kayak along with a grace and strength that makes my hair curl.

'Is it?' I reply, feigning surprise. 'Oh yes! It is! God damn it!'

'Did you know they were out here?' Cara says, voice laced with suspicion.

'No! No, I didn't!' I lie, like the absolute toad I truly am.

'Do you want to turn back?'

Oh my. She believes me.

It's a good job that I'm facing away from her, otherwise the bloom of red shame that suffuses my face would be obvious for her to see.

'No! No, it's fine,' I tell her. 'I promised I wouldn't let those two affect what we do, and I don't intend to start now!'

Ribbit.

'Okay. Shall we just ignore them then?'

'Yes! Let's just go where we want, and not worry about what they're doing!'

Ribbit.

The lying toad and his trusting, lovely girlfriend continue to kayak towards the end of the long pier that our water bungalow sits on – paying absolutely no mind to what Mr Tiny White Shorts and the Evil Harridan are up to.

No mind at all.

None whatsoever.

I am not constantly sneaking glances over at what they're doing, trying to manufacture a way I can get closer to them . . . without making it obvious that I want to get closer to them. I can't prove that I am as manly as Ray unless he—

she—

can see me doing it, can I?

Luckily, my scheming is made easier when Ray slows the kayak and points a finger down into the water. He's obviously spotted something he wants Amy to have a look at.

Hah!

It's the perfect opportunity to go past them as fast as possible, thus demonstrating my prowess on the water!

I redouble my efforts on the paddle, and the kayak lurches forward at a pace that tests the very limits of my endurance and strength.

So, about three miles an hour, then.

I feel Cara start to paddle harder behind me as well. She's obviously just as keen to power past the other two as I am – though her reasons are probably a lot more to do with getting away from them completely, rather than proving how great she is at kayaking and being A REAL MAN.

Regardless of intent, the plan works, and we cruise past Ray and Amy just as they look up from whatever it was they were studying in the water below.

Both are quite taken aback when we fly past their field of vision.

'Morning!' I cry in a voice that I hope is laced with manly triumph. 'Lovely day for it!'

I smile at them with a grin that the Cheshire Cat would be fucking ashamed of.

Cara says nothing. I can't say I blame her.

But I am *happy*. Truly *happy*.

I have shown Ray just how fast and cool I can look in a kayak. Surely his enormous penis will shrivel in those tiny white shorts now. Surely he will feel incredibly inadequate alongside Amy's powerful ex-husband.

I am basking in the glow of my own pridefulness when out of the corner of my left eye, I see a long yellow shape appear in my peripheral vision.

My head snaps around to see Ray and Amy *catching up with us*.

He's *racing* me. The bastard is actually *racing* me!

No! No! You're supposed to stay back there with a shrivelled penis! You're not supposed to be trying to get *past me*!

Ray doesn't appear to be making any effort whatsoever to keep up. By the serene expression on his face, he could be sat in his favourite armchair, stroking a cat.

As their kayak comes alongside ours, Amy throws me a very quick but deliberate smile that would make the Cheshire Cat give it all up and retire to a small place in the country to raise mice.

I redouble my efforts.

Sadly this does not redouble my speed. I have reached the upper limit of my physical prowess, and no matter how much my ego wants to see my muscles provide it with more power, it's not going to happen.

In fact, about the only change this increase in effort does achieve is to make strange and repetitive noises come out of my mouth at every stroke of the oar.

'*Erng, erng, erng, erng, erng.*'

'Joel? Can we slow down a bit? My arms are hurting.'

'*Erng . . . erng . . . erng . . . erng . . . erng . . .*'

'A bit slower, please!'

'*Erng . . .* Oh, Jesus . . . *Erng . . .* Fuck me . . . *Erng . . .* How is he still going? . . . *Erng . . .*'

We slow right down to a crawl, and watch as Ray powers Amy and the kayak over to a small but perfectly formed sand cay, lying a good hundred yards off the edge of Wimbufushi.

I have two options at this point.

I can suggest to Cara that we go another way, and leave Ray to bask in the glory of victory in his tiny white shorts. This would no doubt please her and lead to a much more relaxed and easy rest of the day. Okay, my ego would have taken a battering, but at least I would have got out of this situation with my body more or less intact.

Or . . . I can continue this farcical game of one-upmanship by following them over to the sand cay, and suggesting a friendly race around the island.

Yes. That's right.

I'm actually considering a race with Ray and Amy around the island, despite the fact that he is clearly much, much fitter than I am. It is a race that the sensible part of my brain knows I have no chance of winning, but if watching years of Formula One has taught me anything, it's that *anything* can happen in a race. Someone with seemingly no hope of winning at all can come through and take the chequered flag ahead of the much better and faster competition.

I could be the Johnny Herbert of this race around Wimbufushi.

With this incredibly stupid thought process filling my incredibly stupid brain, I point the kayak in the direction of the sand cay.

'What are we doing?' Cara asks, slightly aghast that I'm actively heading in the direction of the last person on this island I'm supposed to want to be anywhere near.

'I want to see that sand cay!' I tell her. 'There's no reason to let them stop us going over there, is there?'

'Well, I guess not . . .'

'No! Like you said before, we can't let them ruin our holiday!'

It's deeply unfair of me to bring up an off-hand comment Cara made a few days ago in defence of my idiocy, but if I can drink ashtray water, I can sure as hell rationalise my decisions here in the most unsatisfactory of ways.

I see that Ray and Amy have made it to the cay, and are walking around it slowly. Ray has produced a phone from somewhere and is taking photos of the incredible scenery on offer. Amy is lagging behind a little, and doesn't appear to be paying much attention to what he's doing.

She does pay attention, however, when she sees me and Cara coming closer.

There's a sickly look on her face as I spear our kayak towards the cay, aiming for a spot right next to theirs.

I realise slightly too late that I'm coming in too fast, but there's nothing I can do about it now.

'Hi, there!' I say in the fakest cheery voice I can manage as we get within a few feet of the sand. 'We just thought we'd come and take a— *Ooooft*!' The kayak hits the sand, and our forward progress is immediately arrested. I am instantly flung forward, the wind knocked out of me as I double over with the impact. At the same time, my arse comes off the plastic seat a little, allowing one errant testicle to slide under my thigh, so that when I sit back down again, it gets jammed.

' . . . take a lovely look at this sand cay!' I finish, my voice several octaves higher.

I *must not* let her see that I'm hurt. I *must* make it appear that I meant to park the kayak at that speed. Everything *must* seem deliberate.

'Fucking hell!' Cara exclaims from behind me, but unfortunately I don't have time to check on how she is. I must jump out of the kayak to show Amy and Ray that I am absolutely fine.

With my testicle throbbing to such a degree that I'm slightly concerned I might require medical attention at some point, I throw my paddle up on to the sand, and start to hoist myself out of the kayak. Instead of just swivelling myself around slowly, and standing up beside the damn thing, I instead elect to try something akin to a pole vault dismount by throwing my legs over the plastic rim. Sadly, my trailing left foot gets caught on the edge of the kayak, and instead of jumping out in one smooth motion, I tip out of the kayak in one incredibly *unsmooth* motion, and go headfirst into the drink.

Given that there's only about three inches of Indian Ocean for me to fall into, I end up headbutting the sand cay, as if it had looked at my girlfriend funny.

My girlfriend then lets out a cry of distress, and jumps out of the kayak in the swift manner I was going for, and helps me back to my feet. I splutter madly as I do this, having inadvertently consumed a cocktail of ocean water and sand.

This has not gone well.

But Amy and Ray do not need to know that.

'Ha ha! Always hard to get out of these things, eh?' I cry, spitting sand all over the place.

'I suppose so,' Amy replies in a cold, dead voice. You'd assume she'd take great delight in my hapless exit from the kayak, but she looks like death warmed up.

Oh . . .

Oh, yes. That's right.

The Bolognaise.

I'd temporarily forgotten about my little jape from last night.

Amy clearly hasn't. She looks just like she did on the day after Boxing Day that one year.

'Morning,' Cara says, still holding my arm. 'What a gorgeous little island,' she remarks, raising one hand to her eyes to scan the horizon.

'It certainly is!' Ray remarks, turning from his picture-taking to offer us both a large smile.

I am well aware that I probably look a right fucking state at this point. My face will be bright red with effort and pain, and my hair will be soaking wet and sticking up at all angles, thanks to my brief plunge into the briny.

Ray looks like he's just stepped off the cover of *Good-Looking Rich Bastards Monthly*.

A small, sensible, scared little voice deep down inside of me tries to point out that it might not be such a good idea to challenge this man to anything other than a competition to see who can look the most fat and lost.

The ashtray drinker is having none of it, though. If anything, he's even more determined to have the race now, just to make the mashed testicle worth it.

But I can't offer him the challenge straight off. I'll have to build up to it, *organically*, like.

'How are things for you chaps?' Ray asks, completely ignoring the fact that I've just Inspector Clouseau'd my way out of the kayak. I think this makes me hate him even more.

'Very good!' I tell him, standing up as straight as I possibly can. This causes my testicle to swing dangerously around in my shorts and underpants, sending a jolt of pain up through my stomach. 'Couldn't be better!' I add, sounding more strained than a brickie's tea bag.

'Excellent!' Ray replies. 'Us too. Just taking in a little of the scenery from a different perspective. Always pays to do that, I think. Don't you?'

What does that mean? Is he trying to say something?

I don't see anything in his face to suggest that what he's just said has an ulterior meaning, but it sounded like a very *deliberate* thing to say, didn't it?

My eyes narrow. 'Yes. A different perspective. You're very . . . very right.'

Finding that broad, gleaming smile more than a little disconcerting, I turn my attention to my ex-wife, who continues to look green to the gills. 'Hello, Amy, how are you today?' I say to her blandly.

'Oh, I'm *fine,* Joel. Don't you worry about *me.*'

If Ray is hard to read, Amy is stupendously easy. I have to resist the urge to take a step back. Partially because I don't want to get covered in the vomit that I'm partially convinced is about to erupt from her any minute.

Christ. She does look awful. Maybe I went a little far with my prank last night? I didn't mean for it to make her *this* ill.

'Going out on the water always makes me a little sick,' Cara pipes up from beside me, rummaging around in the pocket of her shorts as she does so. She produces a packet of Tic Tacs and offers it to Amy with a smile. 'Would you like one of these? They help me settle my stomach for some reason.'

For a moment, my ex-wife looks like she's going to smack the box out of Cara's hand, but then her expression relaxes a little and she takes the box. 'Thank you. I do feel a bit queasy.' She shoots me a look. 'Maybe not from sea sickness, though.' Amy pops a Tic Tac and hands the box back to Cara.

Well, this is all perfectly *lovely*, isn't it?

I need to start steering the conversation around to the race – because no, I haven't forgotten about it, unfortunately. I'm Johnny Herbert, remember?

'Kayak much, do you?' I say to Ray.

'Oh . . . yes. A fair bit, I suppose. More of a windsurf kind of guy, to be honest. But I love anything that gets me out on the water.'

Yeah, I bet you do.

'You've got a very . . . smooth action,' I tell him.

'Sorry?'

'With the paddles, I mean. Your action is very smooth.' I mime a bit of paddling to underline my point.

'Oh. Thank you. Yes. I suppose I do.'

I'm trying to get the conversation *organically* to a place where I can actively throw out the idea of a race, but I'm rather afraid I just sound like I'm trying to chat him up.

'I'm sure getting all the way around the island wouldn't be a problem for you, with an action like that,' I tell him, nodding my head sagely.

'Um . . . no. I suppose it wouldn't.'

'Be quite easy for you, given your size.'

Fucking hell. Why don't I just pull down his tiny white shorts, get to work and have done with it?

'My size?' Ray is looking deeply uncomfortable now. This pleases me greatly. Always good to have your opponent a bit off kilter before a race.

'Yes. Your physique,' I clarify. 'I'm sure a lap around the island wouldn't cause you many problems.'

I deliberately don't look at Amy or Cara, because Christ only knows what's going on with their faces right now. It appears from the way I'm talking to Ray that falling out of the kayak has turned me homosexual.

Now, Ray is a very fine figure of a man, and I'm sure if I was gay, he'd be the first on my list to get rejected by, but my motives are not based around a sudden new-found love for my fellow man, they are purely geared towards getting Ray to accept my challenge.

'A lap around the island?' Ray replies, still not sure whether he's actively being chatted up or not by another man, in front of both their female partners.

'Yes. Fancy it?' I say, matter-of-factly.

'Fancy what?' Ray responds, still utterly perplexed by this conversation.

On his left I can see Amy's eyes widen as she realises what's going on here. She always was one to get ahead of the game over most other people.

'A little race around the island,' I tell him, trying as hard as possible not to flex my arm muscles and tighten the ones around my belly as I say this.

Ray's eyes narrow. 'You want . . . you want to race me around Wimbufushi?' The tone in his voice is roughly the same as Gordon Ramsay's would be if a seven-year-old just challenged him to see who can cook the best lobster thermidor.

'Yes!' I crow with excitement, finally getting to the crux of the matter. 'Don't you think it would be fun?'

Ray carefully regards me for a second. 'No?' he ventures.

'Don't be so stupid,' Amy says in a typically derisory fashion.

Cara remains silent for the moment.

'Oh come on!' I say expansively to them both. 'It'd just be a bit of fun. A little light competition on a lovely sunny Thursday morning!'

'It's a crazy idea, Joel!' Amy snaps. 'We're here to relax, not race!'

Oh, so she appears to be doing all the talking, does she? Well, we'll see about that . . .

I affect a look of disappointment. 'Oh well. Shame. If Ray doesn't think he can beat me, then I suppose it's probably right that we don't do it. I'm sure you know what's best, Amy.'

This, my friends, is the kind of thing that leads to pistols at dawn. I've essentially just said that I believe Amy wears the trousers in their relationship. No man alive can ignore such an insult.

Ray nods. 'She is the sensible one of the two of us,' he remarks, completely unfazed by my questioning of his manhood.

What the fuck?

But no man alive can ignore such an insult!

Ray has clearly never drunk water out of a used ashtray before!

'I don't think it's something I'd like to do,' Ray continues in a mild tone, as if I haven't basically just told him he's a big girl's blouse.

'You're on!' Amy snaps, in a bewildering change of attitude that takes us all by surprise.

'I am?' I reply, flabbergasted. A few seconds ago she was dead set against the idea, but now she's well up for it?

'Yes. You *are*,' she responds. 'Ray doesn't need me to tell him what to do. He makes his own decisions!'

Aah. I think I see what's going on here . . .

Amy has realised my rather pathetically concealed gambit. If Ray isn't bothered by my deliberate attempt to question his manhood, then Amy most certainly is.

'I do?' Ray says to her, now so confused by proceedings, he keeps blinking and frowning like someone's shining a torch in his face.

'Yes! You do!' Amy replies. 'And you know as well as I do that you'd beat Joel in a race around the island. That *we'd* beat him . . . So let's have a go, eh?' Amy looks daggers at me. 'Like Joel says . . . it's just a friendly bit of Thursday morning competition.'

Hang on a moment!

We?

She wants to take part in the race now as well?

My plans were for it to just be me and Ray, but Amy wants in?

'*You* want to have a race?' I say, incredulous.

'Of course! Why not?' she tells me, chin thrust out. Then Amy looks past me at Cara. 'What do you say, Cara? Want to join me in showing these men that us women can race just as hard as them?'

Cara is slack-jawed with amazement. She's been quiet this entire time, and just stood there watching this bizarre conversation play out. I doubt she expected to be included in it at any point, and the fact she now is has evidently come as something of a shock.

'I don't want . . . I don't want to have a race,' she eventually says, shaking her head a little.

I turn to her, desperate for her to play along. If Amy is going to be in Ray's kayak, I need her in mine!

'Please, sweetie!' I say to her through partially gritted teeth. 'It won't be fair otherwise!'

Cara stares at me for a moment, wondering how she managed to get herself into this predicament.

And by predicament, I don't mean being stood on a sandy cay in the middle of the Indian Ocean discussing a race in a kayak – I mean dating an absolute cock like me.

'Okay,' she tells me in a voice full of resignation, defeat and not a little horrified bemusement.

'Great!' I exclaim and turn back to Amy. 'So we're all set, then?'

'Yes, we *are*,' she replies with grim determination.

Ray looks like he's just discovered his bottom has fallen off.

'We'll start right by the end of the water bungalows, shall we?' I suggest, pointing over at where the wide wooden walkway terminates. Amy stares over at where I'm pointing with a look of absolute horror on her face. What could possibly be so awful about that as a starting place?

'No!' she immediately responds. 'We'll start right here. First one back wins!'

'Right! Er . . . Yes!' I agree, still wondering what's so wrong with that particular patch of water underneath the walkway.

'Come on, Ray! Let's get back into the kayak and get ready!' Amy tells her partner, who looks at her like she might know where his bottom is, but is just not telling him for some reason.

I turn back to Cara, who looks angry.

And well she might. Half an hour ago she was quite happily laid out on a sunbed, relaxing into her holiday, perhaps for the first time since we got here. And now she's being pressganged into a race she clearly wants no part of.

'What the hell, Joel?' she says to me once Ray and Amy are out of earshot.

'I'm sorry, baby!' I tell her. 'I didn't think Amy would be a part of the race! But if she is, I need you to help me.'

'Race, Joel? Why do you want to race Ray *anyway*?'

Because a bloke I knew at university called Heavy Kev once bet me fifty quid I couldn't drink an ashtray full of water because I was a pussy.

'Because I thought it would be fun?' I venture, knowing full well that wasn't my motive.

Cara lets out an exasperated sigh. 'Is this about . . . about *her*?' she says, her voice lowered.

'No!'

Yes! Of course it is! It's really all about her! I desperately need her to see that I can still be the confident, successful man I once was when we were married! I need her to see that she didn't make me that way!

'Of course it's not! I just wanted to have a friendly little race to make the kayaking a bit more interesting.'

Cara rolls her eyes. 'Right. Well . . . I'll do it. But after this, we do what I want for the rest of the day, okay?'

'Of course!'

And I really do mean that. The rest of Thursday is totally in my girlfriend's control. I just have to get this out of my system first.

'Come on then,' she says in a resigned tone, and goes back over to the kayak, just as Ray is pushing theirs away from the shore.

I take a deep breath to steel myself, and also clamber back into the kayak – taking it nice and easy this time.

Once in it, I also push us away from the shore, straining as I do so. Today really is going to play havoc with what's left of my muscles after the evil massage Amy made me have.

My jaw tightens as I remember what she did.

It tightens even more as we paddle around the sand cay, to come alongside Ray and Amy, who have pointed their kayak in the direction of the sea to the left side of the island.

My heart starts to pound.

This is it.

Time to prove myself.

If I can drink ashtray water, I can race this pillock around a small island.

Heavy Kev didn't get the best of me, and neither will Tiny Shorts Ray.

Let battle commence!

Thursday

Amy – The Battle Of Wimbufushi

How dare he?

How dare he cast aspersions on Ray's abilities!

Joel? Beat Ray in a *race*?

How utterly absurd!

I couldn't let it stand. I just *couldn't*.

Ray would have, bless him. He's so good-natured and kind, he would have just let Joel get away with such an insult . . . but I *couldn't*. Joel needs to be put in his bloody place, and if that means a quick race around Wimbufushi, then so be it!

Quite why I decided to inject myself into it is beyond me, though.

The last thing I need is to take part in any more strenuous exercise.

But damn it, I just saw *red*! I know what Joel is up to. I *always* know what Joel is up to.

He was trying to make *my* man look *bad*. And I can't have that! Not at all!

So, despite the fact that I feel like death warmed up, I am going to take part in this stupid race, and I am going to prove to Joel just how small and pathetic he truly is!

If I don't throw up, that is . . .

Because there's every chance I might, thanks to what I ate last night.

After the . . . *outdoor toileting incident*, I made my way very slowly back to Ray, keeping to the shadows as best I could. I told him I wasn't feeling well, and he came back to the bungalow with me, proceeding to fuss over me until I fell into a fitful sleep.

I had another attack of the galloping runs at about 4 a.m., throughout which I cursed my ex-husband to the lowest pits of hell.

When I got up this morning, the need to go to the toilet had passed, but I still felt decidedly under the weather.

When Ray suggested a morning walk to cheer me up a bit, I was happy to accept. When he saw the kayaks, though, my heart sank.

He *loves* water sports. They're pretty much his favourite past time. So it came as no surprise he eagerly went over to them, hoping to have a go on one, only to discover that there were only two-man kayaks available.

What could I do? I couldn't leave him disappointed, could I? Not when he spends his entire life never disappointing me.

So, despite the fact that I was green to the gills, I agreed to come out with him on a little kayaking excursion, provided we took things relatively easy.

And that's how things went – until bloody Joel and bloody Cara came alongside us.

And now, for some unfathomable reason, I'm about to take part in a race around Wimbufushi island, even though I might yak up all over Ray's back while doing so.

But I just can't let him get away with it.

Joel, I mean.

I can't let him walk away from insulting the best person I know like that.

AND I want some measure of revenge for making me shit over the side of that pier . . .

Does Joel know that's what I had to do? Is that why he suggested we start the race right on top of the place where I . . . made my deposit?

I can't imagine how he would know, but the irrational idea that he followed me over, and sat in the shadows giggling his head off while I crapped on a passing clown fish is something I can't get out of my head.

So, yes.

We will race Joel and Cara around this island, and we will fucking *win*. No matter how terrible I feel.

I watch with a look of loathing on my face as Joel awkwardly pilots his kayak towards where we're waiting for him. He already looks puffed out before the race even begins, to be honest. This should be a breeze.

The only thing that worries me is Cara Rowntree. I can see some pretty well-defined arm muscles under that gloriously tanned skin of hers. She must work out.

I do not, and I fear that I may be at a definite disadvantage, especially considering the state I'm in. Going up against Cara is a huge mistake. There's something about her that screams she's an aggressive type – probably all those arm muscles. She swanned around the office like she owned the place on the times she used to come in, I remember that. Not one lacking in self confidence is Miss Rowntree. A trait that's bound to serve her well in this race, along with those well-defined muscles.

I instantly regret my decision to insert myself into the race, instead of just letting the boys get on with it. I should have stood aside and let Ray mash Joel into the ground, but I saw red, and when that happens, I make irrational and stupid decisions.

Ones I later come to regret. In this case, a mere *few minutes* later.

But I can't back out now – I'll look like a coward, and I can just see the delighted expression on Joel's face if I withdraw from the race. Also, I'm pretty sure Cara actually wants nothing to do with any of it, so if I can inconvenience her a little as well, I will do. This comes from a place of sheer, petty jealousy, I'll happily admit. I've got ten years and ten pounds on her at least, and I don't like it at all.

I didn't like that smug smile she had on her face when she handed me that Tic Tac, either. I could tell she was taking great delight in my misfortune.

My stomach gives a small gurgle as Joel and Cara draw up alongside us. This is probably nerves, but I'm also hoping and praying it isn't anything else. I can't just drop my shorts and shove my bum over the side of the kayak, now can I?

'We all ready, then?' Joel says in that voice he always uses when he wants to sound cheerful, but is really anything but inside.

Gah.

I wish I didn't know him as well as I do. I wish I couldn't read him like a book. But I do, and I can. He was a huge part of my life for so long, whether I like it or not, and all the contents of that book stay with you long after the fact. I know what he's doing. I know he's trying to prove that he's 'still got it'. It's quite exceptionally sad.

'Yes,' Ray replies calmly. He doesn't sound flustered in the slightest. I'd like to think I know Ray as well as I know Joel, and I'm pretty sure that he's as calm as he sounds – but we've only been together for a relatively short time, and I have to confess there are things about him I'm still discovering. He's not a man of many layers, though, I know that much. What you see is what you get. That's the thing that attracted me to him in the first place. Ray is

153

simple to understand, and simplicity is very attractive. He probably is as calm and collected as he appears.

But I can't be *one hundred per cent* sure . . .

I despise the fact that I know the man I hate more than the man I love.

'Excellent!' Joel replies, voice cracking a little at the end. 'On the count of three, then?' He raises one hand. It's shaking slightly. 'One! Two! Three!'

Joel brings his hand down and I feel the kayak surge forward underneath me.

Oh shit. That's right, isn't it? I have to help Ray paddle, don't I? Properly this time, as well. Up until now I've been making half-hearted efforts to dip my paddle blades into the water and at least look like I'm contributing, but I haven't been really. Ray's been doing all the work.

But that's not going to wash now. Ray is by far the stronger, better kayaker of the two men, but I am also by far the weaker of the two women.

I slap my paddle awkwardly into the water and wrench my arm back. The instant I do I feel a sharp stab of nausea suffuse my being. Unbidden, images of half-digested beef Bolognaise enter my mind, and the nausea grows.

Oh, Christ. Am I going to be able to do this?

From my left-hand side I see Joel and Cara starting to catch Ray and me.

Yes! Yes, I *can* bloody do this, because that man *cannot win*!

I grit my teeth together, try to ignore the nausea, and attempt to copy the long, strong strokes Ray is easily pulling off in front of me.

This is partially successful, and we move into a relatively healthy lead.

I turn my head back to look at Joel, who is a picture of suffering. His face is beetroot red, and every time his right arm sends the paddle back into the water, he winces painfully. Behind him, Cara now looks quite determined. What she's determined about I don't know – maybe it's rethinking her relationship with my ex-husband. One can only hope.

Regardless, she's making a lot more effort than I am, and is therefore powering them both back towards us again.

Oh God!

I'm letting Ray down!

'You okay back there?' he asks me, hardly out of breath at all.

'Yes! Yes, I'm fine! Just trying to keep up with you!'

'You're doing fine! Just remember . . . long, strong strokes!'

'Yes!'

Long, strong strokes. Long, strong strokes.

Just keep them long, strong and strokey, Caddick. You'll be fine.

And for a few minutes I am.

As we come alongside the island and start to kayak down its length, I do start to get into something of a rhythm. The nausea goes to the back of my mind, and my concentration levels go up. This doesn't seem to correlate much with a faster pace from the kayak, but at least I feel like I'm psychologically contributing something, rather than just being a dead weight.

All I hear is the sound of my paddle hitting the surface of the water, and sliding beneath.

Swoosh, it goes.

Swoosh.

Swoosh.

Swoosh.

Swoosh.

Swoo—

Thwack!

My concentration is broken completely when my paddle connects with something, making an almighty clattering noise.

I look over to see that Joel and Cara have drifted very close to us. So close that Joel's paddle has just hit mine.

'Oi! Get away!' I scream at him, desperately trying to restore my rhythm as I do so.

I was just starting to get into it there . . .

'*You* get away!' Joel roars back, also stabbing his paddle back into the water on the other side of the kayak.

I do much the same thing, which means that when we both go to swap sides with our paddles once more, we inevitably try to stick them in the same patch of water, and they clash again.

'Fuck off!' I bellow. 'Move out a bit!'

'You move in a bit!' he screams back.

'No!'

Thwack!

'You've got all that bloody ocean on your side!' I tell him, blood pressure rising like a volcano.

'It gets too deep! We can't go out beyond the white buoys!' he whines.

Thwack!

'Don't be such a scaredy cat!'

'Stop being so bloody stubborn!'

Thwack!

Up front Ray decides to take matters into his own hands and steers us closer to the shore.

Dammit! That's given ground to Joel! Why did he do that?

It also means that it's given Cara a chance to bring their kayak level with ours. She's now really got her head down, and is motoring along like someone who's suddenly decided they want to win.

Get back into the groove, woman!

Yes!

I will indeed get into the groove! Just like Madonna once told me to do back in the Eighties . . . although, to be honest, I always thought that song was a barely concealed bit of innuendo about her vagina.

Regardless, I try my hardest to concentrate again, as the two kayaks briskly race towards the other end of the island.

And it works.

With me humming 'Into the Groove' under my breath, we start to increase our speed again – this time with me definitely contributing something to proceedings.

I've just reached the bit of the song where Madonna is letting me know that dancing can be such a sweet sensation, when I feel the kayak slow considerably.

Ray must be flagging!

Oh no! I'm not doing enough! I'm not paddling hard enough!

I redouble my efforts, the cords of my neck muscles starting to stand out as I wrench the paddle back through the water.

'Amy!' I hear Ray exclaim ahead of me, but I ignore him. I have to concentrate on my strokes!

Swoosh.

Swoosh.

'Amy!'

Swoosh.

Swoosh.

'Amy! Dugong!' he cries, lifting his paddle out of the water completely.

What is he doing? We have to keep paddling!

Joel's kayak comes alongside again. They're catching us!

'See, cow!' Joel screams at me.

'Fuck you!' I scream back.

Yes! I can see that you've caught us, you utter bastard! And don't call me a fucking cow!

'See cow!' Joel cries again, this time pointing ahead of him.

'Stop calling me a cow!' I roar back at him.

Ray has now actively stabbed his paddle down into the water, causing us to veer sharply off to the right, towards the shore.

What is he doing?!

'Dugong, Amy!' he exclaims again.

Dugong?

What the hell is he talking abou—

Then I see it . . .

Breaking the surface of the otherwise calm ocean water is a massive grey lump – the back of a sea creature that in any other circumstance I would be delighted and privileged to get a look at.

I have to yank my paddle out of the ocean with all of my might to stop it whacking the poor creature. The water is so clear that I can see its enormous head turned up towards me, its placid eyes regarding me with a look of endless patience.

'Sea cow!' Joel cries again, and I understand what he's actually saying this time. There's an excited, boyish expression on his face as his kayak passes by, on the other side of the majestic animal.

We've all stopped paddling now. Partially so we don't stab them into the dugong that's calmly making its way along the bottom of the shallow sea, and partially because the sight of it has taken us all by complete surprise.

This is one of the most endangered species on our planet, and here we are – lucky enough to see one in its natural habitat. Probably one of the very few left in this area of the world.

For a moment, our race is completely forgotten about, as we all slide serenely past the grazing creature, watching it with awestruck expressions on our faces as it moves beneath us.

'That's amazing,' Ray says, staring down into the water.

'Oh God, isn't it lovely?' Cara remarks, doing the same.

Tears actually prick my eyes.

It's a big, fat greyish brown lump, with a face only a mother could love, but it's also one of the most beautiful things I have ever seen.

The kayaks glide by it, and as they do I can't take my eyes off the dugong, until the angle is too sharp to be able to see it anymore under the surface of the water. That's when I look up, and Joel's eyes meet with mine.

For the first time in years, there's no malice or hurt in our combined expression. We both know we've just experienced something incredible – and for the briefest of moments, our anger towards one another disappears.

The look goes on between us for slightly longer than it probably should, before I feel the kayak surge underneath me again, as Ray gets back to the race.

I break away from looking at my ex-husband's awestruck face, and try to get my head back into the competition.

For a good twenty feet, neither kayak gets up much speed as we all try to process what we've just seen. But as we get further away from the dugong, and start to come past the other end of the island, the reality of the race reasserts itself.

So much so, that by the time we're paddling alongside the other row of water bungalows, the run-in with the majestic sea cow is firmly pushed to the back of my mind.

. . . though I have a feeling that when all is said and done, seeing it will be one of the strongest memories I will have of this holiday, whatever else happens.

Ray is now glancing over at Joel every once in a while to check where their kayak is in relation to ours – and unfortunately, they're pretty close. That's thanks to Cara's fitness levels, and Joel's stubborn streak.

I swear that man would die just to prove a point.

Looking at him I can see that he's obviously not enjoying this race one bit. All his talk of friendly, light-hearted competition was of course a load of old cobblers. This was, is, and always will be about him measuring the size of his dick against Ray's.

The fact of the matter is that they both own penises of roughly the same size, but I wouldn't tell either of them that, because even saying a man has a penis roughly the same size as another man is taken as an insult, for reasons I cannot fathom for the life of me.

Mind you, I'm not sure Ray would care all that much. He's so laid back about almost everything in life, I have to marvel at the fact he doesn't walk around with permanent back ache. Going from the maelstrom of neuroses and stress ticks that Joel is, to the calm, steady demeanour that Ray cultivates was both a shock and a relief.

I was intensely glad to find a man who doesn't make my life more hectic than I can handle. I recognise that I have my own set of strange mental quirks that don't play well with others, and Ray has been a calming influence on them, whereas Joel just exacerbated them at every opportunity – deliberately or otherwise.

I'm so pleased to be living a life without Joel Sinclair causing me constant stress and emotional drainage.

. . . or rather I *would be*, were it not for the fact that I'm currently getting splattered in the face by Indian Ocean water, as I paddle like a mad thing, in a race I actually want no part of.

Oh, and I've also just thrown up.

A few moments ago, while I was talking about Joel's penis.

I didn't mention it, as there wasn't much to it, to be honest. Barely visible. I'm breathing so hard and am so covered in sea water that a little bit of unstoppable vomit is hardly worth the bother of detailing.

It just came out as I was ducking the paddle into the water on my left, while simultaneously taking another huge, ragged breath.

I should be horrified by this, but I'm not. All I can think about is beating Joel, and winning this race. That's where my mind is at, as Ray starts to shift the kayak around to the right, and we head to the end of the water bungalows. The ones that you can see the sunset from on the veranda . . .

Aaaargh!

'Faster, Ray!' I demand of my fiancé. 'We've got to get ahead again!'

'Okay, sweetheart!' he calls back and starts to paddle harder.

Our kayak surges once more into a healthy lead as we round the island, and start to head back in roughly the direction that we came.

This side of the island is a lot busier with people than the other. This is largely due to the fact that the gorgeous coral reef that surrounds the island is most easily accessible from this side. This means there are quite a lot of guests snorkelling their way through the water, forcing us to head further out into the deeper ocean to avoid them.

This is the last thing I need as I'm getting increasingly more and more tired. The waves out here are a bit choppier, which makes the paddling harder. If we weren't a good two thirds of the way through this race, I would probably be thinking about giving up.

The fact I'm getting weary means that Joel and Cara have closed the gap again.

'Push, Ray! Push!' I encourage feverishly, not wanting us to lose our lead.

'Trying as hard as I can, sweetie!' he cries back, trying to sound as positive as possible about the situation. It's quite clear that I'm the dead weight in this kayak, though. Just like Joel is in the other.

Speaking of whom, he's now covered in snot.

Yep, there's a glistening trail of nose production streaming across his cheeks now.

Joel always gets snotty when undertaking exercise.

We went through a short post-Christmas weight-loss program one year that largely consisted of eating the blandest food imaginable, and going for a daily jog.

You haven't seen true horror until you've seen Joel Sinclair's face after a two-mile run in six degrees. There's something about physical exertion that gives him a runny nose. It looks like someone's rubbed a bag of slugs across his face.

It appears he suffers from the same problem in hot temperatures too, as he currently looks like the same person's been at him with a bag of tropical sea slugs.

Mind you, I now have vomit over my cute blue bikini top, so who am I to judge?

Cara is covered in neither vomit nor snot, but even she looks like she's been through the wringer. It doesn't matter how young and beautiful you are, you still look a mess when you've had sea water thrown at your face for fifteen minutes.

I can't see what Ray looks like, but I can picture the look of good-natured determination on his face. It'll be the same one he employs when bargaining with a client over the price of a new yacht. Or when he's approaching orgasm.

Actually, come to think of it, Ray isn't the most expressive of people in the facial department. Being that laid back all the time isn't commensurate to a lot of animated facial expressions.

I'm happy to take that over what the hell is going on to my left, though. Joel is doing enough animated facial expressions for all four of us and the rest of the island's inhabitants combined. His lips are wide open, and his teeth are gritted. His eyes are bulging out on stalks and keep looking over at Ray, his thinning hair is flapping about like kelp in a tropical storm, and those trails of snot are getting longer by the second.

You might not want him to be your teammate in a kayak race, but if you're commanding a navy about to go to war with a pirate horde, you could do a lot worse than superglue him to the front of your biggest ship. Those pirates would turn tail in terror if they saw that grisly visage coming at them. I know I fucking would.

And would you look at this?

As we fly past the beach full of snorkellers and get more or less halfway down the island's length, we're breaking out into a decent lead again.

This is because Joel, despite all his effort, and the look of terrifying desperation on his face, is starting to flag badly. And even Cara's efforts are now not enough to prevent Ray and me getting further and further ahead.

As we head in the direction of the main pier that passengers from the boat plane disembark from when they first arrive on Wimbufushi, I have to resist the urge to crow in triumph. We are going to win this race, and we're going to do it by a country mile if we keep up this pace!

'Aaargh!' Ray cries out and immediately stops paddling. His left hand flies to his right bicep as he does this.

'Ray! Sweetheart! Are you okay?!'

I've never heard Ray cry out in pain like that. All thoughts of the race are extinguished as something far more important has replaced it – instant worry over my fiancé's health.

'It's my arm!' he tells me, still nursing his bicep and wincing.

I barely notice as Joel and Cara go flying past us.

'What's happened?' I ask Ray, my voice full of concern.

'Think I've pulled something!' he replies, breathing out heavily. 'Not the first time. Did it windsurfing about seven years ago. Same place!'

'Oh no!'

'Probably shouldn't have pushed myself so much!'

I am instantly consumed with guilt.

This is all my fault.

I'm the one who persuaded Ray into having this stupid race, all because I was mad at Joel. *And* I'm the one who's constantly been pushing Ray to paddle harder to make up for my inadequacies.

All just to beat Joel . . .

Hang on a bloody minute! This isn't my fault! It's HIS! It's bloody Joel's! *Again!*

We wouldn't be in this race at all if it wasn't for him being such an arsehole. My poor Ray would be fine if it weren't for him!

And just look at him now, would you?

Look at him gloat as he flies into the lead!

Look how he stares back at us, knowing that we're done for!

Look how that snotty grimace has turned into a snotty grin of triumph!

Look how his head wobbles back and forth in the uncontained pleasure of the moment!

Look how he and Cara spear the kayak directly into one of the pylons holding the main wooden pier up, because Joel hasn't been paying attention to where he's going . . .

The kayak hits the wooden pole just off-centre to the right, scraping its entire side down it.

Both Joel and Cara lose their paddles, as they also clatter into the thick wooden pole.

Cara lets out a scream, as does Joel. It's hard to tell which one is more high-pitched.

Their kayak, still being propelled forward by their previous frenzied paddling, steers itself off to the right, and back out into deeper water. I can see a large gash down the side of the fibreglass, and water beginning to pour into the kayak's cockpit.

'Jesus Christ!' Joel screams, as he starts to ineffectually bail water out of the kayak with his cupped hands.

'We have to help them!' Ray says, painfully grabbing his paddle from the water beside him.

'What?' I exclaim. 'No! You're hurt! There's nothing we can do!'

'I'm fine!' he tells me, though the fact his face has gone a pallid grey colour tells me he's lying. 'We have to stop them before they drift past the red buoys!'

'The what?'

'The red buoys Jarvis told us about! We're not supposed to stray that far out into the sea at this point, because of the plane!'

'The plane?'

'Yes! That one!'

Ray points into the blue sky at a small black speck, barely visible at this distance.

'Oh shit,' I reply, understanding what he's saying. Joel and Cara are drifting out into the lane that the plane the rich folk come to the island on uses to land, with no means of controlling their fast-sinking kayak.

'Come on! Help me paddle!' Ray commands, and starts to push our kayak towards where Joel and Cara are now both crying for help and bailing away at the influx of water.

Then, from somewhere unidentifiable, Bonnie Tyler starts to sing.

You know the one.

Do do do doooooo . . .
Do do do doooooo . . .
Do do do doooooo . . .
Do daaaaaaaah . . .
Do daaaaaaaah . . .

I'm not sure where *all* the good men have gone, Bonnie, but I can point *one* out to you at least. He's sat right in front of me, paddling for all his worth, over to my *worthless* ex.

I wouldn't necessarily class Ray as a streetwise Hercules, but he's definitely doing a great impression of a white knight right about now.

And it's a good job he's doing so, because Joel and Cara have indeed drifted past the red buoys, and are currently sinking slowly, right in the lane that the boat plane lands in.

Neither of them appear to have noticed this latest dreadful turn of events, as they are clearly still trying to cope with the last one. Sadly, their efforts aren't proving very useful, as no matter how much bailing out they've done, the kayak continues to sink at an alarming rate of knots. The whole front end is pretty much in the water now, and Joel is waist deep.

'Help!' he screeches, flailing his arms around like one of those things you see outside a used-car dealership. 'We're sinking!'

His grasp of the blindingly obvious is as firm as always, it seems.

Instead of panicking, Cara is just sat quietly behind Joel, staring up at the sky in a display of absolute resignation that you have to admire.

'It's okay, we're here!' Ray says in a soothing tone, as we get closer. 'We can help get you out of the way.'

'Out of the way?' Joel wails, his face a mask of confusion. 'Out of the way of what?'

I know I shouldn't take such extreme satisfaction in my next move, but I just can't help myself. After all, I'm in as much comparative danger as Joel is – being sat alongside him – but at least my kayak is in fine working shape, and being piloted by a man who can get me clear of the danger zone in no time at all, even with a pulled bicep muscle.

I point an arm up at the rapidly growing shape of the Wimbufushi Island Resort and Spa boat plane, full of posh people who would never deign to use something as lower class as

166

a speedboat to reach their tropical getaway. 'That, Joel. *That*,' I explain. 'There's a plane coming right at you.'

The blood drains from his face in a most satisfying manner.

A bit like it did from my face when I realised I had to have a poo in public.

Ray pulls our kayak alongside theirs and tries to yank the front end out of the water with his good left arm. This doesn't do much, given Joel's bulk. 'You'll have to jump out, chap,' Ray tells him, earning him a look of panicked bewilderment.

'Get out of the fucking kayak, Joel,' I repeat slowly and loudly.

When you've got a boat plane aimed at your face, you shouldn't really talk slowly. It is a time most definitely reserved for speaking *quickly* – but the chance to really make my ex-husband feel as small as possible is too good to pass up – even if it does increase my chances of getting a propeller up the backside.

Joel stares at me for a second, before sliding out of the kayak, allowing Ray to try to lift the sinking end of the thing again. Unfortunately too much water has entered it now, so he's got no chance.

'You'll have to both abandon the kayak,' he tells them. 'Swim away, and you'll be fine!'

'I'm . . . I'm too knackered to swim!' Joel admits, barely keeping his head above water.

'Okay,' Ray replies. 'Then hold on to our kayak and I'll steer us out of the plane's path.'

Cara immediately nods and tips herself out of the kayak, grabbing the back end of ours just behind me. There's a small loop of white rope on the pointy bit that she can easily grab on to, answering the question of why it's there in the first place, I suppose.

Joel splutters and slaps his way around the sinking form of his kayak, and brings himself alongside Ray. He then grabs hold of the side of our kayak, making it list heavily.

'Careful!' Ray warns, as he tries to compensate for the dead weight.

I know how you feel, sweetheart. I had to do it for years.

Given that Joel has parked himself on Ray's left-hand side, my fiancé then has to start awkwardly and painfully paddling just on the right-hand side, which starts to send us all around in a slow, pathetic circle.

I immediately try to lend a hand by doing a bit of paddling myself – being careful not to hit Cara over the head as I do so.

Don't get me wrong, there's probably a part of me that would like to clonk her on the head, but I resist the temptation like a proper adult.

Given how weak I feel, my paddling really doesn't help matters much, and all we do is start to go around in a slightly larger pathetic circle.

Even I'm starting to feel a little panicked now. The plane is getting close enough to both see and hear properly, and isn't making much effort to change its trajectory.

'Oh God, the plane!' Joel cries. 'The plane! The plane!'

'Yes, we can see the fucking plane!' I shout at him, as I try to push us forward once more with my weak-wristed paddling.

It's no good, though. Ray is injured, I'm knackered, Joel is a dead weight and Cara appears to have gone to her happy place. We're not going to get out of the way in time. I'm going to be the first person in history to die in a holiday plane crash, and not be in the sodding plane when it happens.

All four of us look up in terror as the boat plane gets closer and closer.

'You fucking twat, Joel,' I say to my ex-husband in a weary voice.

These are not the best final words a person has ever spoken, but they'll just have to do.

Then, having finally seen the calamity unfolding beneath him, the pilot of the plane roars back up into the sky again, missing us by a good sixty or seventy feet.

'Oh, thank God,' Ray remarks, in a display of shocked relief that seems quite out of character for him. I guess this situation must have been pretty damn hairy then, for him to seem so relieved it's over.

Gulp.

'Bloody hellfire, that was close!' Joel says, sounding equally relieved.

'Yes, it fucking was,' I add, trying my hardest not to whack him on the head with my paddle.

Cara remains silent behind me. I think she might have had some sort of nervous breakdown, but I can't be a hundred per cent sure.

Then, on a day of non-stop humiliations, the final crowning indignity occurs, when I look up to see a small rubber dinghy coming towards us, with Wimbufushi's congenial host Azim sat at the prow, an anxious look on his face.

It appears we are being *rescued.*

Oh joy.

'Hello! Hello! Are you all well?' Azim says in a concerned voice, as the guy driving the motor at the back of the dinghy slows it down and comes alongside us.

'Yes!' Ray tells him. 'Although we would be grateful of some assistance getting back to shore!'

'Yes, of course!' Azim replies. 'We have never had to do this before!'

No, I bet you haven't, Azim. I bet that everybody else who visits Wimbufushi is quite capable of going out for a pleasant paddle in one of your excellent kayaks, without vomiting, nearly murdering an endangered species, and getting run over by a plane.

I've never been so embarrassed in all of my life.

. . . well, except when I turned up at Goblin Central five hours late for an important fucking meeting, of course.

Go on. Just smack him with the paddle once. It doesn't have to be that hard.

Oh, but it is *hard*. So very, very hard to remain adult, and resist the temptation . . .

But then, I don't want to give Joel any more ammunition to use against me. He knows me too well. Best I just take a deep breath, try to smile at Azim, and put this bizarre and awful conflict behind me.

It's clearly not worth the bloody hassle, and will only result in more shared misery.

Nearly having your hair cut by a plane propeller should be all you need to tell you that keeping up a course of action is only going to end in very bad things.

I should never have let Joel rile me up. I should never have pushed Ray into this race.

I should have risen above Joel's pettiness. That way, I wouldn't be covered in my own vomit, and about to be rescued from the ocean by a man who can't quite believe he's dealing with such a moronic group of holidaymakers.

That's *it*, though.

I've learned my bloody lesson.

As Azim tows Ray and I back to shore, with Joel and Cara in the dinghy with him, I resolve to not let my ex-husband negatively affect my holiday anymore. For the remaining three days, I will try my level best to ignore both him, and anything he attempts to get a rise out of me.

That way, I may just get out of here alive.

. . . which is not the kind of thing you're supposed to wish for halfway through a luxury holiday in the Maldives, now is it?

Friday

Joel – Emasculation

I think, all things considered, it's probably about the right time to get absolutely fucking pissed.

There aren't many occasions in life when this seems like the best course of action, but taking into account what's happened to me recently, I can see no other possible avenue of pursuit that would be as effective.

When you've comprehensively been shown up in front of your girlfriend by another man – especially one in Tiny White Shorts – there's very little else you can do to make yourself feel better than climb into a bottle.

Yesterday was a *disaster*. A five-star disaster, with sea views, a spa bath, and twenty-four-hour room service.

And to think that for a moment, I thought I'd actually *won*.

As Mr Tiny White Shorts stopped paddling and started cradling his injured arm, I felt a surge of triumph go through me.

This lasted for precisely twelve seconds, before we hit that fucking pole and everything went to shit.

Twelve seconds.

Twelve seconds of triumph, surrounded by abject defeat.

That'll be what I'll call my autobiography, if I ever get the chance to write it.

And that abject defeat came to a conclusion when I had to be rescued by Azim – another competent, well-put-together man who makes me look like a towering idiot.

At least he isn't having sex with my ex-wife, I suppose.

Azim was very gracious about the destroyed kayak. I tried to say I was sorry about the damage, but he just waved my apologies away with a laugh. There was a brittleness around the edges of that laugh though, showing that even someone as well trained in the arts of hospitality as Azim cannot entirely conceal his true feelings *all* of the time.

I was frankly glad to say goodbye to him and trudge back to the water bungalow. I was even more glad that Ray and Amy went in the other direction. If they'd have been going to the same place as us, there's every chance I would have suggested to Ray that we race to see who got there first. One last opportunity to prove that I am not the single most beta male that has ever walked the face of the planet.

Mind you, I could have beaten him by a hundred yards and it still wouldn't make up for the fact that ten minutes prior to that I was hanging on to him for dear life and screaming like a little girl.

Good bloody *grief*.

Cara's been quiet ever since we got back to the bungalow. I suppose I can't blame her. I forced her into a stupid race she wanted no part of, and nearly got her killed – first by drowning, and then by plane attack. No wonder she hasn't wanted to talk to me much. She's probably re-evaluating our entire relationship – and wondering how she managed to get stuck with a man in his late thirties with a slight paunch and extremely fragile ego, when she could easily find a man in tiny white shorts, if she so desired.

. . . okay, I'm obsessed. I realise that now. It's funny how nearly having a boat plane embedded in your skull can really help you get to grips with your own neuroses.

I'd have to have no self-awareness at all to not appreciate how jealous I am of Ray Holland. I look at him and see everything I'm not.

He's taller, better looking, better built and better mannered.

He's also managed to make a relationship work with Amy Caddick, which is no mean feat. Certainly one I was not capable of.

The question of when that relationship started still plays on my mind, though, I can tell you that.

From what I remember, Ray Holland became a client of Rowntree Land & Home a good three or four months prior to the disaster of Goblin Central. And did Amy have a lot more contact with him than I did?

Why, yes, she absolutely *did*. At the time I thought nothing of it – I was just glad that we'd landed a good sale, given how much commission it paid us. But all these years later, knowing what I know now . . . I have to wonder what was going on between them, right under my bloody nose.

I have no proof of any shenanigans, of course. But can I rule out that shenanigans might well have happened? Can I say for certain that my already problematic marriage wasn't made much worse the day Ray Holland walked into our offices, and asked Amy and I for help in buying his next home?

No, I cannot.

And here he is, in what seems like a very comfortable, happy relationship with Amy – while I flounder around in the depths with Cara, with a rapidly sinking feeling that makes the one I felt in the kayak seem inconsequential by comparison.

I used to be like Ray. I used to be the confident one. I used to be the one in control of his life. Right up until Goblin Central happened. Ever since then and the subsequent divorce, it's been an uphill battle. All because of Amy. All because of what she took away from me . . .

Throughout the whole of today, I've tried to put all of this stupidity out of my head, and just relax. I've failed at this *spectacularly*.

We're now into the second half of this holiday, and so far – other than a very pleasant few hours on the sun beds yesterday morning – it's been about as relaxing as a Red-Bull-soaked rollercoaster ride. I'm well aware that it's my actions that have caused this, so I've done all I can today to make sure Cara is as happy as possible. This is all well and good for her, but it's left me stressed out and tense. I'm so desperate to make up for yesterday that I'm doing everything in my power to see that Cara is well taken care of, and that's not conducive to my own sense of well-being.

I've waited on her hand and foot all day, and left her in as much peace as I can, without making it seem like I'm being inattentive. This appears to have been successful in the respect that by early evening Cara looks blissfully chilled out, but it doesn't mean she's talking to me that much more than she was this morning, when we both woke up with the horrors of yesterday still lingering fresh in our minds.

Is she still just in stunned silence about the whole thing?

Or is this some sort of precursor to the breakdown of our relationship?

I have no idea.

Cara remains pretty quiet throughout dinner this evening, only speaking to me when I try my hardest to start a bland, inoffensive conversation – largely about the food we're eating. I should just force the issue, and confront her ongoing coolness towards me, but I have to confess I'm just too scared to do so. I'm terrified that if I do push it, everything will unravel completely, and I will discover that she does indeed want out of this relationship, and just hasn't voiced that thanks to the fact she's trapped on this island with me for another three days.

In the midst of this evening angst, I see Amy and Ray come into dinner looking quite happy and relaxed with each other. They clearly had a better day than I did. They also both pointedly ignored me like the plague, which is much to be expected, given the circumstances. I have no idea what they've been up to today, but it quite obviously doesn't consist of either giving the other the cold shoulder.

Given all of this, and given that I see no way of rectifying my issues anytime soon, you can hopefully understand that by the time dinner is over, I am in the mood to get good and drunk.

Happily for me – or perhaps incredibly *un*happily, depending on who you ask – Wimbufushi Island Resort and Spa is all inclusive, which means I have access to an unlimited supply of booze.

Therefore, once dinner is over, and I have finished off the last of my profiteroles, I suggest to Cara that we move from the restaurant over to the monstrous and extremely comfortable main lounge bar of the island, which is called Blue Horizon.

Unlike the tiny Reef Bar, which is designed to look as much like a hastily erected beach bar as is humanly possible without actually being one, Blue Horizon is meant to come across as the most luxurious drinking establishment possible – and boy does it succeed in that.

Built underneath a gigantic domed roof, the circular lounge is dominated by the enormous edifice of the bar itself. The rows and rows of drink bottles stretch all the way up to the ceiling on glass shelves that wrap around the thick central pole that holds up the roof, and can only be reachable by ladder or Spider-Man.

Think of a drink . . . any drink.

It's here, trust me.

If you have a hankering for a kumquat-infused vodka, then look no further. If you've always fancied a fermented yak milk and lime cocktail, then this is the place for you.

I just intend to throw as many Sin Cities down my neck as possible – but what else can I possibly do to entertain myself, when my girlfriend is not really speaking to me?

She seems quite content to sit here quietly in the booth we're occupying in a cool, dark corner of the lounge, sipping on her Manhattan – which must mean that she's not so sick of my company yet as to want to get completely away from it.

I'm going to take that as a good sign, in a day of signs worse than the ones that tell you dangerous rock falls are ahead.

By the time I have finished the second Sin City, my nerves have calmed considerably, and when the third one is dispensed with, I'm starting to actually feel relaxed for the first time today.

You see?

Getting drunk *is* a good idea, isn't it? You can tell by the way I'm sat here smiling at nothing.

Even Cara seems to be enjoying herself. She's on her second Manhattan, and has actually just engaged me in a proper conversation for the first time since I asked her if she'd like to go kayaking. Okay, it was only to ask why I thought there were large speakers and a PC monitor being set up on the other side of the circular lounge, in front of the enormous OLED TV that often plays music videos for the entertainment of the bar's patrons, but it's a conversation starter nonetheless, and better than stony silence.

'I'm not sure,' I reply, looking over at where a couple of Wimbufushi staff are erecting two tall columns of speakers, with the monitor in front of them on a plinth, facing away from us. Underneath this, a small computer is being tucked on to a shelf in the plinth.

I may say that I have no idea what's going on, but deep down inside me, there's a small part of my soul that has just started to do cartwheels.

It knows what those speakers and that monitor means, even if my conscious and half-pissed mind doesn't quite yet.

Let's see how long it takes for the rest of me to catch up . . .

'Maybe there's a band playing tonight?' Cara wonders. 'I forgot to look at the island's activities for today.'

I nod sagely. I also didn't bother to look at the island activity roster today. It's a white board nailed up in reception that changes information on a daily basis, letting us all know what's on the schedule. It's a convenient way to find out what trips, activities and entertainment are on that day, when you can't be arsed to look in your welcome pack.

I've been so concerned with my relationship, and strange obsession with Ray Holland, that I forgot to even glance at it. It's a little hard to get excited about scuba-diving lessons when your ego is being slowly torn to shreds.

'Well, I guess we'll find out what it is pretty soon. There's quite a few people congregating around it now.'

And indeed, that's precisely what's happening. There are a plethora of squat wicker tables set up in front of where the speakers are, surrounded by deep, comfortable wicker armchairs. These are rapidly filling up with holidaymakers, all of whom look quite expectant. Some even look a little nervous.

That little part of my soul that knows what's going on is running around like its hair is on fire, because it knows what's coming.

One of the Wimbufushi staff then erects two microphone stands just behind the monitor, and everything falls into place.

Karaoke.

It can only be karaoke!

. . . or bingo.

But can you see bingo being played here on one of the Maldives' most luxurious island resorts?

No, neither can I.

Far too tacky for such exalted clientele. I doubt anyone within a thousand square miles wants anything to do with clickety click or two fat ladies.

You'd think the same would hold true for karaoke, but for some bizarre and unexplained reasons, the popularity of it extends right up and down the social spectrum. From the poorest, most down-trodden of households, to the mansions of the rich and famous – everyone likes a bit of karaoke! And it's therefore perfectly reasonable to expect to see it occurring in a place like this.

'Cool!' I exclaim, staring at the microphone stand.

I say this because I have now caught up with that small, excited part of my soul, and know full well what the future now holds.

I fucking LOVE karaoke. It's a bizarre and odd obsession of mine that I've never been able to move past, no matter how much I try.

To clarify, though, I only love karaoke when I'm *drunk*. I can take it or leave it if I'm stone cold sober. The drunker I am, though, the more I'm into it.

Because I have not been that much of a drinker across my adult years, I have actually conducted karaoke on only *three* occasions. On each and every one of those occasions I have been comprehensively blotto.

They are, in chronological order, my mother's fiftieth birthday, the Christmas my uncle got a karaoke machine as a present, and my wedding reception.

I have never completed an entire song.

At my mother's birthday I got about sixty-five per cent of the way through 'Killing In The Name Of' by Rage Against The Machine before I fell off the stage. The Christmas ordeal of having to listen to me destroying 'I Wish It Could Be Christmas Everyday' was ended when I inadvertently yanked the plug out of the wall, while kicking my legs up like the last chorus girl in the shop.

And at my wedding, I was dragged off stage by an equally drunk Amy Sinclair née Caddick, who thought that her married life probably shouldn't start with her new husband attempting to sing, *'My milkshake brings all the boys to the yard,'* at the top of his voice.

So, I have never finished an entire song when performing karaoke, and it's been a thorn in my side ever since.

'It's karaoke, Cara!' I tell my girlfriend in an excited voice. 'They're setting up for a nice bit of karaoke this evening.'

'Oh. I've never done karaoke. Always fancied giving it a try, though.'

'Really?'

'Yes.'

'Stay right there.'

I jump to my feet, and make a beeline for the guys setting up the equipment. If Cara has never done karaoke, that is an oversight that must be rectified immediately!

'Hi there,' I say to the first bloke I manage to distract from his work. 'How the hell are you this evening, my friend?'

'I am very well, sir,' he replies, a bit taken aback by my enthusiasm.

'You look like you're doing a very fine job setting all of this stuff up . . . er . . . ?' I trail off, looking at him expectantly.

'Hassan,' he replies, obviously quite surprised that I want to know his name.

'Hassan! Nice to meet you, my friend.' I point at the speakers. 'All of this . . . it's is for karaoke, yes?'

He nods his head and offers me that patented Wimbufushi hospitality smile. 'Yes indeed, sir.'

'Great! How are people putting their names forward to do it?'

'Speak to Rajesh over there, sir.' He points to another Wimbufushi man, this one dressed in white trousers and a dark blue shirt with sequin dragons down the lapels, standing over by one of the speakers, chatting to a couple of his colleagues.

I say thank you to Hassan, giving him a friendly pat on the back as I do so, and make my way over to Rajesh, who has the most closely cropped beard I've ever seen, and a fair amount of product in his hair. All of this screams master of ceremonies to me.

As I approach him, I see the massive TV on the wall burst into life with the legend *Couple's Karaoke* on it, in large, friendly letters.

Hah! *Perfect!*

'Hello there!' I say to Rajesh, interrupting the conversation. I tend to get a bit interrupty when I've had a few drinks. It's not one of my good points.

'Good evening, sir!' Rajesh says, looking like he's incredibly happy to see me. I'm sure he's not, though. 'What can I do for you?'

'Well, Rajesh, I'd really love to be a part of the karaoke tonight. How do I put myself and my girlfriend down for it?' I ask in an expectant voice.

'Very easy, sir.' Rajesh beams. 'Just give me your names and I will put you on my list.'

'Thanks very much!' I reply, shaking Rajesh's hand vigorously.

I then give him my name and Cara's, which he pops on to an iPad, and then I walk at an excited pace back to Cara.

'What have you done?' she asks, when I plonk myself back down on the chair.

'I've put us in for the karaoke!' I tell her.

Cara's eyes go wide. 'You didn't!'

'I did! It'll be fun! You said you've never done it before, so here's your chance!'

Cara giggles. Actually *giggles*. This is the most positive I've seen her towards me all day. 'What song will we sing?'

'Oh. I'm not sure,' I reply, then wave a hand. 'I'm sure they'll let us choose one when we get up there.'

'Okay!'

I'm so pleased Cara looks this animated and happy. Thank God for the miracle of karaoke, eh?

A few minutes later, Rajesh takes to the 'stage' and introduces himself.

'Welcome, everyone, to tonight's very special karaoke session,' he tells us. 'Those of you who know the island well will know that we're famous for our karaoke nights, and we're so pleased you've joined us all for this very special Randomiser Karaoke evening.'

Wait . . . what? Randomiser Karaoke?

'It'll be lots of fun getting you on stage to sing songs that our computer picks at random for you.' Rajesh chuckles. 'You're all very brave for putting yourself forward for it!'

'Randomiser?' Cara says with a doubtful voice.

I wave a hand again. 'I'm sure it'll be fine,' I tell her, trying to avoid the look on her face.

Rajesh then taps away on his iPad – which is obviously connected by strange and technological means to the karaoke system – and on the TV screen behind him *Trevor & Sandra* appears.

From over to my left, Trevor and Sandra roar their approval at seeing their names come up first (they look like they've had their fair share of Sin Cities as well) and come over to stand next to Rajesh, who greets them with a huge smile, and then leaves the stage for them to occupy on their own.

'Evening!' Sandra says in a broad Essex accent.

Trevor and Sandra are quite clearly working-class folks done good, and are the couple I saw chatting to Ray and Amy on the speedboat to the island.

Trevor has got a beer gut you could bounce pennies off, and is covered in amateurish tattoos – and Sandra's definitely *had some work done.* They scream salt of the Earth from every single pore, and I guess the used-car business or scrapyard is doing very well for itself, hence why they are here on Wimbufushi.

Let's see what song they get to sing . . .

I see Rajesh playing with the iPad again, and the TV starts to randomly flash through several dozen song titles while a synthesised drum roll plays.

There's a loud clash of electronic cymbals, as the flashing names stop on 'I've Got You Babe' by Sonny and Cher.

I have to roll my eyes. Maybe this 'randomiser' isn't quite as random as Rajesh made out, given how clichéd and obvious that song choice is. I don't think Cara and I will have much to worry about.

'Oh, I would have liked to do that one,' Cara says, a little disappointed.

'Don't worry, I'm sure we'll get something similar,' I assure her.

The first chords of 'I've Got You Babe' start up, and Trevor and Sandra ready themselves.

When Sandra starts to sing, I immediately call over a waiter to go and get me another Sin City. If everyone involved in this event has a voice like hers, I'm afraid the only things that are likely to survive are the cockroaches and the hard of hearing.

Trevor's not much better. His voice drones like a fully laden bomber.

'Oh dear,' Cara remarks, wincing.

By the time 'I've Got You Babe' has mercifully finished, I have my fourth Sin City in front of me.

By the time the *fifth* comes, another four couples have had their turn, all by varying degrees of awfulness. Bao and Chun really did a fucking number on 'Endless Love'. 'Ebony and Ivory' did not live together in perfect harmony once Larry and Chad got their hands on it. Sasha and Mitchell should be drowned before they're allowed to sing 'Islands in the Stream' again, and 'Don't Go Breaking My Heart' is now some kind of auditory nerve agent, thanks to the efforts of Reginald and Susan.

I'm starting to wonder when Cara and I are going to get our turn. The evening is wearing on, and if I drink too many more of these Sin Cities, I'm not going to be able to hold the microphone up the right way.

I try my hardest not to let out a groan when I see Amy and Ray walk into the lounge, and move towards the back.

Can't I just have one evening where those two don't turn up to spoil everything?

Amy looks horrified at the prospect of having to watch karaoke. I assume this is because her last run-in with it involved dragging my inebriated backside away from the mic, before I could do any more damage. Ray looks like he's enjoying it, though.

Oh shit . . . what if they are one of the couples doing a routine tonight as well?

My blood runs cold.

What if we go on *right after them*?

I know for a fact that Amy can bang out a tune when she feels up to it, and I bet Ray has a set of lungs on him to match those biceps.

Gah . . .

It'll be like yesterday all over again!

I should pull us out of this whole thing before it gets to that. I'll just get up now, go and see Rajesh and wipe our names off the list. That way we (I) won't have the indignity of not being able to compete with Amy and—

'Joel! It's us!' I hear Cara exclaim with slurred excitement. She's on her fifth Manhattan of the evening herself.

Oh *shit*. Too late.

On the huge TV screen, our names have flashed up in those big, friendly letters. They don't look half as friendly now, though.

I see Ray and Amy take seats at one of the only spare tables left in the lounge, quite close to the back wall. Good. At least they won't be in obvious eyeshot.

I get to my feet and put on a fake smile.

Even in my drunken state, I know I don't want to do this anymore. The last thing I want is to perform badly in front of my ex. I did enough of that in the fucking kayak, and the memory of it has not been diminished in the slightest by the heroic amount of hard alcohol I've consumed this evening.

'Come on! Let's go!' Cara says, grabbing my arm.

Great. This is the first physical contact I've had with her all day, and it has to come at the expense of whatever's left of my self-worth. I either disappoint Cara by pulling out of the karaoke, and risk a return to the coldness I've endured all day, or I go and make a fool of myself, knowing full well that Ray and Amy are probably waiting in the wings to do a much better job of having a public sing-song than I am.

I allow Cara to drag me to the karaoke mics, my heart hammering all the while.

I was really looking forward to doing this – until I saw Amy. Now I'm shitting a brick, despite the five Sin Cities.

'You okay?' Cara says as she takes a mic off its stand.

I nod and give her a smile, if only because it's lovely to hear her concerned about my welfare. I just can't let her down now by not going through with it.

I grab the other mic off the stand, and look down at the monitor in front of us. Rajesh has already pulled the virtual lever, and the song names are rapidly rolling over one another to the accompaniment of the drum roll.

I roll my eyes when it stops on 'The Time Of My Life' by Bill Medley and Jennifer Warnes. I then let out a high-pitched whine when at the bottom, in brackets, it adds, *Gender Swap Version*.

What the fuck?

The song's first few notes begin, and I look at Cara in confusion. What does it mean by gender swap?

On the screen in front of us, and mirrored on the massive one just behind us, the first lyrics of the song appear like this:

Her: Now I've had the time of my life . . . no, I never felt like this before.

'Fuck! Do I sing this bit?' Cara asks, looking at me and then over at Rajesh – who smiles, nods and beckons her to start.

'Yes! I think so!' I reply, watching as the colour of the words on the screen starts to change from bright green to bright red from left to right, to indicate that they should be sung.

Cara splutters over the first few words, but by the time she reaches the end of the first line of lyrics, she's caught up magnificently, and has – it has to be said – a rather lovely singing voice.

The audience actually give her a bit of a clap, which is very nice of them. I can't see Amy and Ray at the back, but I have a feeling there's probably not much clapping going on over there.

Then, on screen, it changes to show me that I'm supposed to start singing the Jennifer Warnes bit. I, Joel Sinclair, who at the best of times probably has a singing voice that can strip the paint off a nuclear silo, am now required to mimic a woman's singing.

Ah, fuck it.

If I'm going to have to do this weird gender swap thing, let's have some fun with it, eh?

I repeat the same lines that Cara just has, only in the worst falsetto voice I can manage. This is *shriekingly* hideous to listen to, but at least it's deliberately so, rather than my normal singing, which is equally awful, but in no way intentional.

Instant, loud and raucous laughter swells into the air from the audience, and I have to stifle a loud, drunken chuckle. Well, it's nice to see my efforts have not gone unappreciated.

I continue through the next couple of lines, with the laughter still ringing in my ears.

Now I remember why I like karaoke so much! I'm entertaining the people!

Okay, it's not the way karaoke is necessarily intended to entertain, but I'll take it!

It really helps that Cara has such a nice voice. It works in perfect counterpoint to whatever the hell it is that I'm doing. Going from her in-tune, lovely pitch to my weird Monty Python-esque falsetto is as hilarious as it is incongruous.

And Cara is enjoying herself *immensely*. She can barely keep it together every time I sing. It's fabulous to see such a huge smile on her face. I don't think I've seen her look this happy the entire time we've been on the island.

Who'd have thought a bit of Medley and Warnes would do the trick?

We might not quite be having the time of our lives, but it's certainly a lot of drunken fun, and that's good enough for me, for the time being.

When we hit the chorus, and both Cara and I have to sing together, it takes the performance to a whole new level. So much so that we start to dance around one another with our arms linked. I don't remember Bill and Jen doing the Dosey Doe in the video to the song, but it feels completely appropriate in this context.

The audience continues to lap all of this up, and I can even hear a few of them joining in with the singing when we hit the chorus for the second time. Everybody on planet Earth knows the lyrics to the chorus of this song, even if they don't bloody want or need to.

Cara and I are a *hit*.

. . . and I bet Amy is *hating* every second of it.

I'm currently the centre of attention – in a positive way for once – and I bet that is sticking in her craw like a sideways chicken bone. I'm making a point of not looking in her direction, but I can just see the expression on her face in my mind's eye.

Hah! See, Amy? See how I don't need you to have fun, or do well at something?

And I bet Ray – good old happy-go-lucky, wife-stealing-from-under-my-fucking-nose Ray – is sat there tapping his foot along, with a big, handsome, goofy smile on his face. That'll annoy her even more.

This vision warms my heart as we hit the saxophone break.

What also warms my heart is how much my girlfriend is having fun. It may be the five Sin Cities talking, but she's never looked more beautiful than she does now – with her hair plastered to her forehead with sweat, her arms and legs flailing around to the greatest saxophone solo ever recorded, and loud cackles erupting from her mouth like a braying horse.

I have never sat through all of *Dirty Dancing*, because obviously not, but I know enough about it to know that there was some serious lambada action going on between the overwrought interpersonal drama.

I figure that while the saxophone is going, I might as well attempt to recreate the dance from the movie with Cara for the delight and edification of our audience.

I sidle up to her and put my arms around her neck, indicating to her that she should put her arms around my waist.

She steps away from me with a pointed expression on her face.

Oops.

Have I gone too far?

'Oh no, mister!' she says in a breathless voice. 'You're the girl here, remember?'

And then she closes the gap with me again, but forces my hands around her waist, while she loops hers around my neck.

Heh.

Fair enough. This is the gender-swap version after all, isn't it?

Cara and I then proceed to drunkenly lambada, while the instrumental plays itself out. This largely consists of stumbling back and forth in front of the monitor, occasionally bumping our crotches into each other awkwardly. Whoever decided this was a sexy dance must be a right masochist.

As the saxophone reaches a crescendo, Cara loosens her grip around my waist and dips me.

Yes, that's right, she actually *dips me*, so I have to arch my back and drop my head backwards. The timing is perfect. As the sax stops, and everything goes quiet for that bit in the song where everyone can get their breath back, we hold the dipped position like we were born for it.

The crowd *loves* it. So does Cara.

I'm not sure how I feel about it. I couldn't care less about being the dipped person in the equation, but I'm not sure I can stay like this for long before my back gives out. I am neither as young nor as flexible as the woman in the film, and while Cara is a strong girl for her size (the way she powered us around in the kayak is testament to that) I'm pretty sure she's not as strong as Patrick Swayze, so I'd better come upright again fast, before my spine gives out and we both crash to the floor.

I receive the mother of all head rushes as I stand up again, but that's all the damage that's done. My back is thankfully fine.

Bill Medley is telling us all once again that he's had the time of his life, this time with no backing track. It's so incredibly earnest.

From over near where Cara and I were sitting I hear some-body scream, 'Do the lift!' I think it might be Trevor, or possibly Sandra – she sounds like she goes through forty B&H every day of her life, so it's perfectly possible to mistake the two.

I laugh and wave my hand dismissively.

'*Do the lift*,' he/she says.

Is he/she mad?

We all know what *the lift* is, don't we? Even those of us like myself who have never sat through *Dirty Dancing* know all about that bit at the end when Swayze lifts the girl by her waist, while she does her best impression of a jumbo jet.

'Do the lift!' Trevor/Sandra calls again, this time being joined by some of the other karaoke fans watching us.

I mean . . .

It would be one hell of a way to round things off, wouldn't it?

I have never finished a karaoke song in my life, and if I'm going to finally do so, it'd be nice to mark the occasion with something spectacular . . .

And Cara has already demonstrated that she is happy to play the part of Patrick Swayze. What's to say I can't carry on being Jumbo Jet Girl and finish this performance off with a real showstopper?

Yes. I have indeed taken leave of my senses. Thank you so much for noticing.

Scientists posit that there could be multiple realities layered over our own. The inflationary theory of existence states that count-less individual universes could have been created at the time of the Big Bang.

It's a truly fascinating concept.

I bet you all the fucking tea in China that no matter how weird and wonderful the physics are in those strange parallel universes, none of them would allow for all thirteen stone of me to be lifted successfully above my nine-stone girlfriend's head.

And yet, right here in *this* universe, five Sin Cities are telling me it's perfectly possible, and the absolute best way to bring the house down at the end of a marvellous performance.

I start nodding and gesticulating to Cara as the song starts to wind itself towards its conclusion. She in turn starts shaking her head and backing away from me.

This is the worst possible thing she could have done, as it gives me a run up.

As everyone in the lounge sings the last couple of choruses for us, I step away from Cara by a few more feet, as she continues to back away, towards the giant main TV screen.

'Do it! Do it!' the crowd start to chant.

The bastards want blood, and they're not going to be satisfied until they get it!

Well, that's just fine by me!

Nobody is going to upstage Cara and I tonight. Not Trevor and Sandra, not Bao and Chun, not Larry and Chad, and *definitely* not Amy and Ray!

'The Time Of My Life' reaches its crescendo, and I start running straight at Cara, screaming 'Arms up!' as I do so.

The poor girl is so taken aback by my commanding drunken tone that she does as I ask, and her hands go above and slightly in front of her head, ready to receive me as I jump gazelle-like into the air.

Now, you may have noticed that I couldn't jump like a gazelle if you popped one in a hand-made teleport machine with me, and spliced us together in one gloriously hideous lump.

Especially not when I've had a skinful.

But I'm committed now. There's simply nothing that can stop me attempting to jump into the air like Superman on his way to a bank robbery, and have Cara lift me over her head like a graceful jumbo jet.

. . . all except Cara that is, who – being still partially in control of her faculties – jumps out of my way at the very last instant, squealing in terror as she does so.

This means that when I do launch myself off the ground like Clark Kent responding to another dastardly Lex Luthor plot to take over the world, I am not gathered lovingly up in my girlfriend's outstretched arms, but instead fly face first straight into the TV screen.

The heavy, flat crunch that accompanies this is far louder than Bill, Jen and the entire happy crowd of the Blue Horizon lounge.

'The Time Of My Life' therefore does not conclude this evening with its usual repetitive wind down. It instead comes to a very abrupt and decisive halt with all thirteen stone of Joel Sinclair meeting the lower third of a sixty-five-inch flat-screen telly at a speed that does neither of them any good whatsoever.

Tell you what, though . . . nobody else will be able to follow my performance tonight, I am entirely right about that. There's something very *final* about a fully grown man flying into a TV screen, I think you'll agree. Unless someone wants to try to upstage me by karate kicking the entire bar to pieces, this karaoke session is fucking *done*.

Cara cries out in shock and alarm as I slide down on to the ground, leaving the TV screen above me blackened and covered in a spiderweb of cracked lines.

From somewhere far off and very distant I can hear Trevor and/ or Sandra start to laugh raucously.

Ah well, at least I've sent them home happy, I think, as I slide into temporary unconsciousness.

Friday

Amy – A Split Second

He came around about two or three minutes later.

With blood running from a freshly smashed nose, my inebriated ex-husband let everyone in the bar know that he was okay. He was given a round of applause that even I had to begrudgingly admit he probably deserved. The way he flew straight into that television was quite something. I don't really have the words to describe it. They probably haven't been invented yet. But when they are, they will be long, difficult to pronounce and only used on extremely rare occasions.

We all had to clap at the sheer unlikelihood of him getting away without major injury. He'll have a sore nose for a while, but that's probably about it.

What concerns me most is my reaction to seeing him fly into that TV screen.

For a moment there, it genuinely looked like he could have done himself a serious injury. There's something both very dramatic and quite terrifying about watching someone crash straight into something that is ostensibly made of glass. Especially someone you know well.

I did not laugh like the funniest thing ever had happened when he did it – unlike some of the drunken people in the lounge, who found the whole thing hilarious.

No, I leaped to my feet and immediately started to rush forward.

I was so far at the back of the lounge, though, that by the time I'd even closed half the distance, Joel was already surrounded by people fussing over him.

This brought me up short, and it suddenly hit me that I was not the right person to be helping him, even if my gut reaction was to rush over.

I'm not his wife anymore.

I haven't been his wife for a long time.

And I *hate* him.

I should be doubled over with laughter at the sight of him potentially hurting himself badly . . . but that was not how I reacted at all.

It only took a few moments to shake myself out of the panicked need to see if he was okay or not, but I was acting on autopilot for those few moments, and had no real control of myself.

Ray then joined me, also looking pretty concerned. We may both have good reason to think Joel Sinclair is the biggest idiot that has ever graced God's green earth, but that doesn't mean either of us wants to see him crash into a sheet of glass.

We hung back a little as we watched Cara, Rajesh and the rest of the Wimbufushi staff tending to Joel where he lay on the floor in front of the broken TV.

I have to say it was with some relief that I saw him slowly get to his feet, helped up by everyone around him. He looked dazed, confused and bloodied from the smashed nose, but other than that, Joel looked like he'd got away with his crazy drunken antics without permanent injury.

I guess I shouldn't be surprised that things ended this way.

Joel has *never* been good around karaoke. The only reason he didn't break his neck at our wedding reception was because I pulled him off the two-foot stage before he had a chance to fall off it. Nobody – and I do mean nobody – should be inflicted with Joel singing Kelis's 'Milkshake', no matter how much they've had to drink across an entire wedding day.

I wouldn't have let him run at me the way Cara did either, but then I'm older, wiser and more cautious than she is.

Mind you, I'd never have got up on stage to sing that song with him in the first place. I'm just not that . . . crazy? Brave? I don't know.

Ray and I left the lounge shortly after Joel was walked away to be treated in the island's small medical centre, which lies somewhere in the depths of Wimbufushi.

As we strolled back to our bungalow, I couldn't help but reflect on my reaction to seeing Joel fly into the TV.

I continued to reflect on it throughout what remained of the evening, and I continue to reflect on it even now – at two o'clock in the morning, when I should be fast asleep.

I am *disturbed*, you see.

Disturbed that even under all the rage I feel towards Joel for what he did to me two years ago, there is still a part of me that quite clearly cares for him.

You don't leap out of your seat with your heart in your throat when it looks like someone you don't really know has hurt themselves badly.

Or do you?

Maybe I'm just a very, very nice human being, full of compassion for my fellow man. Maybe I would have leaped up in the same way, even if it had been that tattooed guy Trevor who had run face first into the screen.

Maybe . . .

But what's keeping me awake now is the prospect that I only reacted the way I did because it *was* Joel. Followed swiftly by the horrible question: would I have done the same if it had been Ray?

Not that Ray would ever do something as foolish as that, but still.

And then there was that *moment*, wasn't there?

The one with the dugong – where Joel's eyes met with mine, and for the first time in years there was no sign of malice in them whatsoever. That wasn't Today Joel and Today Amy looking at each other. That was the Joel and Amy of *Yesterday*. The two people who loved each other very much and would leap out of chairs in an instant if the other one looked hurt.

Oh, good grief.

Is it any wonder I can't bloody *sleep*?

I shift the thin covers off, and sit up. Beside me, Ray is softly snoring and looks incredibly content about everything in the world. He's quite beautiful when he's like this. There have been times when I've just spent a couple of seconds watching him, with a big dumb smile on my face.

Joel looks and sounds like a dying camel when he's sleeping.

And here I am again . . . back to thinking about my bloody ex-husband. What the hell is going on?

I get out of bed and pad my way over to the front door, pulling on a t-shirt and jogging bottoms as I do so. A bit of night-time fresh air will make me sleepy. It always does.

As I quietly open the front door, Ray turns over and farts. Hearing Ray fart is quite a rare occurrence. He's not one for being demonstrative about his bodily functions.

Unlike some other men I could mention . . .

Gah.

Fresh air, woman. Go and get some.

Taking the key card from the cabinet at the side of the door, I go through and close it softly behind me.

Outside, it's *glorious*.

There aren't many places on this planet where it's wonderfully warm and calm at two o'clock in the morning, but the Maldives is certainly one of them.

And just look at that sky!

I still marvel every night at how incredible the stars are here. You can see so many of them. If nothing else, this little starlit sojourn will give me the opportunity to look at that properly in peace.

And boy is it *peaceful*. I can't hear anyone or anything, other than the soft lapping of the gentle water beneath my feet.

Anywhere else, this would feel a little creepy. The complete absence of humanity, and the absolute darkness can do that. But it's a little hard to do creepy when you're on a Maldivian island. They're just too damn warm, pretty and serene.

I get to the end of the walkway that leads to our bungalow and firmly walk left. I have no intention of looking at the stars above my head anywhere near where I had to take an outdoor shit.

This instantly reminds me of why I despise my ex-husband so much, and why it's so strange for me to feel any concern for him whatsoever.

Grumbling to myself, I make my way down the main walkway leading back to the island proper, and arrive at the beach just as a soft wind picks up, giving me a thrill down my back, as my toes dig into the soft sand.

Well . . . this is quite *marvellous*. I feel like I have the whole island to myself.

Where will I go?

If I head left, it will take me down the more populated side of the island, where the bars and restaurant are. There's a chance I might bump into someone, and I would really rather like to be on my own for this entire walk.

Going right takes me down the far less busy side of Wimbufushi, with only the beach bungalows of the resident guests to worry about. Much better.

This way also gives me a chance to come close to where we saw the dugong yesterday, and I would dearly love to see it again, even if it's only a black shape cresting the waves in front of me. That'd do. Just to know it's still there, and still happily grazing for food as the island's inhabitants sleep off theirs.

The soft wind continues to caress my skin in a way that I would dearly love to experience every night of my life, and the sand beneath my feet remains soft and yielding. I'm aware that the darkness has heightened my senses somewhat, and that's just fine with me. My eyes get all the fun during the day. It's nice to give the others a go in the driving seat.

It takes me only a few minutes to reach the rough middle point of the island. Wimbufushi really is tiny. It's here where I decide to stop and look out to sea.

There's no moon again tonight, and the water is calm, so I can actually see the starlight reflecting off the water. Can I even begin to describe how incredible that simple thing is? To see the light from stars a million miles away, caught in the rippling shimmer of the night-time ocean?

Probably not. Best I just stand here and admire it, instead of trying to trap it into things as crude and unsuitable as words.

I take a deep, long breath, and close my eyes.

What an *exquisite* moment.

For the first time, I actually feel incredibly pleased that I couldn't get to sleep. If I had drifted off as normal, I wouldn't get to experience this, and that would have been a terrible thing.

If only the reason for my sleeplessness had been something nicer than thoughts of my ex-husband.

Still, never mind about him. He's probably safely tucked up in bed with Cara, snoring away like a camel with adenoids, and farting like a dugong that's wolfed down way too much seaweed for one night.

'Lovely, isn't it?'

'Bloody hell!' I scream, heart jumping into my throat.

I whip my head around to see that someone is sat up the beach from me, just under the overhang of a palm tree.

Oh, how fucking *special*. I'm going to get murdered in the Maldives.

That'll be what they call the ITV docudrama they make about it. *Murdered in the Maldives: The Story of Amy Caddick and Her Run-in with the Coconut Killer.*

'It's okay, Amy. It's only me.'

'Joel?!'

'Yeah. Who else?'

He stands up, brushes sand off his board shorts, and walks down the beach to join me. There's a look of resignation on his face. There are also small white tubes of cotton wool shoved up his nose, and even in the starlight, I can see that both eyes look a little black.

'I don't fucking believe it,' I say, hand on my chest.

'Don't you? We seem to keep bumping into each other, no matter how hard we try not to.' He looks up. 'Somebody up there clearly doesn't like us very much.'

I roll my eyes. 'There are just stars up there, Joel. The fact we keep running into each other is entirely down to us.'

He gives me a quizzical look. I return it with a long-suffering one.

'Why are you here on the beach tonight?' I ask him.

He shrugs. 'I don't know. I just couldn't sleep because my nose really hurts, so I thought I'd have a walk, and came down here because I—'

'—wanted to see the dugong again,' I finish for him, which makes his blackened eyes go wide with surprise.

'Yeah, that's right. How did you—'

I roll my eyes. 'Because, while I hate to admit it, there are things about us that are quite *similar*, Joel. We both loved seeing that big, fat, beautiful thing, so it's no wonder we'd both want to get another glimpse of it.'

'At exactly the same time, though? In the middle of the night?'

I cock my head. 'Alright, I concede it's a bit strange, but I'm not going to entertain the idiotic idea that there's some god or higher being shoving us together for its own amusement.'

'Sounds pretty believable to me.'

'Well, you believe a lot of strange things, Joel. Including thinking that it's a good idea to jump into a TV.'

His face takes on a maudlin expression. 'You saw that, did you?'

'Well, of course I saw it. It'd be a bit hard to bloody miss.'

He doesn't need to know about my kneejerk concern for him. That would do neither of us any good.

Joel's fingers gently touch his nose, making him wince.

'Leave it alone. You'll only make it worse.'

Oh God!

What is *wrong* with me? I still sound like I give a shit!

'Okay,' he replies, and for an instant I am transported back five years, to a time when this kind of conversation was appropriate.

'I guess I'll leave you to it, then,' I say, wanting to get away from this unwanted wander down memory lane as fast as possible.

I don't move an inch however, clearly indicating that I actually want him to be the one doing the leaving.

'Okay.'

'Though I was enjoying the view.'

'Right.'

'But maybe it's best we're not here together. One of us should certainly leave.'

'Okay.'

Aaargh! Why can't he pick up on any bloody signals! *I* don't want to leave. I want *him* to leave! I want to stay here and watch the stars on the water for a little longer. I don't want to have to go away just because I don't want to be around Joel. He's already ruined my sunsets. I don't want him ruining my starlight!

'Don't you think you should be in bed resting, though?' I say. 'That does look painful.'

'I keep rolling on to it,' he says forlornly. 'Every time I do it sends a stabbing pain up into my brain.'

'Yes, well, that's probably your body's way of telling you not to act like such a bloody idiot.' I'm annoyed now. I've got over the shock of seeing Joel at this ungodly hour, and am comprehensively irritated by his presence.

'Alright, Ames. Give it a rest, will you.'

That's the first time anyone's called me Ames in years. Mainly because it was only ever Joel who called me it.

'*You* give it a rest, Joel. Your constant need to be the centre of attention always results in this kind of thing. You nearly got me killed yesterday with that bloody kayaking.'

'You didn't need to do the race,' he says sullenly. 'It was between Ray and me.'

'Oh, for crying out loud. Ray wanted no part of your need to massage your ego, Joel. He's not that kind of man.'

'And what kind of man is he?' Joel says with a sneer. 'The kind that nicks someone's wife out from under them?'

I stare at him. 'Don't be so *stupid*, Joel. Ray and I didn't get together until long after you and I split. Ray isn't the kind of man to do something like that. And I'm not that kind of woman. He's very honest. And kind. And hard working. And . . . *reliable.*'

Don't go there, Amy. Don't say it. Just walk away and don't let this conversation escala—

'Unlike some men I could mention.'

Oh for fuck's sake. Carry on, then. Don't say I didn't warn you.

Joel's face changes from largely self-pitying to highly irritated. 'What's that supposed to bloody mean?'

My hands go to my hips. 'You know *exactly* what I mean!'

He throws his hands in the air. 'Are you on about Goblin Central?'

I cock my head to one side. 'Well, you weren't exactly *reliable* back then, were you?'

'Aaaaarggh! That wasn't my fault!'

'Then who's fault was it?'

Oh, Jesus Christ. Here we go again!

The same argument. The same anger. The same *bullshit.*

I want to just run away from it – because the definition of insanity really is doing the same thing over and over, expecting different results – but I can't.

I can't be the one to back down.

The problem is, Joel thinks exactly the same.

'Not *mine,* Amy! I did what you told me to! I arranged that meeting just fine! *You* must have accidentally changed the appointment time after I'd made it!'

'No! No, Joel! I did no such thing! I was always the one who was careful about that kind of thing. It's *you* who were disorganised, Joel! *You* who were reckless!'

'No, I wasn't! I'm not like that!'

'Oh no? Tell your fucking *nose* that, Joel! You've got two miniature tampons up it! I'd say that's a healthy indicator that you're a bit of a reckless idiot, wouldn't you?'

'I did not get the appointment time wrong!' he shouts.

'Yes, you did!' I retort at the same volume.

A light comes on in one of the beach bungalows up in the island's dense foliage.

'Oh for the love of God,' I snap in a lowered voice, looking over at it. 'I'm not doing this anymore with you, Joel.'

'No! No! You don't just get to walk away from this!' he replies in an angry stage whisper.

'What more is there to say?' I hiss back at him, as we both move further down the beach, so that we're right on the water's edge, and hopefully far enough away from the bungalows not to disturb anyone else.

'I want to hear you admit that I didn't screw up! That it could have been you!' he demands.

'But it *wasn't*!'

'It must have been, because I put the right time down!'

'No, you didn't!'

'Yes, I did!'

'No! No, you fucking didn't, Joel! *You* screwed up! Just like you screwed up earlier, and smashed that TV to pieces! You're the one who fucks things up here, not me! *You* messed up the meeting!'

'No, I didn't!'

'Yes, you did!'

'No, I fucking didn't!'

'Yes, you fucking di—'

From about ten feet away in the water, we both hear a loud, animalistic *harrumph*. It's the sound of a clearly irate large sea mammal, not happy about having its night-time grazing disturbed by two extremely angry humans.

We can't really see much of our friendly dugong in the gloom, but the stars provide just enough illumination to know that it's him.

'Oh my God,' I say, and this time the whisper in my voice is driven by amazement rather than rage.

'He's back,' Joel remarks, sounding equally astonished.

'Yeah,' is all I can reply, as I watch the dugong spin slowly around to face us. I can't see his face, but I know there's probably a look of ancient wisdom on it that I couldn't fathom if I had all the time in the world.

The dugong harrumphs again, right at us, as if he's chastising Joel and I for ruining such a gentle night with this stupid argument that's been had a thousand times before.

This isn't the place for that, the harrumph seems to say. *This is a place for peace and quiet. And eating sea grass.*

Okay, I'm the one who eats the sea grass. I don't expect you to join me. That would be a bit ridiculous – and there's really not enough of it to go around these days anyway. It's a bloody miracle I'm still here, quite frankly.

Fundamentally, though, what I'm trying to say is that you two silly humans should just both give it a rest. Your loud voices are not conducive to easy digestion, and this sea grass is hard enough on the bowels at the best of times.

Dugongs can convey an awful lot of information in one long harrumph, I'm sure you'll agree.

Both Joel and I are completely silent. There's not really much else you can do when you're being told off by a dugong. It's a little hard to make a counter-argument against an animal that's all but extinct. It would just feel wrong. On behalf of the entire human race, it's probably best we just stand here and take it, given what we've done to all of his blubbery mates over the last few decades.

Eventually, the dugong grows tired of giving us a disapproving eye and sinks back below the surface of the water, no doubt satisfied that it's got us to shut up.

Both of us continue to just stare at the empty patch of water where the dugong was for a few moments.

Joel is the first one to break the silence, in quite an unexpected fashion.

'What the hell happened to us, Amy?' he says in a quiet voice that's heavy with regret.

I sigh equally heavily in response. How exactly am I supposed to reply to that? 'We got *lost*, Joel. We made stupid mistakes and got lost,' I tell him, not really able to be any more coherent.

I'm still referring to Goblin Central, of course, but to pretend that it was the only mistake in our marriage would be churlish. The rot had started to set in long before then.

Hell, if I'm being brutally honest, getting together in the first place was probably our biggest mistake. One that Joel is also cognisant of, as I discover when he speaks again.

'I keep . . . I keep thinking . . .' he says, still in that hushed tone, ' . . . that we should have never . . . got together. Just stayed *friends*. Business partners. We would have been far better off. Things wouldn't have got so fraught. Things wouldn't have . . .'

'Wouldn't have hurt so much,' I finish for him, closing my eyes and thinking back to how I felt when I had to leave Rowntree Land & Home.

'But . . . but . . .'

'But what, Joel?'

'But I couldn't help *loving you*,' he eventually says, voice cracking a little.

My shoulders drop. 'No, Joel. Me neither. Even though I look back and wish I hadn't, I couldn't help loving you either.'

He turns to face me, and suddenly I'm very aware that there isn't that much space between us.

'I never meant for any of it to happen,' he says, now speaking quickly. 'I didn't know you'd have to *leave*. I didn't want that. I *never* wanted that!'

'Neither did I.' I can't help but allow a little steel back into my voice, even if I really don't think it'll help matters right now.

'It wasn't the same after you left,' he continues, still talking in almost a babble. Joel is clearly getting some stuff off his chest. 'Things haven't been great. *I* haven't been great. Not since you . . . were gone. I'm under . . . under a lot of pressure, and . . . it's not been easy for me to . . . cope.'

No.

No, Amy Caddick.

You do not feel sympathy for this man.

'At least you got to stay in your job, Joel,' I remind him, but the steel has melted a little. This is clearly not a man happy with his lot in life. And can I honestly say the same thing? I work for the man I love, in a job I enjoy.

. . . okay, selling small- to medium-sized boats for a yacht company doesn't quite have the same thrill as selling gigantic, expensive mansions, but it's a *good* job. Well paid. Pretty easy. Nice office. Lovely boss.

It's *fine*. It's a *fine* job.

. . . oh, who am I fucking kidding? I miss being a high-end real estate agent every bloody day. And if I'm honest with myself, part of the reason I miss it so much is because working with Joel *was* great. It was exciting, fulfilling and profitable – in multiple senses of the word. That's why it hurt so much that it all fell apart and I was forced out. And that's why it hurt so much that Joel was so bloody disorganised, and screwed up so badly with Goblin Central. Why did he let us down like that? Why wasn't he as careful and as protective of our relationship as I was?

Joel's shaking his head now, quite slowly. I think there might be tears in his eyes, but the starlight might be telling me lies. 'It's not a job you'd still want, Ames. Things aren't . . . good at the agency. The old man is getting increasingly strange, and Michelle has hired some young, cheap new talent that are more concerned with how good they look for Instagram than selling houses.'

I wince. Michelle Hardacre – the one-woman human resources department of Rowntree Land & Home – is someone for whom the word 'employee' is something that applies to everyone else, but not her. It was only Roland Rowntree who seemed to keep her in check, and if he's not on the ball anymore, then her reign of terror has nothing to stop it.

'It's getting harder and harder to . . . to compete,' Joel tells me. 'Things have been really going downhill since . . .'

He leaves it hanging. He doesn't need to say much else. I know exactly when *since* was. It was the day I managed to stop myself from crying like a baby until I was in my car and a good two miles away from the office.

The look on Roland's face when he told me he was letting me go. It's seared into my conscious brain, and will float there until the day I shuffle off this mortal coil.

But apparently I don't actually have Joel Sinclair to blame for my departure – not if what he's saying to me now is anything to go by.

I just have him to blame for the catalyst that led to my exit – which is bad enough as it is. But I genuinely don't believe Joel is an *evil* man. Disorganised, yes. Reckless, certainly. Prone to thought-lessness, without a shadow of a doubt.

But I don't think he'd deliberately force me out of my job. Not anymore.

'Well, I'm sorry about that, Joel,' I tell him, trying to maintain a cool tone of voice. 'But what goes on at Rowntree's is not my concern anymore.'

'More's the pity. I swear that place would have fallen apart if it wasn't for us. And then you were gone, and it did.'

I turn to face Joel for the first time. 'Then why didn't you treat *us* better, Joel? Why didn't you act like it was that important?'

'I did! I really did!'

So why did you cock up the appointment time in our calendar?! I want to scream at him, but what good would it do? Just spark off the argument again, and I don't want to upset the dugong's digestive system any further, if I can possibly help it. There's only about ten of them left, and I don't want to be responsible for edging them closer to extinction by giving one of their kind fatal indigestion.

'We had something special,' I eventually elect to say, trying to keep things as neutral as I can. 'Both at work and at home.'

Joel then takes a step forward. I am painfully aware that there's barely a foot of space between us now.

'Yes, we did,' he tells me. 'And I have no idea how we managed to throw it away.'

I stare him straight in the eyes. 'Like I said, Joel – we got *lost*. For a while there we were totally *together*, and everything was easy – but then we *weren't* anymore, and it's almost impossible to know where you're going at that point.'

'You always did have a good turn of phrase, Ames,' Joel says ruefully.

'Well, maybe sometimes. When I'm in the right mood and standing under the star—'

Joel kisses me.

My eyes go wide and my back stiffens as he does it.

But then, for a moment . . . for the absolute *briefest* of moments . . . both relax again, and I allow it to happen.

Then my hands come up and push him away hard.

'Bloody hell, Joel!' I exclaim, trying to catch my breath.

'Sorry! I'm sorry!' he says, his own hands up now, as if to ward me away.

'I can't believe you did that!'

'No, neither can I!'

And I can't believe I didn't push him away immediately . . .

'I, er, I think I'm going to go now,' I tell him, taking a very conscious step backwards.

'Yeah, okay. I will too,' he replies, trying to look everywhere but into my eyes.

I don't want to look at him either.

What the hell was that?

Why did he kiss me?

And why didn't you push him away?

I did! I bloody did!

Not straight away, girl. Not straight away.

It doesn't matter. It doesn't. It was just a split second. Nothing to worry about. Nothing to think about anymore.

I just need to get away from here, and forget this ever happened.

'Joel? What are you doing?'

I look past Joel to see that we've been joined by a third person.

It is, of course, Cara Rowntree – whose grandfather's sad face as he fired me will haunt my memories for the rest of my days.

'Cara!' Joel exclaims, turning to her.

Jesus Christ. How much did she *see*?

Did she see Joel kiss me?

The starlight doesn't give off much illumination, but would it have been enough for her to see him do it? And to see me not push him away for that split second?

How close was she? Has she been standing there the whole *time*?

Oh fuck me, these are not questions I want to consider. I have to get out of here.

'Hello, Cara,' I say to her, trying to keep my voice as bland as possible – as if I haven't just locked lips with an ex-husband I'm supposed to hate and despise. 'Hope you're well.' I turn back to Joel. 'Goodnight, Joel,' I say, continuing to affect that carefree, completely disinterested tone. 'I hope you enjoy the rest of your walk.'

Yes. That's it.

We're just two people who happened to bump into each other briefly on a night-time walk. Nothing more than that. That's all you saw, Cara. Nothing else.

I don't wait for a response from either of them, but instead turn on my heel and start to walk back in the direction of my water bungalow and the sleeping Ray.

Ray!

Good, kind, wonderful Ray!

It meant nothing!

I pushed him away, I really did!

Not straight away. Not for a split second.

It doesn't matter! I was just in shock. I didn't know what was happening!

Shocked people don't let their shoulders relax.

No! It meant nothing! Joel and I were over a long time ago. He betrayed me. He ruined what we had. Not like Ray!

So why did you do it?

I didn't do anything!

This internal war with myself lasts all the way back to the bungalow, and I have to take a couple of deep breaths outside the front door before I go back inside.

'Amy?' Ray says in a muffled tone as I close the door behind me. My heart leaps into my throat. It's the first time that's ever happened when he's called my name.

'Yeah?'

'Are you okay?'

'Yes, I'm fine!' I tell him as I walk back across to the bed. 'Just couldn't sleep, so I went to get a little fresh air.'

'Oh . . . everything okay?'

'Yes! Absolutely fine. Go back to sleep, sweetheart. I'm totally fine.'

'Okay.'

Ray rolls over and says no more.

I sit down on my side of the bed and stare into space for a second.

The second turns into a minute before I know what's happened.

I then force myself to lie down. It's now coming up to three o'clock in the morning, and I really should try to get some sleep.

I should never have left the bed in the first place.

. . . *but I didn't do anything* wrong.

It was *Joel*. It was Joel who was at fault. *He* kissed *me*.

In the past, it's always been very easy for me to blame my ex-husband for the trouble I've found myself in. After all, he is reckless, disorganised and thoughtless.

But this time, try as hard as I might, I can't pin the blame for what's just happened solely on him.

Because there was a split second.

A split second brought on by a dugong, a soft, warm, night-time breeze, and the stars reflecting off the surface of the calm ocean.

And maybe the realisation that Joel Sinclair isn't quite the monster I've built him up to be in the past two years.

BUT.

It doesn't matter. I just need to forget about it. The man I love is sleeping next to me as I speak . . . not standing around in the middle of the night with two mini tampons shoved up his nose because he's an idiot.

That split second only happened thanks to residual memory. The memory of a marriage that had some wonderful times as well as some awful ones. And the *most* wonderful of those wonderful times were the ones we had together here on this island.

Yes.

That's it.

In that split second, I wasn't Amy Caddick *right now* – I was Amy Sinclair *back then.*

But she's gone again now.

I can go to sleep, safe in the knowledge that all of that is in my past.

That Joel Sinclair is in my past.

. . . okay, he's also about half a mile away with a potentially broken nose, but he's still *in my past.*

Eventually, sleep does come – but it's a fitful one, full of dreams about things I thought long forgotten, and memories long buried. All dredged up from my subconscious by that split second I should never have allowed to happen.

Mind you, one dream does also involve me riding a dugong naked through a Chinese restaurant, so I'm not going to read *too* much into it all.

That way, inevitably, lies madness.

Saturday

JOEL – INTROSPECTION

'Aaaaarghh!' I scream in pain.

This is happening because my girlfriend Cara has just flicked me on the end of the nose.

Without warning, she has just reached out her hand – her brow furrowed with understandable rage – and flicked me right on the tip with her middle finger.

The bolt of pain that stabs into my brain is as terrible as it is deserved.

'Bloody hell!' I exclaim, as both hands fly up to my nose, to protect it from any more incensed flickage.

'Don't lie to me, Joel!' Cara spits, hand hovering in front of her face, with thumb pressed over her tight middle finger. 'There are other parts of your anatomy I can flick, you know!'

'I'm not lying!' I wail, now trying to debate whether it's worth sacrificing some of the structural integrity of the barrier erected around my nose to send a protective hand down to cover my crotch. 'I didn't arrange to meet up with her, I swear!'

'Really? Because it's a hell of a coincidence, isn't it? That you just *happened* to be walking along the beach at *exactly* the same time she was . . . in the middle of the fucking night!'

'It really was a coincidence, I promise! It was the dugong!'

'The what?'

'The dugong! I only went back to that bit of the beach because I wanted to see if it was still there, and she was apparently doing the same, so we both just ended up in the same place, and—'

'In the middle of the fucking night!'

'Yes, in the middle of the fucking night. But it wasn't planned, I swear!'

Cara's eyes blaze. 'Did you have sex with her?'

My eyes bulge, and my mouth opens to form a response, but such is the enormous horror of the question just posed to me that I am unable to speak. Instead I just make a strange noise at the back of my throat that I can only describe as 'Geeb' as my head vibrates back and forth under the intense gravitational pressure brought on by such an apocalyptically huge enquiry.

'Well? Did you?'

'Geeb.'

'Joel!'

'No! Of course not!' I whine.

No, I just kissed her. That's okay, isn't it? I completely lost control of myself and was for a moment transported back to a better, happier life, in which kissing Amy Sinclair was one of the highlights of my day. But I don't know if you'd understand, if I told you that, Cara. I should be one hundred per cent honest with you right now, but I don't think I could get across to you the reasons why it actually happened. I don't think I could explain . . . the history. *I don't think I could be honest with you about the whole thing, because I don't know how honest I'm being about it with* myself.

'Are you sure?'

'Of course I'm *sure!*' I tell her. 'Why would I do something like that? I *hate* Amy. You *know* that!'

'You were married to her for a long time, Joel,' she says, eyes narrow.

'And that was a *long time ago!*' I reply.

'Not that long.'

Cara's obviously right about that. It certainly isn't long enough for me to forget what it was like to kiss Amy . . .

That's why I did what I did. In the heat of the moment, in the gloom of the beach, with five Sin Cities still partially sloshing around inside me, I just lost myself in the past and did something incredibly stupid.

It wasn't just you. She liked it.

Did she, though? I thought – just for a second – that she responded, but then I could have been very much mistaken.

Rather than make me feel better, the idea that Amy wanted it too – however briefly – actually makes me feel ten times *worse*. Far better to put the incident down to a moment of weakness on my part, and leave it at that. The implications of any emotional connection still lying between us don't bear thinking about.

'Look, baby, I swear to you. There was nothing going on there, other than two people meeting accidentally.' I shake my head. 'Do you really, honestly think I'd want to meet up with her like that? After everything that's happened on this holiday? After everything that happened two years ago?'

Which are all very good points. There is no chance that I'd deliberately arrange some sort of secret meeting with Amy, with our respective other halves only yards away. If for no other reason than she would have laughed right in my face.

I just wanted to do something other than lie in bed listening to my nose throb.

. . . yes, I know you can't technically listen to pain, but when something hurts this much, you'd be forgiven for thinking that you can.

So, I went for a walk – and I did want to see if the dugong had come back. Unfortunately so did my ex-wife, which has led to this early morning argument.

Funnily enough, Cara didn't say a damn thing to me last night, after I followed her back to the bungalow with my tail between my legs. She just climbed into bed and went to sleep. I actually thought I might have got away with my momentary lapse of judgement. Amy certainly tried to help in that regard with her cold pantomime before she left. She gave off absolutely no indication that we'd been kissing a few moments beforehand.

What's this 'we' business, my laddo? It was all down to you, stupid.

I managed to get some sleep, thinking that things might not be as bad as I feared, and that Cara didn't see me committing the heinous act.

But then this morning arrived, and it became quite apparent that I hadn't got away with a damn thing. And if Cara didn't actually see me kiss Amy because of the darkness that surrounded us, then she certainly knew something had been going on. How could she not? Amy and I were standing *very* close together – closer than two people who are supposed to despise each other, anyway.

Cara stares at me for a second, digesting my words, before turning away and walking on to our veranda with her arms crossed.

I heave a heavy, deep sigh and go after her, trying to construct my next sentence very carefully. The guilt and shame I feel are so all encompassing that I'm finding it hard to think. I should know what to say at a time like this. After all, I've made a career of being able to say the right things at the right time. That's how I managed to sell so many houses. You have to have the gift of the gab to convince someone to part with more money than you or I will probably ever see in our lifetimes for a new luxury pad.

Mind you, I don't sell houses anymore, do I? It's been *months* since I had a decent sale on my commission sheet. In fact, the only things I've been able to secure the sale for have been a dreadfully dull detached house in the suburbs of Kent – something built in the late 1980s out of beige bricks and exhaustion – and a houseboat on the Thames. A fucking *houseboat*.

I used to make multi-million-pound deals with all manner of minor and major celebrities and business people, and now I'm reduced to flogging houseboats. Okay, it was rather a lovely one, and certainly wasn't cheap for the artist who bought it, but when compared to some of the properties my younger colleagues have been securing, it's kind of pathetic.

They've started calling me Captain Pugwash, because of it. And Steamboat Joelly.

Not to my face, of course. I am the most senior member of staff at the agency, other than Roland and Michelle – but I know they're calling me those names behind my back.

And I can't even blame them for it – not really. Not when I used to be the one making up the nicknames for everyone.

But mine were *funny*, dammit. Amy certainly seemed to think so, anyway. Which was just as well, as she was the only one who ever got to hear them.

And I never gave any of my *colleagues* nicknames – just the clients who bought the houses from us, or the vendors who were selling them. I never wanted to make fun of the people I worked closely with.

That doesn't appear to be much of a problem for the people I work with now. They're quite happy to take the piss out of Joel and his amazing inability to sell a fucking house anymore.

In fact, just about the only person who has come to work at the agency in the past year or so who doesn't treat me like yesterday's tin of tuna fish has been Cara.

We became friends straight away when she joined as a new agent, and I was more than happy to show her the ropes. I'd seen her a couple times around the office over the years because she was Roland's granddaughter, but it was only when she took the job eight months ago that we actually got to know each other.

I can't pretend it didn't make me feel good to help her. She was so enthusiastic. So willing to learn from me.

In many ways she reminded me of—

Well, no one that I need to mention at this juncture.

Our friendship became something else after about three months, despite my protestations. I knew I was too old for her, but she was having none of it. She firmly ignored the advances of the younger men around her at work and made a bee line straight for yours truly.

I can't pretend it wasn't the best thing that had happened to me in *years*.

And she's been amazing ever since. Supporting me when others were whispering about me behind my back. Helping me to keep my spirits up throughout this long, lean period I've been having. In many ways, she's rescued me from a long, slow slide that I might have never been able to stop on my own.

Even though she's never admitted it, I know she's had words with her grandfather about me. His attitude towards me has improved considerably since I started dating Cara. He dotes on that girl, and I think he'd do anything to make her happy.

My ego feels utterly pancaked by this notion, of course. I am a proud man (as evidenced by my idiotic desire to race a man far fitter than me around an island in a kayak) and I can't pretend that having my arse saved by someone else isn't something I hate. But I am deeply grateful for her intervention anyway.

I truly sometimes wonder if Cara is the reason I still have a job at Rowntree Land & Home. It certainly isn't because of the fucking houseboat.

And how do I repay that support and kindness?

By kissing the woman who is responsible for my decline, that's how. By locking lips with someone who did everything she could to destroy me in an acrimonious divorce that left me in dire financial straits.

Jesus Christ, what the hell is wrong with me?

I can't find the right words to say to my girlfriend – that's what's wrong with me at the moment.

I stare at her shoulder blades and the back of her head for a second as I try to think of the right thing to say. The right words to make her feel better. To make *me* feel better.

'The only thing I think of when I see Amy's face is pain, Cara,' I eventually say in a low voice.

This is good, though. This is most definitely the truth – and somebody very clever once said it will set me free, so I think I'll keep up with it.

'The last thing I'd want is to go back to her, and not be with you.'

Also very, very true.

'She . . . she put me in a hole two years ago, and you pulled me back out again. I don't know what else I can say.'

Cara slowly turns. As she does, she shakes her head. 'That woman really messed you up, didn't she?'

'Yes,' I say, shoulders sagging.

'All because of one stupid appointment.'

'Yes . . . no . . . I don't know. It wasn't *just* that, not by any means, but that was what blew everything up. And it's been an explosion that's been going on in my soul for years now. And the only thing that's stopped it burning me to a crisp has been you.'

Aah . . .

There it is.

The gab.

The old Joel Sinclair gab, making a triumphant return at a time when it's most needed.

Only, I don't think it is really the gift of the gab. I think – no, I *know* – that I'm being one hundred per cent honest. I owe Cara so much for supporting me, and making my life a better place to be during the aftermath of my marriage breakdown. She doesn't deserve a man who would repay that kindness with a moment of such weakness.

'I can't pretend that those six years with Amy didn't happen,' I continue. 'But I can absolutely assure you that you are the only woman I want to be with, Cara.'

I suddenly feel exhausted. Probably with good reason. I've had no more than three hours' sleep, and this argument started before breakfast, so I'm operating on fumes here.

I'm hoping and praying I've said enough for it to be over, because I don't think I have the strength to say anything else. My mental reserve tank is empty.

'Oh, Joel, what the hell am I going to do with you?' Cara says, and hugs me.

I'm so astounded by the swift change to her demeanour that for a second I just stand there with my arms open, letting her do all the hugging – but then I reciprocate, wrapping my arms around her waist and squeezing her tight.

'I don't know, baby,' I reply, voice thick with emotion. 'You know what I'm like.'

'Yes, I do. You are an incredibly wonderful man, who's just been broken by the things that have happened to you,' Cara tells me, sounding about as emotional as I feel. 'But I'm here to fix you, Joel. That's my job,' she finishes, and hugs me even tighter.

I am *incredibly* lucky. *Stupendously* lucky. Far too lucky for an idiot like me, that's for certain.

I've treated Cara *horribly* on this holiday, and I really don't deserve her forgiveness – but I'm extremely happy to be getting it anyway.

The question is, what the hell am I going to do to make it all up to her?

Thankfully, Cara now comes up with one suggestion to get the ball rolling. 'Can we please stay as far away from those people as possible, for the rest of this holiday?' she says in a determined tone.

'Yes! Of course we can!' I reply.

Frankly, if she'd asked me to get Sonic the Hedgehog tattooed on both butt cheeks I'd probably have agreed. Steering clear of Amy and Ray will be a piece of piss. It's something I want to do anyway. I don't want to be around Amy. Not one bit.

Shit, I haven't wanted to be around Amy for *two years*, but now I have even more of reason to avoid being in her vicinity. There are obviously . . . *feelings* still there I didn't know I had – despite everything that's happened and despite everything she's done. It's a very good idea to make sure those feelings stay exactly where they should: buried deep down under a ton of neuroses and doubt, rather than being exposed to the world.

Cara nods and smiles. There's a vicious edge to it. 'Okay, that's great. I just want to punch that *bitch* every time I see her.'

Right then . . . so that's another good reason to keep Cara away from Amy. There's every chance it might result in some sort of cat fight between the two of them that I'd probably have to try to break up. And the state my nose is in, I don't want to risk that.

'Easy, tiger,' I reply with a note of mock fear in my voice. 'We don't want to get you too riled up!'

Cara's brow furrows. 'I can't help it. When I think about what she's done. Blaming you for the appointment change, when it could just as easily have been her fault. Making your life a misery for so long afterwards. Being so horrible to you in the divorce . . .'

I nod. 'Yeah, I know. I know.'

So why on fucking Earth did you think it was a good idea to kiss her, you pleb?

Both Cara's anger and her words have hammered home what a fool I was to do that last night. How the hell could I even consider it? Amy is the bad guy here. She's the bloody enemy.

You don't kiss your enemies.

You never see Batman giving The Joker a nice, big, sloppy one, do you?

There isn't newsreel footage of Churchill planting a lovely peck on Hitler's cheek.

Mary Berry has never passionately embraced Ainsley Harriot.

. . . look, I don't know for a fact that Mary Berry and Ainsley Harriot are sworn enemies, but at the same time I'm absolutely *sure* of it. Don't ask me why, it's just a hunch.

I'm also pretty sure that Paul Hollywood and Delia Smith can't stand each other either, but then nobody likes Paul Hollywood. His name is Paul *Hollywood*, for crying out loud.

Basically, what I'm getting at here is that all of the celebrity cooks are at constant war with one another, in a never-ending conflict that will last down through the ages of man. Armageddon will come and go, and the survivors will have to decide whether they join the ranks of Antony Worrall Thompson's standing army, or sign up to Prue Leith's plucky band of resistance fighters.

You think Jamie Oliver is just a fat-lipped Essex boy, with a face only a mother could punch? When the day of judgement comes, you'll see his true colours – as he's storming Marco Pierre White's last remaining bunker. He'll emerge from the drifting clouds of self-raising flour, carrying his ceremonial ginsu knife, with a look of bloodlust in his eyes that can only be sated with the lifeblood of a Michelin-star chef – who sounds like he should be French, but is actually British.

That's weird, isn't it? *Marco Pierre White*. He sounds about as French as a baguette stick surrendering to the Germans, but apparently he's from *Leeds*. What the actual fuck?

'Joel? Are you okay?'

Yes, thank you, Cara, I am perfectly *fine*. It's just that I'd rather occupy my brain with a fanciful and entirely ridiculous war between celebrity chefs than continue to deal with the repercussions of kissing my hated ex-wife. It's so much easier, a lot more fun, and far more visually stimulating.

Who wants to spend their entire time feeling a constant surge of guilt, shame and self-recrimination, when you can instead picture Heston Blumenthal engaged in bloody hand-to-hand combat with Rustie Lee over the last packet of organic couscous?

'Joel!'

'Yeah! Yeah! Sorry. I'm just happy that you're not mad at me anymore. And a little stunned, if I'm honest.'

She shakes her head and rolls her eyes. 'It's hard to stay angry at you when you look so *vulnerable*, Joel. Your poor nose must be hurting so much. I'm sorry I flicked it.'

'That's okay. Probably deserved.'

'I should go and flick Amy's nose instead. And that boyfriend of hers.'

Cara then starts to flick the air beside her vigorously, pouting again for all she's worth.

I guess her still being angry isn't such a great thing, but the fact it's now firmly aimed in another direction than at my person is something of a relief.

'I think it's better that we just steer clear of them, like we agreed,' I say, blinking rapidly at the sight of her continuing air flickage.

Cara's hand drops again, and she loops them both around my neck. 'Agreed. No more Amy and Ray. From now on, for the last few days of this holiday, it's just Joel and Cara.'

'Absolutely.'

Cara then kisses me.

It's not a kiss that suggests we'll be leaving the water bungalow for breakfast any time soon.

And it's a kiss that makes me forget all about the one I engaged in last night.

. . . for the time being at least.

I'd like to say that the rest of the day is spent in relaxed bliss with my girlfriend, but I'd be lying.

It's easy to promise that you'll steer clear of your ex-wife and her lover, but it's not such an easy thing to actually do when you're still trapped on a tiny tropical island with them.

I am in a constant state of cat-like readiness.

The second I so much as see a flash of blond hair and a pair of tiny white shorts, I will be up and running.

The problem with this is that people who look like Amy and Ray aren't exactly in short supply around here.

Wimbufushi is absolutely busting at the gills – in as much as a tropical island known for its laidback luxury can be busting at the gills with anything – with middle-class white couples.

You only truly become aware of this when you have to concentrate on it, so you can avoid another run-in with people you don't like, and another potential argument with someone you do.

Everywhere I look there are rich white people lounging around, while a lot of hard-working brown people do everything they can to keep them happy, well fed and writing good TripAdvisor reviews.

It's . . . a little *uncomfortable*, if I'm honest.

What's even more uncomfortable is that I'm painfully aware of the fact that I am one of those well-fed white people . . . who will most certainly be writing a glowing TripAdvisor review, if only to assuage some of the misplaced guilt I'm feeling.

'Joel!' Cara calls, breaking me out of my thoughts.

She's had to do a lot of this recently. I am spending altogether too much time in my own head. This is quite a common failing of mine, but it's supposed to be something that happens back at home, where I could do with the escape – not on holiday in the Maldives, which should be the place I've escaped to.

'You going to catch this or what?' Cara says, indicating the frisbee that we've been throwing back and forth to each other in the waist-deep ocean water.

I drag my eyes away from the beach, and my near constant scanning of its inhabitants for Amy and Ray, and put up both hands to indicate that I am ready to receive.

Cara lobs the frisbee, and does it with such gusto that it goes flying over my head, out into the deeper water. 'Sorry!' she exclaims, although she doesn't actually *look* all that sorry.

While Cara seems to have forgiven me my trespasses of last night, I don't think she's going to *forget* about it for quite a while . . .

This was proved to me earlier when she slapped me on the arse during our frantic bout of morning love making. It's the first time she's ever done that, and I'm not entirely sure I approve. She definitely enjoyed it, though. I could tell from the flash of angry delight in her eyes as she did it. I let it go this one time, but if I'm about to descend into a relationship where I am – to use the popular parlance – going to be made 'her bitch', I may have to have words.

Cara is certainly showing me up at frisbee. This is third time the damn thing has gone sailing over my head, making me go fetch. This has two consequences. One, it makes me wish I'd never suggested a little light frisbee action, and two, it gives me more chance to scan the island in front of me for the two people in the world I want to see least, as I wade back to my place.

This time, Cara has flung the frisbee further out than ever, and it's bobbing around a good thirty feet away from me. This will take a while to recover.

Still, this does mean that my back is turned to the beach, which stops me from searching it for a while.

My task of retrieving the frisbee is made somewhat easier when two small children come floating past on rubber rings. They are – in complete contradiction to my observations earlier about the island's guests – both of Middle Eastern descent, and looking like everything in the world is exactly where it should be. The giggling is at such a high level, it's a wonder they don't pass out from lack of breath. The older of the two – a brother of about nine or ten – is frantically paddling both his rubber ring and the one his younger sister is sitting in, that's tied to his, at a fair head of steam. He definitely looks like he's got a grip on the fundamentals of how to paddle successfully better than I did the other day.

I feel as if I should warn him about passing dugongs, but then I'm a bit wary of calling out to random, passing children in swimsuits, for what should be blindingly obvious reasons.

He has absolutely no issues with communicating with me, though.

'This your frisbee?' he says, as he scoops it out of the water and waggles it in my general direction.

'Yeah!'

He smiles, and tosses it back to me in a flat, perfect trajectory that flies straight into my hands like a fucking arrow from a bow.

The kid then returns to paddling without breaking his stride or speed. It's quite majestic.

I despise children.

'Thank you!' I tell him, as I watch them steam away from me, heading for the other end of the island. Hell, the pace he's going, he could probably get home before his parents would have a chance to miss them both.

I turn back, and my heart jumps into my mouth when I see a flash of blond hair on the beach. It returns to its rightful place in my chest, though, when I see that the blond hair is attached to a woman in her fifties and a few pounds north of two hundred.

'Well, throw it back, then!' Cara says, arms outstretched and making beckoning signals with her hands. She really has taken to this frisbee stuff with some aplomb.

I wonder why this is, right up until she once again flings it back towards me, this time sending it a good thirty feet past me in the direction of the beach.

Sigh.

I guess I should just put up with it. It's probably better than getting my arse slapped.

The frisbee is now dug in the sand, just where it meets the gently lapping water. At least this doesn't require any more wading to reach. There's something incredibly undignified about *wading*, especially for a man like me – in his late thirties and sporting a small paunch. The small paunch is ignorable most of the time, I'm happy to say, but there's something unforgettable about it when it's the thing thrust out in front of you as you make your way through the water. When the paunch leads the way, the paunch is undeniable.

I heave another sigh as I bend over to pick the frisbee up.

I know what I'm doing here – engaging in my favourite pastime of You're Too Old and Fat to be Dating This Woman. Whenever

I'm not feeling sure about myself, or my relationship with Cara, this is what I tend to do. Regular as clockwork, every time we have even the mildest of disagreements, or if she seems unhappy about something to do with me in any way, shape or form, I will drop into this melancholic examination of my shortcomings.

I don't think I'd realised the extent of this habit until we came on holiday.

Perhaps it's the close proximity to a woman who is in the same age group as me that I've had sex with multiple times. Amy and I may be sworn(ish) enemies these days, but once upon a time we were an extremely compatible couple. On the surface, anyway. Only a few years apart in age, and with a similar world view, I never felt like I shouldn't be in a relationship with her. That it was somehow . . . *inappropriate*.

Then compare that to the gorgeous, young and frisbee-chucking woman standing over there in the shallows. My relationship with her feels *wholly* inappropriate. The age gap. The fact she's the granddaughter of my boss . . .

These things conspire to make me question myself at every available opportunity.

Cara may have saved me from tumbling into a deep depression, but she's also made me feel quite insecure about myself.

It's incredibly confusing.

Throw in the fact that she's just about the only thing that's kept me going throughout the pressure I've been under at work, and is it any wonder I do stupid things like kiss ex-wives when I'm drunk, half concussed from jumping into a TV, and fundamentally confused?

I bet Gino D'Acampo is never fundamentally confused.

I bet that little Italian powerhouse of culinary expertise is completely calm and collected, as he plans his midnight attack on Gordon Ramsay's Heathrow Airport restaurant.

Those two have been at loggerheads for years now, I'm sure of it.

And one day, the cold war between them will spill into the hot zone, and then we will witness a battle the likes of which have not been seen since the hosts of Heaven stepped out on to the plains of Megiddo to face the hordes of the Fallen One.

The casualties will be *horrendous*.

'Joel! Throw the bloody frisbee!' Cara shouts at me – once again pulling me out of my strangely constructed, grand-scale military conflict between celebrity chefs.

I don't mean to go off there, you know. It's not deliberate.

I think my brain is just activating a self-defence mechanism every time I start to dwell too much on things it doesn't want to think about.

Good, brain. Well done, you.

I do then indeed hurl the frisbee back at Cara, feeling a combination of guilt and smugness when it sails over her head, and she's the one forced to go fetch.

Then, in my peripheral vision, that fat woman with the blond hair moves slightly on her lounger and my heart climbs back into my throat again.

Good bloody grief. I am a man on the edge.

I'll frankly be glad to get away from this supposedly relaxing, tropical island.

What is it people say?

You need a holiday to get over a holiday?

Well, in my case, it's that I need a holiday to get over the constant fear of rejection, self-analysis and a subconscious that's preoccupied with celebrity-chef conflict.

It doesn't quite roll off the tongue the same way, but in my case it is one hundred per cent more accurate.

Unlike Cara's aim, which now sends the frisbee back out into the deep water again.

I resist the urge to sigh. I think I've done quite enough of that for one morning.

And I need to stop the constant picking at my neuroses too. It's doing me no good whatsoever.

I bet whatever Amy is up to right now, it doesn't include this kind of thought process. She never doubted herself as much as I do. It just isn't in her psychological make-up.

No. Whatever she's up to, you can guarantee it won't involve feeling bad about herself. That's just not in her DNA.

Saturday

AMY – THE BIG BANG

Oh God.

I am a monster.

A heartless, shameless, morally bankrupt *monster*.

As I sit here on the couch, staring down into the azure waters through the thick glass floor panel in front of me, my mind is full of recrimination and shame.

It was a split second, woman.

I know!

But do you know how much can happen in a split second?

A bloody shit load, that's what!

I looked it up on Google.

For instance, in far less than a split second, our entire universe expanded hundreds of times, from the subatomic level to several light years in diameter. That sounds like quite a lot, wouldn't you say? Quite the accomplishment for such a short period?

By the time the universe reached the split-second mark, neutrinos had ceased interacting with baryonic matter, and leptons and antileptons had managed to remain in thermal equilibrium.

I have no idea what *any* of that means, but it sounds jolly impressive, doesn't it?

The fact that the leptons and antileptons had remained in equilibrium must be testament to their staying power, if nothing else. You'd think with all the banging going on, that keeping your balance would be fucking impossible.

I truly wish I was more like a lepton.

In a split second last night, my equilibrium was thrown off completely . . . and shows no sign of returning any time soon.

When Ray rolled over and gave me a very sweet kiss on the tip of my nose this morning, I wanted to cry. I honestly did. He then gave me a longer, deeper kiss that stirred other emotions in me. Emotions that got squashed almost immediately when I thought about what I did on the beach last night.

How could I let Joel kiss me?

How could I let him get away with that?

I should have kneed him in the balls. That's what I should have done.

Instead I just stood there for the time it took the universe to expand to ten light years across, and let him do it.

And now I am so wracked by guilt I can think of nothing else.

A reef shark swims across my field of vision, and for an instant I wish I could swap places with him.

I bet reef sharks don't have to worry about this kind of stuff. I bet they don't obsess over what they get up to during incredibly short periods of time, or look things up on Wikipedia while their other halves take showers – completely unaware of the universe-sized infidelity that their partners are guilty of.

You need to tell him.

What?

You need to tell him what you did.

No! No, I can't do that!

Yes, you can. You must.

No. I can't.

And I don't *need* to either. It was just a split second. That's all. It doesn't matter how many leptons and antileptons stayed in equilibrium, it was just a split fucking second.

It didn't mean anything.

Then why are you sat here like this, wishing you were a bloody shark?

It's fine. It's okay. I just . . . I just need to do something to prove to Ray how much I love him. I just need to . . . reconnect with him.

What are you banging on about, woman?

Yes. That's right. Banging.

Pardon?

Banging. That's a great idea, thank you.

What?!

I'll seduce Ray . . . right here and right now. When he gets out of the shower. That'll show him just how much I love him.

You've gone fucking potty.

No, I haven't! It's a great idea. I love Ray with all of my heart, and after that stupid split second last night, I need to show him that – I need to show *myself* that – and the best way I can think of doing it is by making love to him right here on this couch.

So, not by a heartfelt conversation where you lay things out honestly to him and trust him to understand?

Don't be so stupid. Sex will do the trick. It always does. I can show Ray just how much he means to me by . . . by creating a second Big Bang.

Oh dear Lord.

Just shut up, will you? I'm upset, feeling guilty . . . and unfortunately I'm also horny. It's an odd combination, and I need to do something with it.

Go on, then. Just don't say I didn't warn you . . .

232

Right.

I have to make myself look *sexy*.

This means changing from these sleep pants into something small and thongy. I could also do with removing this rather baggy white t-shirt, and putting on something nice and tight instead. And I have to do this all in the next minute or so, as I'm sure Ray will be out of the shower very soon.

I'm sure the universe was probably creating all the elements needed to cook a sherry trifle by the time a minute had gone by, so I shouldn't have any problem making myself look sexually appealing in the same time period.

And indeed, once those sixty seconds have elapsed, I am back on the couch in a black thong, and a tight black vest top that may produce a fair degree of side boob, but also hugs my body in a way that feels good.

I then spend another few moments putting myself in an alluring position. This generally consists of lying out on the couch, with one leg bent seductively and my back arched slightly. If I stay like this too long I'm likely to throw out a disc, but Ray will hopefully emerge before that happens.

And indeed, Ray does not let me or my back down. Out he comes from the rear of the bungalow, with a towel wrapped around his waist, and nothing else.

Oh yes.

That'll do.

That'll do *nicely*.

Ray has the kind of physique that comes naturally to a man who's spent his life on the water, doing lots of extremely active sports involving jibs and keels. You don't get fat when you're tacking and jibing all the bloody time, let me tell you that.

There is nothing *less* sexy than referencing nautical terms, however, so I'll move on to thinking about how much I love that his stomach is washboard flat, rather than the reasons for it being that way.

'Hiya,' I say to him, twirling a few strands of hair in one finger, and trying to ignore the bloom of slight pain currently settling in nicely around my lower spine.

'Hello,' he replies, noticing both my positioning and my outfit with an upraised eyebrow.

Ray looks a little surprised because I am not by nature, a 'morning type'.

Some people just love to have sex right after they've got up, but I can't usually think of anything worse. If it's not mug-shaped and containing tea, I don't want my mouth anywhere near it for the first hour of my day.

But this morning is very different, because I woke up feeling an abject guilt about a minor (universe-sized) indiscretion I committed last night, and want to do something to assuage my guilt.

Ray doesn't look to be complaining. In fact, I can see just how much he's not complaining by what's happening to that towel.

'Wow. You look incredible,' he tells me, coming to sit on the edge of the couch, and running one hand up and down my raised leg.

Hnnnrrrrr.

'Thanks,' I reply. 'You look pretty good yourself.'

'What's brought this on?'

I kissed my ex-husband in the time it took the universe to form!

'We're on holiday, Ray. It's warm and gloriously sunny. That always makes me feel . . .'

Guilty! Horny!
Both of the above!

' . . . good.'

He smiles. 'Well, okay, then. That's great. That's definitely something I can get behind.'

My turn to smile. It's the sexiest one I can conjure up, so I hope it's good enough. 'That's great to hear. Why don't you get *behind me* on this couch?' I suggest, rolling on to my side and shifting towards the edge.

Ray obliges and things then start to happen.

Good things.

Nice things.

Things that make me feel so much better, in so many, many ways.

I'm once again looking down through that glass floor panel into the cool, clear waters beneath me, but this time I'm doing it while my mind is entirely occupied with happy thoughts.

This is *much* better.

And because Ray is the grand physical specimen we spoke of earlier, he is quite willing and able to move me into different positions on the couch that I am more than happy for him to put me in.

After a few minutes of that, though, I decide it's time for me to take the lead, and I push Ray off the couch, on to the floor. I want to get . . . er . . . better purchase on him, you see, and I can't really do that while we're on that big squishy couch. I need a hard surface to . . . um . . . properly build up a head of steam.

Ray gasps in surprise as his back meets the cool glass floor panel.

'Too cold?' I say, as I climb aboard his luxury yacht.

'No, it's fine. Feels kind of nice, actually.'

This is just as well, as I'm at the point now where any pause to change position will not go down well with the complicated parts of me that are starting the long climb up the hill towards Orgasm Town.

Oh yes, this is going *marvellously* well.

So well, that I'm now sweating like a pig. The temperature in the water bungalow has got to be in the high twenties as the sun climbs into the morning sky, and this has been a very active session thus far, given how keen I am to rock Ray's world this morning. My skin feels like a furnace.

I pull off my vest, allowing Ray his first proper look at the girls, which seems to please him mightily.

As he continues to please himself mightily, I have to slam both hands down on to the surface of the glass panel on either side of his head to steady myself.

The glass feels wonderfully cool underneath my palms – Ray was absolutely right – and I am suddenly filled with a strange notion.

What would that feel like on my boobs?

Because they are extremely hot and sweaty now. Along with the rest of me.

'I want to lie down on my front,' I tell Ray in a breathless voice.

He looks up at me, a little surprised. I'm sure he thought we were getting to the final act, and to have me pull a twist on him this close to the denouement is quite unexpected. 'Okay,' he says. 'Back on to the couch?'

'No. Right here.'

I slide off and when he moves away, I lay myself down on a section of the glass panel that's still lovely and cool to the touch. The panel isn't large enough to accommodate my whole body – just the top half – but that's more than enough for me. A thrill of pleasure suffuses my entire being as I do this. I was right. The glass really does feel quite wonderful again my bare skin – even if it does squeeze my boobs more than a fair bit. A price worth paying, I can assure you.

Another pleasurable thrill immediately follows, as Ray climbs on board and starting jibbing and tacking for all he's worth.

I close my eyes and after only a few moments, I feel myself getting to the point of no return. This really is quite spectacular.

I continue to lie there with my eyes closed as Ray does his thing, blissfully empty of coherent thought and complex emotion.

I've often thought that one of the best things about sex is how *simple* it is.

Simple is *good*. Simple is easy to cope with.

But you know what isn't easy to cope with?

Opening your eyes and looking down on two children in rubber rings directly below you, that's what.

For a moment – a (ha!) *split second* – my brain refuses to comprehend what it's witnessing.

Don't be bloody stupid, Amy.

There's no way two small children are looking up at my mashed tits and gormless pre-orgasm expression. That would be a horror show of such vast and all-encompassing embarrassment that it would make the size of the known universe seem tiny by comparison.

As Ray carries on doing something that is wholly inappropriate given the new reality we find ourselves in, I blink a couple of times in terror, wishing away the two stunned onlookers with the sheer force of my will.

Nope. That didn't work. They're still there. And still bearing witness (or should that be *baring* witness) to my squished breasts.

Thank Christ the glass panel only extends as far as my belly button – because *can you only fucking imagine?*

Anyway, time to scream, I think.

'Ray! Ray! Get off!' I cry at the top of my voice. As I do this, I push back as violently as I can, causing my boobs to squeal painfully across the glass.

Excellent. I set out to seduce my fiancé so that I'd feel better about a stupid mistake I made last night, and instead I've managed to turn my tits into do-it-yourself squeegees.

This torrid day will now forever be linked with the sound of high-pitched squealing. I'll never be able to look the window cleaner in the face again.

'Bloody hell!' Ray exclaims, as he's rudely interrupted close to the conclusion of his activities.

There's nothing I can do about that, though. Two small children have witnessed my squeegee boobs and now I must die in a corner somewhere.

'What's the matter?!' Ray says, watching as I frantically gather up my vest, covering my squeegees with it.

I point down through the glass. 'Children!'

'What?'

'There are children!'

Ray leans his head back over the glass panel. 'Jesus Christ!' he wails, as he sees the little boy and girl, who are still paralysed with what I can only assume is abject fear. 'Clear off!' Ray demands, thrusting a finger out. I look down to see the boy go even more wide-eyed than he already was, and immediately start to paddle frantically away from us.

'How the bloody hell did they get under there?' Ray asks, peering down as he watches them go.

'I don't know!' I wail, my voice one big tremor of embarrassment and shame.

Ray sees the fraught expression on my face, and immediately shifts over to give me a hug. 'It's okay, Amy. Don't worry. They didn't . . . they didn't see much.'

'They saw my bloody *squeegees*, Ray!' I reply, pushing him away.

'Your *what*?'

I stare at him for a moment before bursting into tears.

These are not, I should hasten to add, tears brought on by the fact that two small children have just inadvertently been exposed to my chest. I am mortified at the idea of that, obviously, but it doesn't really warrant such an explosive response. A flaming red face and a desire to only ever have sex again in the dark, possibly – but not the massive crying fit that's just come over me all at once.

No.

I am obviously in this state because the shame I feel about what's just happened pales into insignificance alongside the shame I feel about kissing Joel.

Because that's what I fucking did, friends and neighbours.

I kissed my bloody ex-husband last night on a starlit beach, and there's not a damn thing a black thong, a glass panel or squeegee boobs can do about it.

I could slather my naked body in cocoa butter and slide down the side of the fucking Louvre Pyramid at the height of rush hour, and it wouldn't be worse than that fucking *split second.*

'Amy! What's wrong?!' Ray cries, trying to hug me again. But I push him away. He shouldn't have to hug me. I don't deserve to be hugged. I deserve to sit here half naked with tears rolling down my cheeks.

I deserve to be thoroughly miserable and ashamed of myself, because I thought I could paper over such a colossal act of betrayal with sex.

Told you so.

Piss off!

'Amy! Talk to me!' Ray says, utterly shocked by my sudden and frightening change of demeanour.

I take a deep, sobbing breath and look him square in the eyes. 'I kissed Joel!' I squeal, feeling every atom of my being wanting to separate itself from the rest of me all at once.

'You did what?'

'We were on the beach last night!' I sob. 'Talking about . . . *everything.* And he . . . and he kissed me! I don't know why!' I run a hand across the underside of a nose that is now primarily composed of runny snot and tears.

'And you kissed him back?' Ray is angry now.

It's the worst thing I've ever seen.

I pause, thinking for a moment about what to say next. 'I let him do it, Ray!' I wail. 'For a split second I let him kiss me!'

His face crumples in confusion. 'But you said *you* kissed *him*?'

'I did!'

'But then you said *he* kissed *you*?'

'Yes! And *I let him do it*!' If I wail any louder, Azim will be down here with a fire extinguisher, a medical kit and a very concerned expression on his face.

'For *a split second*?' Now Ray sounds more confused than angry. I don't know which is worse.

I still sound like a blubbering mess, because that's exactly what I am. 'Yes!'

'But you didn't kiss him back?'

'Well . . . I . . . Er . . .'

Ray might have a point here, damn him. I've worked myself up into hysterics over this whole thing, but that one question is forcing me to re-evaluate what happened somewhat.

'No . . . I guess I didn't kiss him back.' I wipe the tears out of my eyes. 'But I let him do it, Ray.'

'For a split second, though?'

'Yes. About the time it took for the universe to expand to make a sherry trifle.'

'Pardon?'

'Nothing. Ignore me.'

A few moments ago I pushed Ray away, but now I need to hug him more than I have ever hugged another human being in my entire life.

My lip trembles as I shift myself across the floor to sit closer to him. 'I'm so sorry, Ray. I'm so, so sorry.'

He regards me for a second, his face lined with thought. 'Are you trying to say that your ex-husband sprung a surprise kiss on you, and it took you no more than a second to push him away?'

I nod, and then sniff.

He reaches out and puts an arm on my shoulder. 'Do you really think you actually have anything to apologise *for*?'

I look in his eyes and ponder the question.

And for the first time since I did push Joel away, I think about what happened in a calm and rational manner.

I've been an *idiot*.

I didn't do anything wrong, did I?

Unless you want to criticise the speed of my reflexes. Because as soon as I realised what was happening, I *did* push Joel away. I did not kiss him!

'Oh bloody hell,' I say with a heavy breath, and hang my head.

'You were married to the guy for four years, Amy. I'm surprised you managed to fight him off that quickly.'

'What do you mean?'

Ray holds up both hands, palms open. 'This isn't a fantasy world, Amy. You don't just stop having feelings for people you've spent a large chunk of your life with – no matter what happens between the two of you. Love is a really weird thing. I don't doubt that you love me, but I'd be a child if I thought that meant you had no feelings left over for Joel. That's not how the world works.'

'Isn't it?' I reply, genuinely shocked by both this viewpoint, and the way Ray is putting it across.

'No, of course not. That's why you wanted to come back to this island, wasn't it?'

'What? No! I just wanted to come back because it's such a lovely place!'

'But part of the reason it was lovely was why you were here. It was your honeymoon.'

'Yes, but my love for it has nothing to do with Joel!'

'Doesn't it? Because it's okay if it did. You loved him back then. I'm sure you had a wonderful time with him here.'

'Yes, but it all went so horribly wrong, and I wanted to . . . wanted to . . .'

'Come back with me?'

'Yes!'

'And recreate how you felt back then?'

'No! Feel *better* than I did back then! I love you, Ray! I love you so much more than I ever loved Joel!'

Ray shakes his head and smiles. 'We haven't been together long enough for you to know that yet, Amy. But I'm hoping that you will do. The same goes for me. In the meantime, pretending that you never loved anybody else, or me doing the same, is very silly, don't you think? Like I say, this isn't a fantasy. This is the real world. And in the real world, nothing is ever that black and white.'

Can we get a vicar in here right now, so I can marry this man right on top of the glass panel I've just squeegeed with my boobs?

'Oh, Ray, please hug me!' I tell him, shifting close into him.

'Of course,' he agrees with a huge smile, and envelops me in his arms.

The guilt that's permeated my entire body has dropped away like a suit of heavy armour.

While I still regret the whole incident with Joel, I do feel like it's not something I need to feel quite so bad about. Ray is perfectly correct – I *did* love Joel Sinclair once, and if it took me a second to push him away, I'd say that's pretty good going, considering all of the shared history we have.

And I can't even be angry at Joel for instigating the kiss in the first place, because if what Ray says is true for me, then it must be true for Joel as well. He loved me as much as I loved him. Can I really criticise him for having a moment of weakness in a place where we were very much in love the last time we were here?

A sudden, but wholly necessary, shift in my outlook occurs at that moment, while Ray has his arms wrapped tight around me.

I realise that it's okay to still have feelings for Joel – because we *were* married and because, for a brief time, we *were* happy.

I know how angry and betrayed I felt about what happened with Goblin Central and the aftermath – I still feel it now in every fibre of my being. But the only reason I felt so incredibly hurt was because I *loved* Joel. And maybe the reason why I've acted so strangely on this holiday is because those feelings are still there – buried deep – and that has made me feel both guilty and frustrated with myself for that being the case.

I think the kiss was probably the catalyst for bringing all of it to a nasty head, and Ray's way of looking at things has been the lance that's popped the boil.

'That's why he did it,' I say in a quiet voice.

'Sorry?'

'That's why Joel kissed me. Not because he wants me back or anything . . . but because he still has those lingering feelings for me. That's why we've been at each other's throats on this holiday.'

'Probably. If you didn't still care about each other a little, it wouldn't have bothered you to be around each other so much.'

I then give Ray a kiss that goes on long enough for me to feel like I'm human again.

'What's that for?' he asks with a chuckle.

'For being so insightful,' I reply, honestly.

He smiles. 'No one's ever called me insightful before.'

'But you are.'

'Well, maybe. I think it's more that I've spent a lot of time on my own in a boat. You get a lot of time to think when you're on your own in a boat.'

'I bet you do,' I reply, laughing back at him.

'Do you . . . do you want to go talk to him?'

'Joel?'

'Yes.'

'No, I don't think so. I understand everything you've said, and I feel a lot better about what happened, but none of it means I want to be friends with him. He still contributed to me getting fired from a job I loved.'

Ray nods. 'Fair enough. I don't blame you for feeling like that at all.'

'Thanks.'

'We'll make sure that for the last couple of days of this trip, we steer clear of both Joel and Cara.'

'Yes.' I hold up a finger. 'But if we do bump into them, I will try my very hardest not to be as angry or upset. Because there's no need for me to feel that strongly about it all anymore.'

'Quite right.'

'Now. Do you think we can get up off this floor? My bum has gone very numb.'

Ray laughs and climbs to his feet, offering me a hand up.

. . . the second hand up he's given me this morning, when you get right down to it. I think I can face my pent-up anger towards Joel Sinclair a lot better now.

There's something else that's pent up in me too. Something that got ruined on its way to not being pent up any more by two kids in rubber rings.

'Ray? Can we go back to bed for a little bit?'

244

'Oh, are you feeling tired?'

I shake my head. 'No, Ray. Not really.'

It is a much calmer and more content Amy Caddick that sits back on the couch looking down at the crystal-clear waters again, while Ray takes another shower.

Her mind still loops back to the kiss on the beach last night, but it does it now in a far more abstract and disconnected way.

I still wish it had never happened, but I don't feel like it was the world-ending occurrence I did a mere hour or so ago. All thanks to Ray Holland, and his hitherto undiscovered ability to parse human emotions in a frighteningly reasonable manner. I knew I loved him for being the man I thought he was – strong, sensible, dependable and straightforward – but this revelation that there are much deeper currents to Ray Holland's personality reinforces my love for him even more.

I really do have to get out on a boat more on my own. It would clearly be very good for my mental health.

The thing I'm wondering most about now is whether Joel has had a similar conversation with Cara to the one Ray and I have just had.

Did he confess what he did to her?

Did they arrive at a happier, more content place because he managed to get it all out in the open, the same way I eventually did?

I'm going to say probably not, because, let's face it – the only reason I was pushed into honesty was because I flashed my boobs to a pair of aquatic minors.

Unless Joel did something similar, I doubt he managed the same level of honesty. He's not that brave.

Mind you, this is Joel Sinclair we're talking about. If there's an opportunity for him to accidentally expose himself to a complete stranger, he'll run headlong into it like it's a flat-screen TV.

Gah.

None of that is my problem, though. I can't fix Joel's problems for him. I can only fix my own. If his relationship with Cara has been affected by what we did last night, then there's not a damn thing I can do about it.

You could go talk to him. Tell him what Ray told you. Tell him it's okay to still have feelings for you. It might help him out as much as it's done for you.

Both hands tighten on my knees.

No.

I won't be doing that.

Because there's still Goblin Central. There's still my job. There's still the look on Roland Rowntree's face. There's still moving out of the house I loved. There's still months and months of stress, hurt and betrayal.

No.

Joel can handle his own affairs. I don't feel the need to get involved.

The most I can do for him is to better understand the feelings I still have for him as my ex-partner and ex-husband. That will make things much easier for us both to deal with, if we're ever thrust together again like we have been on this holiday.

I very much hope that doesn't happen, though.

I think Joel and Amy have been thrust together more than enough for one lifetime – and more than enough for one holiday, thank you very much.

'Want to go for a late breakfast?' Ray says, coming around to sit next to me after he's popped a shirt on. This one has fruit on it. Coconuts and bananas.

I very much want to spend the rest of my life with a man who can wear a green Hawaiian shirt with coconuts and bananas on it without looking like a complete maniac.

'Yes, that'd be lovely,' I reply and, for the first time, the prospect of it doesn't come with a small tightness in my chest because we might bump into Joel and Cara. I will mark this as definite progress.

I feel like I'm finally starting to come to terms with my past – and that's all thanks to the coconut-and-banana-wearing present. Despite exposing myself to children, I'm quite glad everything went the way it did this morning. It's been a painful but necessary step for me – both mentally and physically.

I'm extremely glad to have had my perspective shifted to a far more level-headed one, but really could have done without having to have my boobs shifted up around my earlobes to bloody get there . . .

Joel

You know when you're really looking forward to something big and exciting, but when it actually rolls around, you could probably just do without it?

We've all been there . . .

Maybe it's a big day out, or an important birthday.

Possibly it might be going on a faraway holiday you've saved up for, or a day trip to somewhere a bit closer that you've never been to before.

It could be a night out with lots of friends that you were just so *happy* to be included in when the Facebook invite came in, but now the day is actually here, the thought of getting dressed up, going into town and getting blasted is something that fills you with an obscure *dread*.

You were *super* glad to be invited and included, but when you get right down to it, a nice evening in front of Netflix, with that packet of untouched wine gums you've had in the cupboard all week, sounds like an infinitely superior way to spend your evening.

Well, that's the way I feel right now, only instead of wanting to avoid a night on the tiles, I want to avoid a night under the ocean – or at least the time just before night falls, anyway.

You see, today marks the grand finale of our holiday here on Wimbufushi, and consists of a snorkelling trip to one of the outer reefs, conducted as the sun is going down.

This sounds *super* romantic and lovely when you're looking at the resort website a month before it happens – how could it not? The chance to swim among the reefs, enjoying the fish and the other aquatic life, as the sun sets gloriously around you, is a prospect that sounds mighty wonderful. Add the fact that there's a champagne supper thrown into the equation and you should be looking forward to an evening out that is unparalleled.

. . . but I'd rather just lie here and watch *Stranger Things*, while chewing on a rounded-off oblong of black gelatine, if I'm honest.

I'm exhausted, you see.

This luxury, all-inclusive holiday in the Maldives has really taken it out of me.

I feel like I've done a seventy-hour week. Seventy hours of panic, stress, tension and upset over the presence of a single human being and her oh-so-perfect boyfriend.

And I just *know* they're going to be on the snorkelling trip this evening as well.

I don't know this for *definite*, of course. I haven't seen the actual manifest of guests who will be attending – but I think we've reached the point now in proceedings where all of us can be *one hundred per cent* sure that they will be doing it, haven't we?

Oh, yes.

The chances of the two of them *not* being on the snorkelling trip are about the same as the chances of me going back to work next week to find that I now miraculously have the unending respect of all of my colleagues.

In fact, I'd be willing to bet an entire month's wages – of the job I can no longer stand, but have no choice but to continue with because I have mortgage and maintenance payments – that when we get to the boat this evening, Amy and Ray will be right there alongside us, as they have been through this entire fucking holiday.

I am not a religious man, and I do not necessarily believe in things like fate or karma or serendipity – but I have become absolutely *convinced* that there is indeed some sort of malevolent entity looking down on me right now, guiding my movements and throwing me into these situations for their own sick amusement, and the amusement of their followers.

I discovered on Google this morning, during some idle surfing, that there is a word that means the opposite of serendipity.

Zemblanity.

Perfect, isn't it?

A word that describes a deeply unpleasant circumstance, which has come about thanks to some ineffable, otherworldly design.

I'm sure you'll agree that it absolutely encompasses the last week of my life to a bloody *tee*.

I have had zemblanity forced into every orifice of my being over the last seven days. I am so incredibly stuffed full of zemblanity that if you decided to punch me in the stomach (because why the hell not at this stage, eh?) I would no doubt throw up zemblanity all over you.

And it is because I am pretty much *drowning* in zemblanity that it makes me so sure that if Cara and I do go on the snorkelling trip together tonight, we will be doing it right alongside Amy and Ray.

I have not tried to put my feelings about zemblanity and its effects on snorkelling excursions to Cara. I feel that way probably lies madness.

This is because my girlfriend is very much looking forward to it.

The lure of evening Netflix and wine gums is not something she embraces, as she is in her twenties – and I'm sure the prospect of a nice wine gum in her mouth is completely abhorrent to her.

Young people do not enjoy wine gums. They are only the provision of those who are approaching, or have passed, the age of forty.

I'd imagine Cara would treat wine gums in much the same way as I would consider Werther's Originals – things to be only sucked by old people. They mark the slide into entropic dotage, and should be avoided at all costs.

God knows what kind of sweet people who like Werther's Originals are afraid of popping in their mouth. Whatever it is, I'm assuming it will come laced with embalming fluid, just to get a bit ahead of the game.

Anyway . . . the point here is that Cara is excited about the snorkelling, and if I tell her of my concerns, I will bring on *the pout*. I do not want to bring on the pout again. I have done that far too much this week.

The last thing I want to do is mention Amy to her again, in any capacity. There has been a fragile but happy peace between us these last twenty-four hours, and I do not want that ruined by talk of zemblanity and the likelihood that her snorkelling adventure will be marred by its influence.

Therefore, I find myself in the situation of knowing that I am careening towards another unpleasant encounter, but unable to do a damn thing to stop it.

There will be no Netflix and wine gums for me tonight. Only sea water and zemblanity.

As the day ticks down to what increasingly feels like some kind of staged denouement to these bizarre and unlikely seven days on Wimbufushi, I try my level best to remain calm. I do this by lying in the sun a lot, with a mindfulness app playing on my iPhone, through my EarPods.

I had to choose a mindfulness session that didn't include any gentle, relaxing music in it, because that would just remind me of the plinky plonky and Suha's massage from hell. Instead, I elected to listen to a nice man telling me all about how my mind is like the blue sky above my head, which should be as free of clouds as possible. An uncluttered, mindful brain is a happy one, he takes great pleasure in telling me.

From the sound of him, this is not a chap who has ever had a run-in with zemblanity.

He *does* sound like a chap who has had a run-in with millions of pounds thanks to the popularity of his mindfulness app, so it's no wonder he sounds so bloody content.

However, the app just about keeps me calm for the whole of the afternoon, so I guess he's earned my contribution to his vast profit margins.

When we get to five o'clock, however, as Cara busies herself packing all the essentials for our trip into her voluminous beach bag, I can feel the tension start to rise again.

'Do you need anything else?' she asks, popping a pair of her shorts into the bag. 'I've put in a towel for you, and another t-shirt.' Cara sounds excited and upbeat. She's only about an hour or so away from swimming between beautiful coral reefs at twilight, and she knows it.

'No. I'm sure that's all fine,' I reply, trying to look as enthused as she obviously feels.

'What's wrong?'

'Pardon?'

'You look like someone about to go to the gallows.'

'Oh. Sorry. I guess I'm just a bit nervous about the snorkelling. Deep water in the dark isn't something I've faced before.'

This is not altogether untrue.

I've seen movies. I know what kind of stuff lurks in deep, dark water. Stuff with teeth and tentacles, that's what.

'Ah. It'll be fine. This is snorkelling for people of all ages. I doubt we'll actually be going anywhere that isn't completely safe and easy to get around. We're not going to get into any trouble.'

In a week full of mishaps, bad timing and hideous mistakes, this comment will prove to be the most *inaccurate* of them all . . .

But I don't know that right now. Hence why I'm actually able to manage a genuine smile. 'I'm sure you're right.'

Cara gently pats me on the arm. 'Just think about that champagne and the food. That'll get you through it.'

Normally I'd agree with her completely, but I don't feel hungry at all . . . for some reason.

When we leave the water bungalow I do so with a heartfelt look back at the widescreen TV. This tells you just how much I want to stay here and watch Netflix. I should look at widescreen TVs with horror, given what happened between me and one a couple of days ago, but instead the look I give it is *wistful.* I could probably get all the way through a whole packet of wine gums watching season four of *The Crown.*

But instead of Olivia Colman in a tiara, I have Cara in a bikini. It's testament to my stress levels about tonight that I would actually like to watch the former more than the latter.

I don't spend the whole walk across the island to the jetty looking for signs of blond hair. I don't want to make it look too obvious to my girlfriend that I'm worried we might see Amy.

Cara looks entirely unconcerned. Her attention is firmly fixed on the excitement of looking at clown fish as the sun sets behind her. Let's hope she can retain at least some of that enthusiasm when she sees my ex-wife.

There's no sign of Amy and Ray as we hit the wide jetty that leads down to where a large catamaran is moored, coloured in the same white paint and blue stripe as the Wimbufushi speedboat. The catamaran has a large open section at the rear, full of comfy-looking seats, and a cabin in front of that where I assume all the driving goes on.

There's a line of people waiting to jump aboard, but I don't see them in the queue either.

A bloom of hope springs into life in the depths of my chest.

Maybe . . . just maybe, I'm going to get *lucky* here.

My assumptions over the continuing zemblanity that mars my life may have been in error!

After all, here we are, now in the line for the catamaran, and there really is absolutely *no* sign of Amy or Ray. I look behind me and can't see them walking towards us. I study the line ahead of us closely, and they are definitely not there either.

Wow.

I wonder what's stopped them coming on the trip? Maybe they've got into a huge argument about something and don't want to spend time together out on the ocean?

A very small, petty part of me takes pleasure in the prospect of this.

Strangely, though, I'm not pleased at the idea of an argument between them making Amy upset, but rather that it might knock that smug smile off good old Ray's face.

Amy was – how do I say this? – quite *nice* the other night on the beach. For the first time in years we had a decent adult conversation, all thanks to that dugong. It brought back memories of the person she used to be – which is of course what led to that stupid kiss. I deeply regret doing that, but I don't regret seeing a side of my ex-wife I haven't for a very long time. The intelligent, thoughtful side, that always played counterpoint to my impulsiveness. Her being that way softened my anger towards her a bit, I can't deny it. Enough for me to be unhappy at the idea of her getting into an argument with her partner, anyway.

Ray, on the other hand: *fuck* that guy. *Seriously*.

I'm still not entirely sure he wasn't moving in on my wife when I was still married to her, despite what she told me on the beach the other night, and I don't trust that warm, convincing smile as far as I could throw it. Nobody can be *that* upstanding. It'd give you chronic backache in no time at all. I'm also deeply jealous of him – as has been readily established – so I have *double* cause to wish him ill. And the idea of him getting all upset and bothered by an argument with Amy fills me with gross and petty pleasure.

Regardless of the reason, the two of them do not appear to be coming on this snorkelling trip, and that makes me very happy. Maybe I can relax and enjoy a little paddling around in the evening light, with Cara by my side, looking down at all the fish and coral.

Azim and a couple of the other Wimbufushi staff are now allowing us to board the catamaran, letting us know that there will be a safety briefing once we are on board. It looks like there are about twenty or so of us on this trip, which is a decent amount for an island with such a small amount of accommodation.

I give Azim a sheepish hello as we pass him. I haven't forgotten about the damage I did to his lovely TV, and I doubt he has either. Not that he shows that in any way, as I receive just as broad and welcoming a smile as anyone else.

I look back one more time at the few people behind us in the queue, and there is still no sign of Amy and Ray.

Brilliant!

I have to roll an internal set of eyes over my silly obsession with zemblanity.

Of course there is no malevolent spirit hanging over me, making my life miserable. Of course I am not cursed with the opposite of whatever serendipity actually is. I am an ordinary man in an ordinary world, where things just happen from time to time that you really wish hadn't.

There's no such thing as zemblanity – and the proof of that is when I step aboard the catamaran, there is no sign of Ray or Amy among the passengers. They are not on the boat. Everything is okay. I don't have to—

'So you say it produces fifty horsepower, even though it's a hybrid? That's amazing! What knots are you getting? Fifteen?'

Footsteps

A knock at the door.

I swing the door wide open.

Zemblanity – for some reason dressed in chef's whites and carrying a machine gun – stands there with a stupid grin on its face.

'Hi, Joel!' it says in the cheeriest of voices. 'I certainly *do* exist! And here I am, on your doorstep to fucking *prove* it!'

From a pocket in the chef's whites it produces a party blower, puts it to its lips and blows. The noise the blower produces is a sound half like a dugong burping and half like a wail of despair.

I look around to see Ray emerging from the catamaran's forward cabin, with both the captain and Amy in tow. The captain looks highly animated by the conversation he's having with a man wearing a bright green shirt covered in fucking coconuts. Amy looks less enthralled.

'Yes! I would say we hit fifteen knots on a regular basis!' the captain replies to Ray, extremely happy that someone has taken such a huge interest in the way his boat runs.

'That's fantastic!' Ray replies. 'I never would have thought a hybrid could achieve that kind of speed at such a constant rate!'

Much like I would never have thought that life could screw me over at such a constant rate, I suppose.

There's part of me that should want to run and hide before Ray or Amy actually sees me, but that part of me has had quite enough of all this bullshit, thank you very much, and prefers to let things play out naturally.

Therefore I just grimace and wave at the both of them when they spot me standing close to the cabin's entrance.

'Oh! Hello there, Joel!' Ray says in that irritatingly confident manner of his.

'Ray,' I reply, with a languid nod of the head.

Now that zemblanity has once again deposited the contents of its bowels all over my head, I appear to have swum into a calm lagoon of acceptance.

There's almost something quite *freeing* about the secure knowledge that the next few hours of your life are going to suck. It takes away the fear of expectation.

'Hi, Joel,' Amy then says, and her tone of voice is actually quite pleasant.

I feel quite happy to return it in kind. 'Hi, Amy. I hope you're well.'

From beside me, I hear Cara huff.

It is a huff that conveys much. First off, it's all about the displeasure of seeing Amy. There's no noticeable evidence that she is upset at seeing Ray, though. Then, on top of that, is the displeasure of hearing me being *civil* to Amy. This is almost a greater aspect of the huff than the first part. Thirdly, and lastly, there is an element of disbelief around the edges of the huff, about how we have all been once again thrown together this way.

I should have sat Cara down and had a nice long chat with her about Mr Zemblanity and his party blower. That would have cleared it up.

My girlfriend says nothing else to her favourite couple in the world, and instead marches off towards the back of the catamaran where there are still a couple of spare seats.

I look down at the floor. This is mainly to avoid Ray and Amy's immediate reactions, before they've had time to get control of their faces again.

'Do excuse me,' I say in the tones of one who has finally reached acceptance of his lot in life, and is just going through the motions from now on.

I head over to where Cara is sat, with her beach bag on her lap and a look of gold-plated chagrin on her face.

'Did you know they were going to be here?' she asks me, as I slowly deposit myself next to her.

For a moment, I consider telling her all about the maniac in the chef's whites, but decide against it, as I don't want her calling the men in equally white coats.

'No. No idea,' I reply.

Cara punches her hand down on to the bag. 'Every bloody thing we do . . . *she's* there. Everywhere we fucking go . . . she's there *too*.'

'Yep.'

'I really, really hate that *bitch*!'

'Yeah. I get that.'

Cara stares at me. 'Why aren't you *angrier* about this? This trip is going to be ruined now!'

I shrug my shoulders. 'I'm tired, Cara. Too damn tired.'

'For God's sake, Joel!'

I turn a little in my seat and put my hand on her shoulder, giving it a gentle squeeze. The second I do this, I am transported back to the first boat trip we took on this holiday, when we realised Amy and Ray were coming to Wimbufushi as well. Cara squeezed my leg in the same sympathetic manner back then.

'Look, I know it sucks,' I tell her. 'But let's try to make the best of it.'

'I don't *want* to make the best of it!'

'I know. But what choice do we have?'

Cara goes to respond again, but the truth in my words is undeniable. The catamaran has left the jetty, so we are committed to staying on board now. We can either thrash about and complain, or just accept our fate.

The pout Cara produces at this moment would sell for millions in a perfume advert. 'The champagne had better be bloody good,' she eventually mutters.

It might well be, baby . . . but it won't be anywhere near as good as the wine gums.

It takes the catamaran fifteen minutes to putter slowly out to the section of reef we're going to be snorkelling around. As it does, the sun starts to get lower in the sky, and a cheerful young man called Harry gives us our safety briefing. I'm sure Harry has a much more interesting Maldivian name, but this is probably a case of having things dumbed down for us.

If I go away from this holiday with one thought (aside from all of the stuff concerning my ex-wife, of course) it will be that I don't feel like I've really visited 'the Maldives' at all. I have no idea about the country's culture or people, even after having been here for a whole week. There's something I find undeniably sad about that.

When the briefing is over, Harry and his two work colleagues hand out the snorkelling equipment. I can see that Ray has gone back into the catamaran's cabin to continue his conversation with the captain. This leaves Amy sat on her own close by, fiddling with the strap on her flippers. She looks a little lost, sitting there all by herself.

Stop it.

She doesn't deserve *that*.

The catamaran then comes to a halt in a patch of deep blue water that looks much like any other, except when you lean over the side, you can see that just below you is a forest of coral, far larger and more elaborate than the ones reachable from the beach on Wimbufushi.

Following Harry's instructions, we all pop on our flippers and snorkels. We are also offered the opportunity to use pool noodles to keep us afloat. I'm a pretty decent swimmer, though, so I turn this down, as does Cara.

'So, everyone!' Harry says, stood at the back of the catamaran where a wide set of steps leads down on to a small deck area that's mere inches above the water. 'We will all now drop into the water, and then I will take you on a tour of the reef, across the shallow section, and out into the deeper water after that.' He holds up a hand. 'And remind me what the hand signal is for if you get into any trouble?'

We all dutifully raise our hands and put our fingers on the tops of our heads, just like Harry taught us during the briefing. There were other hand signals as well, but this one was the most important, so it's no wonder he wants to make sure we all know it.

'Well done!' he says. 'Now follow me!'

And with that, Harry jumps off the side of the catamaran.

He is then followed by the rest of us, and I am instantly reminded of sheep going into the dip. There's an awful lot of flailing arms, legs and pool noodles going on, and I can't help but think that the local fish population must dread this time of the week. You would too, if your otherwise placid day was interrupted by a herd of enormous floundering monstrosities poking you with their brightly coloured tubes of foam plastic.

Cara and I take ourselves off slightly to one side, to make sure we're not at the centre of the heaving mass. I also notice that Ray and Amy have done the same on the other side of the bubbling cauldron of body parts. Ray is, of course, a swimmer *par excellence*. I can see that from the way he moves with utter confidence. Flippers are not things that lend themselves to personal confidence, unless you're extremely comfortable using them. Amy is paddling in one position, while Ray darts in and out of the general area, already looking at the coral underneath him like he's been doing it for years.

Harry gets everyone's attention, and the flailing and thrashing calms down a bit. 'We're going to follow a very specific route,' he tells us. 'Please don't deviate from it. The coral around here is very fragile, and we must be sure to keep to the route marked out so we don't disturb it.'

When he starts to swim away, Cara and I hang back a little, watching where Ray and Amy are. Not a word passes between us while we do this, but it's clear that we both have the same train of thought going on.

Ray, being Ray, is right at the front of the line of flapping tourists, with Amy in close company. I have to wonder whether she's okay with that. Amy never used to be someone who liked to rush things. She's always been the methodical, hang-back-and-appraise-the-situation type. Being up front is not something that comes naturally to her.

Still, at least Ray's enthusiasm makes it easy for Cara and me to hang back. We don't quite bring up the rear – our friends from the karaoke session, Trevor and Sandra, are doing that. All those cigarettes haven't done much for their cardiovascular health, and that means that swimming fast in flippers is quite beyond them. Trevor is gasping for air like a floundering haddock, and Sandra's face is a picture – a picture of Dante's Inferno painted by a psychopath.

You have to wonder why they wanted to come on a snorkelling trip at all.

Still, they make me look good by comparison, which is nice.

For the next few minutes we all happily trawl along behind Harry as he points out some of the weird, wonderful and beautiful aquatic sights beneath us. The sun is still high enough in the sky to provide us with all the light we need. If anything, the golden tones of the slowly lowering sun make everything look even more gorgeous.

The coral out here is larger and more colourful than the stuff close to the island, and my breath is quite taken away by some of their graceful shapes and patterns. The fish are equally lovely to look at. A collection of multi-coloured little darting bodies that pop in and out of the corals at will.

The whole thing is as glorious as it is undeniably *fragile*.

It's enough to make me go home and throw out all of my single use plastic, buy a hemp shopping bag, and start buying my dinner from that Veganthropy Foods company that's all over the place on the TV these days.

We spend a good twenty minutes in this shallower section of the reef before Harry turns to the left, and starts to take us out into deeper water.

Up until this point I have been enjoying this excursion through the forests of coral, but as we approach the edge of the reef's shelf, I start to get a little panicky.

The drop off is . . . *considerable*.

One minute we're about ten feet above the sea floor, and the next minute it drops precipitously off at a near right angle. I feel like I've flown out over the edge of the Grand Canyon, and my bowels don't like it one little bit.

Thankfully, Harry does not take us much further out than a few metres past the edge, but it's enough to allow an extreme sense of vertigo to overtake me. I have to stop for a second and lift my snorkel to catch a proper breath.

'Are you okay?' Cara asks, swimming up alongside me and treading water.

'Yeah! It's just a bit . . . a bit deep!'

'I know what you mean! My heart jumped into my throat when we came over the edge!'

I can see the rest of the group getting ahead of us now . . . being ostensibly led by Harry, but actually being led by Ray, who has gone in front of our tour guide and is happily skirting along the edge of the coral like he was born to do it.

'Trevor! Trevor!' I hear Sandra scream from my right, and whip my head around to see that the plastic-surgery-altered singer of 'I've Got You, Babe' does not in fact have her babe at all, as he appears to have disappeared beneath the waves.

I look back to see that the rest of the group has got even further away from us. We're the only ones anywhere near poor old Sandra and her submarining partner.

I should just call for help. I can't possibly save Trevor myself. That would be a ridiculous thing to try to do. I just don't have it in me.

Do I?

No. I should just scream at the top of my lungs for help, and hope that Ray or Harry get over here in time to save the sinking fat man from a watery grave.

Yes, that's right. That's what you should do. Maybe once upon a time you could have been the hero here, but that was back when you sold mansions and won at life. Now you sell tiny houseboats and lose at everything . . .

Fuck off.

I'm not having that.

Not for a *second*.

263

I swallow hard and look at Cara, pointing in the direction of the others. 'Get their attention! I'll swim over and see if I can help!'

Cara nods, turns to look at where Harry and Ray are still leading the group away, and starts to scream at the top of her voice, her fingers perched atop her head like she was shown in the safety briefing.

As she does this, I motor over to where Sandra is flailing around on her pool noodle for all she's worth. Trevor's noodle is drifting off into the distance, never to be seen again, until it washes up on another tropical beach somewhere across the other side of the planet.

'Where is he?!' I demand as I reach her.

'Down there! He's drowning! He's *drowning*!' she screams.

I plunge my head into the water and can indeed see the top of Trevor's head as it dwindles into the darkness.

I then take the deepest breath I can, and frantically swim downwards.

Thankfully, Trevor is not *too* far under the water, so I am able to reach him before my breath gives out. He's also happily conscious, and thrashing his fat little tattooed arms around as hard as possible. It's not doing much good, because he's also being pulled down by the weight of his rock-hard beer gut.

I get level with him and grab him under the armpits. Then I start to kick my legs as hard as I can, and we start to move back towards the surface again.

Good Lord, I don't want to spoil it, but I do think I might be doing something quite heroic here . . .

I *know*!

I'm as *amazed* as you are.

Such is the upward momentum I've provided to the both of us with my heroic kicking that Trevor begins to rise away from me with a thrash of his pudgy little arms. This is something of a relief, because I think I'm right at the end of my energy reserves.

Still, I think my work here is done. I have done something I can actually be proud of.

Ha! Take *that* zemblanity!

You can stop me having a nice time on holiday, but you can't stop me from—

Trevor's foot smacks me on the top of my head as he hits the surface of the water, and bursts through it like a porpoise who's had a few too many and got a Celtic tattoo put around its blowhole.

This knocks any sense I might have had out of me, along with my breath.

I slowly start to sink back down into the deep again, with what must be the second concussion I've incurred in the past few days.

Ah, zemblanity . . . you just couldn't let me have this one, could you?

I should probably make some sort of effort at this point to not drown.

That is what any sensible, right-thinking individual would do.

But I recently kissed my ex-wife – a woman I'm supposed to hate – because I've completely lost my way in life, so I'm not sure I qualify as someone either sensible or right thinking.

Maybe, just maybe, this is . . . *easier?*

If I don't try to claw my way back to the surface, I'll never have to hear anyone call me Captain Pugwash under their breath again as I pass their desk. I'll never have to feel like I'm out of my depth in a job I used to be completely on top of. I'll never have to look down at my paunch, and wish I could pull off a pair of tiny white shorts. I'll never have to think that I'm far too old and weird to be dating a girl like Cara.

I'll never . . .

I'll never . . .

I'll never . . .

. . .

. . .

And then, he's there.

Like a Greek god. Like a caped superhero. Like the last warrior on the battlefield. Like the Saviour on the mount. Like David Hasselhoff in tiny red shorts, instead of white ones.

Ray spears down through the water with his arms outstretched and grabs me in a rough, manly bearhug. He then kicks his legs a couple of times and we're rising. Rising to the surface, and all those things I'll have to keep coping with, whether I like it or not.

Ray is powering me back to a life I'm not sure I want anymore.

I think, on reflection, it's probably a good time for me to lose consciousness . . .

Fear not, I am only out for a few seconds.

By the time I have broken the surface of the water to find myself surrounded by flailing tourists, an anxious Cara, a very anxious Amy and an *extremely* anxious Harry, I have more or less come back around again. My brain is all over the shop, though. I can't really form a coherent thought or sentence thanks to the minor oxygen deprivation.

Ray continues to hold me in a gentle but firm embrace while we wait for the catamaran to make its way over to us. It is in this moment that I can appreciate why Amy is marrying him. It really is an embrace that makes you feel like nothing in the world could ever hurt you again.

And then, after I've been hauled up on to the boat, and for the second time on this luxury, relaxing holiday to the Maldives, I receive emergency medical treatment. This time sat in a seat on the catamaran, administered by the captain and watched over by about twenty people. This medical treatment largely consists of being gently slapped in the face and given a drink of water, while Harry checks my pulse and asks me if I can breathe okay.

I tell him I can – which is the truth. I don't think I swallowed much sea water. I just feel extremely tired from all the effort of not drowning.

Trevor's fucking *fine*, by the way.

He laughed off his brush with a watery grave, and is currently smoking a fag with his wife on the other side of the boat. He did slap me on the back and call me a cracking bloke, though. He also offered me a good price on a used car if I'm ever in Cheam, which was nice of him.

Cara is sitting by my side, holding my hand, with a look of concern on her face that is likely to freeze in place if she has to adopt it around me many more times.

My lord and saviour, Sir Ray of Holland, stands upright with his arms folded, looking down on me and watching Harry's ministrations, with an expression on his face that suggests a job well done. It's the same expression a gardener would have when seeing how well his potatoes are growing. Amy is hanging back just behind him, trying to look everywhere but at me.

However, when I am overcome by an unexpected coughing fit, she moves forward and sits on the other seat by my side.

Even with the discomfort of hacking my lungs up, I can feel the cringingly awful sensation of having my girlfriend on one side of me and my ex-wife on the other.

'Have another drink,' Amy suggests, and picks up the glass of water from where I'd put it down on the deck.

'Okay,' I reply. 'Thanks.'

'No problem.' Amy looks me in the eyes properly for the first time. 'What you did was . . . very brave,' she eventually says.

'Pfft. What Ray did was brave. What I did was *stupid.*'

Amy rolls her eyes. 'Ray is half fish, Joel. He barely broke a sweat doing that. You once nearly drowned getting my hat out of a canal.'

Oh God. That's right, isn't it? I *did* nearly drown that time we were in Somerset and the wind blew Amy's favourite cap in the canal we were walking beside. I fell in trying to get it back. Luckily it was shallow, and a very hot day.

I chuckle to myself with the memory of it. 'You did get your cap back, though.'

'Yes, and the fat bloke with the tattoos survived, so you did everything right.'

I look up and over at Trevor talking animatedly with some of the other guests, who have grown weary of the entertainment I've been providing them with.

'He did, didn't he? Free to butcher Sonny and Cher songs until the day he dies.'

This makes Amy laugh, and for the briefest of moments – for a mere *split second* – we're just two people on a boat, sharing a laugh after the mildest of near drownings.

And then . . .

'This is all *your* fault.'

I whip my head around to see that Cara is look at Amy like she wants to kill her.

'I'm sorry?' Amy replies, unconsciously shifting back and away.

'I said . . . this is all *your* fucking *fault!*'

'Cara,' I begin, cautiously. 'Don't do this now, I'm fine and—'

'No, Joel! No! I've had enough of keeping *quiet!*' Cara snaps at me, before returning a gaze comprised of the finest quality loathing back in Amy's direction.

I wonder if anyone would mind if I jumped back into the ocean . . .

'You've *ruined* this holiday!' Cara spits at Amy. 'This whole week has been a bloody nightmare because of you and Mr Fucking Perfect here!'

Ray unfolds his arms. 'Now, I don't think you need to—'

'Shut up! Just shut up!' Cara barks at him, which is a bit much. The guy did just save me and my paunch from an early grave. 'I'm sick of being around you! I'm sick of the sight of you!'

Now the other guests, who had temporarily been diverted by whatever shenanigans Trevor was regaling them with, have turned back to the main event, curious about this latest development.

How exquisitely embarrassing.

Cara rises to her feet, as does Amy – who now looks almost as angry as Cara, given that she's just seen her man insulted by the woman who's with her old one.

'Don't you talk to Ray like that,' Amy hisses.

Seriously, if I just push back with my legs, I should be able to slide over the side and into the briny deep, before this really gets going, and we all—

'I'll talk to him however I want, *bitch*!'

Oh, good Lord.

'*What* did you call me?!'

'A bitch, Amy! Because that's what you are!'

'Oh, am I, Cara?'

'Yes! And you always have been! You ruined poor Joel's life two years ago, and now you've nearly got him killed!'

Amy actually takes a step back at this. '*I* nearly got him killed?'

'Yes! He's only been acting weird all week because you've been here!'

269

'Er, now hang on . . .' I say, also getting to my feet. My attempted rescue of Trevor had nothing to do with Amy. I was attempting to do something a bit brave for once.

'No, Joel!' Cara nearly screams at me. 'Stop making excuses, and stop trying to be so *diplomatic*! You know how badly she's affected you! You know how pathetic she's made you!'

My face flames even redder, if such a thing were possible. 'It's not been that bad,' I protest. 'I'm not that bad.'

'Yes, it has! Yes, you are!' Cara disagrees in no uncertain terms. 'It's been a fucking *nightmare*! We came here so you could chill out after all the shit you've had at work, and she's ruined it! Just like she ruined your job in the first place!'

'*I* ruined *his* job?' Amy retorts with disbelief, before pointing a finger at me.

Oh joy. The finger pointing at me has started. It's a wonder it took this long, frankly.

'I got fucking *fired*, Cara! Your bastard grandfather fired *me*, not Joel!'

'Yes! Yes, he did! Because you blamed poor Joel for getting that meeting wrong! Even though it could have been you!'

'No, it couldn't! It was Joel's fault!' Amy rages.

'No, it bloody wasn't!' I shout back at her, instantly angered by the same accusation she's flung at me so many times before.

'Yes, it was!' she screams, now incandescently angry.

Ray steps forward. 'I think we all need to just calm down a little—'

'Shut up, Ray!' Amy, Cara and I all scream in unison.

Cara decides a bit of finger pointing is now in order as well, but thankfully aimed at Amy instead of me. 'I believe Joel! I believe him when he says he got the time right! You must have come along and changed it! He sure as hell didn't do it! He put it down in your work calendar as one p.m.! *You* must have fucking changed it!'

270

'I did no such bloody thing!' Amy insists.

'You must have, Amy,' I tell her. 'I know I didn't do it.'

'Yes! Yes! It was *you!*' Cara says to back me up. '*You* changed the appointment with Lord Ponsonbollocks, not Joel!'

'I did not!' Amy protests.

'Yes, you did!'

I slowly raise a hand, with an outstretched finger that shakes slightly. 'Hang on . . .'

Amy stabs her own finger into her chest. 'I was very careful with all of our appointments! I let Joel do it once, and he fucked it up! He was never good with details, but I always am! Ray will tell you how careful I am with stuff like that, won't you, Ray?'

'Yes, you always are very careful, Amy.'

'Er, just hang on a moment . . .' I repeat.

'Well, you must not have been that fucking *careful* back then!' Cara snaps. 'Because Joel did it right! *You* fucked up!'

'Just wait a second . . .' I say a little louder.

'I never fucked anything up! Your boyfriend did all the fucking up, Miss Rowntree!'

'No, he didn't! He'd never do anything like that, and—'

'Shut up, both of you!' I cry, asserting myself properly for the first time.

Both Cara and Amy fall instantly silent.

Ray *remains* silent because he knows what's good for him.

I look at Cara with a confused expression on my face. 'How did you know I called him Lord Ponsonbollocks?'

She blinks a couple of times. 'Sorry? What?'

'How did you know that's what I called him? I only ever used that nickname with Amy. Nobody else. It was just between me and her. All of my nicknames for our clients were.'

Cara looks flustered. 'Well . . . well, you must have told me it at some point, *Joel.* Obviously!'

271

I shake my head. 'No. I never did. I know I never did, because it' – I throw a quick look at Amy – 'because it hurt too much to think about that type of thing. About the little secrets we had with each other.'

'Well, you must have said it to me!' Cara insists. 'Otherwise, how would I have known it?!'

'The appointment calendar,' Amy says in a dull voice, looking from Cara to me. 'You used to write your nicknames down in our appointment calendar.'

I shrug my shoulders. 'Well, yes. Because it was *private*, and I knew I could get away with it because nobody else had access to it.'

Amy slowly turns back to look at Cara. 'So how did she know you called him Lord Ponsonbollocks, if you never told her?'

'Because she saw it in your fucking calendar!' Trevor exclaims.

'That's right!' Sandra adds. 'She must have seen it!'

For the first time since this argument really got going, I look around to find that we have a rapt audience. Trevor and Sandra look like they're watching a particularly juicy episode of *EastEnders*. Even Harry and the catamaran captain are fascinated by what's going on, and I doubt they even get *EastEnders* out here.

Is there a Maldivian equivalent?

I can't picture what the Maldivian version of the Queen Vic would look like, but they'd probably serve a lot more coconut-based beverages, wouldn't they? They probably wouldn't all looked like a slapped arse, either. It's too sunny and nice out here for that.

Anyway, back to the argument . . .

'It was *you*,' Amy says, her voice now virtually dead. '*You* changed the appointment time, Cara.'

'Don't be *ridiculous*!' Cara says, shrinking back a little. The towering anger that consumed her mere moments ago has been replaced by something even worse in my eyes: *fear*.

'Yes. That's it. There's no way you could have known Joel called him Lord Ponsonbollocks, unless you had seen it written in the calendar,' Amy continues, dropping into the kind of tone Sherlock Holmes would have been proud of. 'You used to come into the office a fair bit in those days. You'd hang around your grandfather a lot.' Amy shoots me a look. 'And my husband.' Her head tilts a little. 'My silly, scatter-brained, reckless husband, who always used to leave his computer on when he was away from his desk . . .'

I can't breathe.

I can't breathe because I'm drowning again.

And this time I don't think Ray is going to be able to save me.

Sunday

AMY – FRIENDS AND PARTNERS

I can barely keep the tremor out of my voice as the horrible truth of it all clicks into place. None of it makes any sense, while at the same time making absolutely *perfect* sense.

It was Cara.

Cara Rowntree who altered the time on the calendar so that we missed that stupid meeting.

But why?

Why would she do such a thing?

'Is it true, Cara?' Joel asks her, his face even whiter than it was when Ray yanked him out of the ocean. 'Did you go into my calendar and change it?'

The silence she responds with is more than enough to convince me that she did.

For a few seconds, Cara Rowntree remains struck dumb, caught between the choice of continuing the lie or defending her actions. She knows her dirty little secret has come out into the open in front of all these people – but let's see if she's stupid enough to keep going with it.

'I did it for *you*, Joel!' she squeals, hands out in an imploring fashion.

Ah . . . good.

No more bullshit, then. That's just as well. I'm sick to death of it.

'What do you mean, you did it for *me*?' Joel replies, and I can see the betrayal writ so large across his face it nearly breaks my heart.

All this time he's blamed me and I've blamed him . . . and *neither of us was to blame.*

That look on his face breaks my heart because it's one I've seen him use on *me*. Hell, it's the same look I've returned back in kind at *him* so many times.

But on this occasion, it is *entirely* justified.

He'd better say or do something soon to retaliate to what she's done, otherwise I'm going to take matters into my own hands and punch her into the middle of next fucking week.

Cara stabs her finger at my face. 'She was no good for you, Joel! I could see that! I saw how unhappy you were with her! How *broken* you were with her!'

'I wasn't broken!' Joel replies in disbelief.

'Yes, you were!' she argues. 'Like a wounded little animal! I saw your marriage breaking down . . . saw how she made you so miserable! I had to do something! I had to save you from her!'

'I didn't need fucking *saving*!' Joel roars back. 'Okay, things weren't that great between Amy and me when you saw us, but for a long time I was *happy*!'

'Were you?' I blurt out.

'Yes!' he exclaims, turning to me. 'Well, most of the time, anyway. I *think*. To start with. It seemed pretty good, didn't it? Those first few years, especially?'

275

I stand there trying to cram six years of memories into (wait for it) a split second. It's not an easy thing to do, and it's even harder to make a general assessment about it all right here and now. There were times when I felt giddily happy about being married to Joel – but all those times very much feel like they happened towards the start of the relationship.

I was certainly happy with him on this silly bloody island six years ago, I remember that.

'I guess so?' I say, being as honest as possible. 'We definitely had our moments.'

Joel gives me a look that for the first time in years has no edge to it at all. It rather takes my breath away. 'We did. Some great moments.' Then he smiles, and it's the smile of the man I once loved.

That smile disappears the instant he looks back at Cara, though. 'You had no right, Cara. No right to do what you did. No right to interfere with my bloody marriage!'

Now Miss Rowntree looks distraught. You'd think that given the circumstances, and the fact that I finally have a definite villain on which to focus my anger, I'd feel good about how bad she looks – but frankly, I'm far too tired of this whole thing to feel that way. About the only emotion I can summon as I look at her shrink back is a combination of pity and regret.

'But I *love* you, Joel!' she pleads. 'I have since the first time we met!' She wipes a snotty hand across her nose. 'You were always nice to me! Always better than the other men! You didn't start every conversation by looking at my tits! You were different! You deserved so much better than Amy. You deserved *me*!'

Oh dear.

Things are rather falling into awful place, aren't they?

Cara did come into the office a fair bit back when I was there. And I suppose I remember her hanging about with Joel – but no more than anybody else? And it never came across that there was any kind of infatuation with my husband. She managed to hide it very well. To me she always just seemed like a granddaughter interested in getting into her grandfather's line of business. A notion borne out by the fact that she did indeed join the agency not long after I'd gone.

. . . after I'd been *sacked.*

Oh my GOD!

A revelation hits me so hard that I'm nearly knocked on to my backside. All this time I thought it was Joel going behind my back to Roland Rowntree to get me fired.

But it fucking *wasn't* Joel, was it?

It was somebody much closer to the old man, with *much* more influence over him!

'Oh, you little fucking *bitch*!' I roar, all the anger rushing back into me as I realise the depths of Cara's Machiavellian deceit. '*You* got me fired, didn't you? *You* told your grandfather he should do it after *you* were the one to sabotage our meeting with Lord Ponsonbollocks!'

'Is that 'is real name?' Sandra pipes up, from where she's stood chewing on one fingernail with the tension of it all.

Snorkelling among tropical fish clearly can't hold a candle to watching a soap opera play itself out in real time right in front of you on the deck of a boat.

'No!' Joel snaps at her. 'His name was Viscount Alastair De Ponsonby Long!'

'Lord Ponsonbollocks sounds better,' Trevor chimes in, chuckling to himself.

'Did you?' Joel says to Cara, trying to ignore the heckling from offstage. 'Did you get Amy sacked?'

'I wanted her to be *far away* from you, Joel! Because she was so *bad* for you! Being around her was hurting you! And I . . . I wanted to be the one who was *close* to you!' she wails, confessing everything at last. 'I wanted to *be* with you, Joel! Because you're a good and kind man! Because you were broken and I knew I could fix you!'

'So you ruined my *life*?' he retorts, voice cracking with the pain and betrayal of it all.

I want to hug him. I truly, truly do. He doesn't deserve any of this. *I* don't deserve any of this. But I can't. It would be completely inappropriate. How would it make Ray feel? Watching me do that?

I turn to look at him and see that his face is a mask of stunned anguish at what's playing out in front of him. He has absolutely no good reason to feel any empathy for my ex-husband, but he does anyway. I'm not going to betray his good nature by hugging Joel in front of him. No matter how much I want to.

'I didn't ruin *anything*!' Cara disagrees at full volume. 'I made your life *better*, Joel. Because I'm better than *her*!' Again with the stabby finger.

Boy, Cara Rowntree really hates me, doesn't she?

Joel takes a step back, which forces him to sit down hard on the seat behind him. I've never seen someone look so dejected in my life. 'We're done,' he says in a quiet voice. 'You and I are done, Cara.' Then he looks at me, and my heart really does break. 'I'm so sorry, Ames. So sorry for all of it.'

The tears are running down my cheeks before I realise they are there.

What a sad, stupid situation.

All the pain, misery and hurt we've both suffered and felt for two years – all brought about by this idiotic little girl with her obsession for an older man.

. . . an idiotic little girl who is now taking steps towards me, clenching and unclenching her hands into tight fists.

Oh crap.

Cara Rowntree may be a silly little girl, but she also has a lot more muscle packed into that tight frame than I do. And now her deceit has been unmasked there's a marked change in her personality for the worse – and potentially psychotic.

'You!' she snarls. 'This is all *your* fault!'

This must count as the worst case of psychological projection in history, but it's not something I have time to consider further at this moment, because I think I'm about to get punched in the face or have my eyes clawed out.

'Cara, just *stop*,' I say, raising my hands.

Hang on, why am I the one being conciliatory here? She's the villain of the piece. I should be the one starting on her!

'Fuck you!' she screams, both arms up as if she's about to slash me with her nails.

Oh, *no*. We'll be having none of that, missy . . .

I move quickly away from Cara, turning my back on her as I push my way past Harry and Faraz, the captain of the catamaran that Ray has made best friends with. Cara gives chase, because that's probably all she's capable of doing now that she appears to have regressed into some sort of animalistic rage.

I attempt to run away from her by skirting around the deck of the catamaran, which is incredibly slippery thanks to all the sea water sloshing about on it.

Our fascinated onlookers get out of my way as best as they can, as I awkwardly traverse the deck – all the time fearing that a woman in her mid-twenties is about to jump on my back and start savaging my neck.

'I'll fucking *kill* you!' Cara screams, underlining the seriousness of the situation.

'Stop that!' I hear Ray cry from somewhere even further behind me.

I only manage to get as far as the other side of the boat before things underfoot become too damn precarious for me to run any further. I may not want to get clawed by Cara, but even that is preferable to breaking a leg by falling over.

I spin back around as Cara quickly closes the gap.

'Now look here, Cara,' I remonstrate. 'You need to stop this! This is very stupid!'

'I'll fucking kill you!' she repeats, indicating that my salient line of reasoning is not getting through *at all*.

Instead, she launches herself at me with all of her might.

Sadly, all of her might is not able to compensate for how slippery the deck is, and rage turns to horror as her left foot goes out from under her, and she stumbles right past my quivering body, slamming into the seat behind me, and tumbling head over heels over the side of the boat and into the ocean, with a loud – and no doubt very painful – clatter.

For a moment, everyone left on deck is shocked into silent immobility.

We can't have all just witnessed an athletic woman in her mid-twenties tumble off the side of a catamaran like the world's worst stuntwoman, can we?

'She's in the fucking drink!' Sandra exclaims, proving that – yes, indeed – we *have* just all seen that very thing.

Everybody then rushes over to the side of the boat, to look down at where Cara is now thrashing around like a lunatic, spitting sea water everywhere.

Ray is by my side, looking down at her with an odd expression on his face. When he sees that I'm staring at him, he turns and regards me with a grave look on his face. 'Well, I'm not bloody saving *her*,' he says in the most matter-of-fact voice I've ever heard him use.

Luckily for Cara, Harry the snorkelling guide has no such qualms, and jumps over the side of the catamaran to render his assistance.

As he swims over to Cara to help her, I look up and behind me to see that the only person who hasn't joined the rest of us watching the rescue take place is Joel. He's still sat down with a look of utter dejection on his face.

I take Ray's hand in mine and look him in the eyes. 'I love you with all of my heart, you know that don't you?' I tell him.

He swallows hard. 'Yes, of course I do.'

'Okay.'

I let go of his hand, and walk carefully back across the deck. 'Joel?' I say as I reach him. 'Joel? Look at me.'

He does this, and it's like staring at a black hole – formed in the first split second of the universe's creation.

'Come here,' I tell him. 'It's okay.'

For a moment he doesn't move. But when I make beckoning gestures with my hands, he slowly rises to his feet, and puts his arms around me. I do the same, and hug him as fiercely as I am able to.

There's passion in that hug.

There's also rage, and frustration, and guilt, and shame, and love, and hate – and a thousand other things I cannot put into words.

But above all, there's forgiveness in it.

Oceans of forgiveness.

A silent, joint apology – carried out with no words or movement whatsoever, while a very silly little girl gets all the attention over on the other side of the boat.

I can feel Joel's breathing slow against my chest and the tension release from his muscles, as we stand there in an embrace that just a few days ago I would have told you was completely impossible.

In the years to come, I will look back on this hug, and it will always be one of the best and most important of my life.

It's often very hard to know when you start a new chapter in your life. But I will always be able to mark this embrace as being the very firm and solid point at which a new one started for me. A better one. One not filled with hurt and anger towards a past love, and equally not filled with guilt and shame towards a current one.

Joel is the first to eventually move away, looking over at where Ray is standing and watching us both with a sad expression on his face.

'It's okay,' I say. 'He understands.'

Joel laughs grimly. 'Does he? Do you think he could explain it all to me then? Because I'm frankly fucking *clueless*.'

I also laugh at this, and the moment – important as it was – is finally broken.

We move away from each other, and both take very deep breaths.

'Well. That's certainly the last time I'll ever go snorkelling,' Joel says, as we look over at where Harry is helping Cara back on to the boat.

Ray moves towards us, taking Faraz gently by one arm as the man tries to pass him. 'I think,' he says, in a tone that rather indicates he won't be listening to any disagreement, 'that we should return to the island now. Given the circumstances.'

Faraz, looking from Ray, to Joel, to me, to a banged-up and bruised Cara Rowntree, gulps and nods his head.

Thank God for that.

If we have to stay on this boat any longer, I'll have to start charging the audience an admission fee. Christ knows what we'd do to top Cara's tumble into the water, though.

I'd have to start riding a dugong around naked, I think – but unlike in my dream, there's not a Chinese restaurant in sight, so that's not going to be on the bloody cards, is it?

The trip back to the island is conducted through what can only be described as the fifth circle of hell. I think the fifth circle is the one all about avoiding the gaze of people you hate, while confined to a small space, isn't it?

Cara sits with Harry, Trevor and Sandra on one side of the deck, while Joel sits with Ray and I on the other. In the middle, a small wormhole has formed, created by the weight of all the contained animosity. I'm hoping it doesn't get any larger, because the last thing we need is eldritch horrors from beyond existence invading our world thanks to a right cow changing a calendar appointment.

This is why I'm making sure not to look in Cara's direction. I don't want to add fuel to the interdimensional fire and bring forth the invasion of Cthulhu and his many-eyeballed pals.

I have never taken such a huge interest in the horizon in my life.

This isn't so bad, to be honest, as the sun is down now, and I can just see the last vestiges of deep blue fading away into nothing. It's as beautiful as it is melancholic.

That's another sunset missed, then.

I look at Joel, who is sitting with his hands between his legs, head down, lost in thought, and playing idly with the sticker on a plastic water bottle.

I want to say more to him, but there's every chance Cara would hear my words, and the last thing I ever want is for Cara Rowntree to hear anything that comes out of my mouth again. Unless it's a well-constructed insult that compares her to some sort of tentacled monstrosity from beyond time. Carathulhu, possibly.

I then watch Joel as his eyes narrow, and he nods to himself.

Oh dear.

He's about to do something very *Joel-ish* . . .

My ex-husband then rises from his feet and walks slowly across the deck of the catamaran to stand right in front of Cara. I would be worried, but I can see the strong set of his shoulders – which is a posture I've not seen him adopt any time recently. This almost looks like the Joel of old, not the Joel of now.

Blimey.

For her part, Cara looks up at him, a sullen expression on her face.

'You lied to me,' Joel begins. 'You manipulated me. You did everything you could to ruin my marriage.'

'No, I didn't, I—'

'Be quiet,' Joel responds, in a low tone of voice that is threaded with pure steel. Cara instantly falls silent again. 'You did all those things, Cara . . . but you wouldn't have been able to do any of them if I hadn't been in a bad place anyway.' He briefly looks back at me. 'If we hadn't been in a bad place. So . . . I'm going to choose not to hate you, Cara. Because I don't think you actually deserve that. You just took advantage of something for your own ends, because you had feelings for me.'

'Yes! I do, Joel! I do have feelings for you! I lov—'

'I said, be quiet,' he repeats, the steel now fully tempered. 'As I say, I don't think you did what you did out of malice. I think you did it out of love. So I don't hate you, Cara. But we are *over*. Do you understand me?'

She looks up at him. And I think for the first time she sees who Joel really is. Because this is the man I once fell in love with, before our marriage started to go south and we sucked all the joy out of each other.

I doubt she's ever met *this* man before in her life.

Cara nods slowly, the misery writ large across her face.

Joel nods again, once more to himself than to anyone else. He then turns and comes to sit down next to me, an expression on his face that I find completely unreadable . . .

I cannot express how relieved I am to climb off the catamaran and get back on to dry land. Mainly because it means I can finally get away from Cara and this incredibly tense situation. Joel may not hate her for what she did to us both, but I sure as hell do. I don't have the emotional connection to feel anything different.

Cara is being helped off the boat by Harry – and I'm sure is playing up her injuries massively for him. While the tumble she took was clearly nasty, I don't think she actually needs the help of three fully grown men to move around, now Azim has joined Harry and Faraz.

Thankfully, this means she's moving at a snail's pace, which lets us get well ahead of her. I don't have to be in her vicinity anymore, and I'm very relieved that this is the case. I really don't want to get arrested by the Maldivian police for beating up an injured woman.

No, far better just to get her out of my line of sight – for the rest of my life.

As I walk down the jetty I am suddenly aware that Joel has no such options available to him. 'Oh *God*. You'll have to go back and sleep in the bungalow with her, won't you?' I say, going wide eyed with horror.

'Yes,' he says, looking dejected. It's obviously something that's already occurred to him.

'Nonsense. He can sleep on our couch,' Ray suggests, looking at Joel. 'I'll go and get your stuff out of there. You can bunk down with us tonight. We have to get up at the crack of dawn tomorrow for the flight anyway, so none of us will be sleeping that much.'

'That's a great idea,' I add, feeling happy that we can at least do something to get Joel away from the evil Carathulhu on his last night on the island.

It further occurs to me that Joel will therefore be sleeping on the same couch I tried to have sex with Ray on because I was guilty about letting Joel kiss me – but there's really not much fire to that thought now.

That was a different woman. One who didn't really understand the way things actually were.

I have undergone a profound change of perspective over the past couple of days. First with Ray's insight into my feelings for Joel, and second with the revelation that Joel was not to blame for me losing my job and my marriage.

That honour goes to the woman behind me, who has just screamed in agony because Azim, Harry and Faraz have dropped her on to the hard wood of the jetty.

The smile that appears on my lips is the biggest one I've been able to muster this entire holiday.

'I'm sorry we can't separate the two of you on the plane, though,' Ray says as we walk along the beach to our water bungalow.

Joel shakes his head. 'Don't worry. I can put up with that. If I can't find an empty seat elsewhere, I'll just stick on some headphones and an eye mask, and ignore her. I certainly don't intend to speak to her anymore, and if she tries, I'll call the steward over and tell him she's an escaped psychopath.'

'Not too far from the truth,' I say, thinking about everything Carathulhu has done.

Joel nods and smiles, but there's no humour in it. His eyes have a haunted look about them that only increases my level of worry for him as we walk together along the beach. He may have summoned up something from deep within him to confront Cara, but whatever it was is slowly seeping out of him now, unfortunately. I don't quite know why.

His head goes down again, and I exchange a glance with Ray that speaks volumes.

It's quite incredible how both of our attitudes towards Joel have irrevocably altered. Where once he was someone to avoid and loathe (on my part anyway. I think Ray only truly extended as far as mild dislike), he's now a friend in need of help.

God.

Joel.

A *friend*.

A friend in need, who I want to help.

What crazy universe is this?

But I have no idea how I *can* help him. None whatsoever – and that twists my stomach into knots. Now that I know my ex-husband was not the architect of my downfall, a lot of the genuine feelings I still have for him are allowed to come out into the open, without being accompanied by negative emotions. I may have fallen out of love with him a long time ago, but that doesn't mean I don't still *love* him.

Bloody hell.

If you could show me something more complicated in human existence than the way love works, I'd be bloody amazed. It makes the formation of an entire universe in a split second seem like a piece of cake.

'It's not the plane I'm worried about when it comes to Cara,' Joel says, still with that haunted expression on his face. 'It's going back into work with her.'

I wince.

I hadn't even thought of that!

That's why he looks so dejected again.

The poor guy not only has to suffer an eleven-hour flight with Carathulhu, but he also has to go to work with her next week!

My stomach is now so twisted that I may never be able to eat the piece of cake that was formed by the universe – right after it invented the sherry trifle.

Bizarrely, I again feel wracked with guilt.

Because *I* get to go home with Ray Holland, and go to work with him next week, in a job I – kind of – enjoy. Even though it isn't a thrill a minute, at least I don't have to do it alongside someone who was instrumental in making my job ten times worse. That's going to be Joel's lot in life moving forward and he really doesn't deserve that.

No more words pass between us as we get back to the water bungalow and go inside. Joel plonks himself down on the couch, while I make us all a nice cup of tea. Ray has wandered off outside to look at the stars, which are starting to come out now that the daylight has completely faded. He looks lost in deep thought.

Once the teas are made, I hand one over to Joel and pop Ray's down on the side table next to the couch.

When he comes back into the bungalow, Ray has a determined expression on his face.

'Joel. I have a proposition for you.'

My heart skips a beat, and I have to sit down next to Joel so my legs don't give out from under me.

I know exactly what Ray is about to say . . . and it's as perfect as it is absolutely amazing.

'Yes, Ray?' Joel replies, looking up at him with his cup of tea clutched in his hands like a lost little schoolboy.

'My yacht business is expanding – not least due to the help Amy has given me with it this past year – and I'm on the lookout for great salesmen who can help me continue to grow. The plan is to move into selling much larger, more expensive boats now, and that will no doubt require more experienced staff.'

'Okay,' Joel says, a bit non-plussed, bless him. He has no idea what Ray is saying, because he has no real comprehension of the kind of man Ray is. A man who I will be very proud to marry at some point in the near future.

'Would you like to come and work for me?' Ray says. 'I've heard all about how well you and Amy worked together before all of the . . . nastiness. It certainly sounds like you know how to sell. You think you can do that with luxury boats the way you have done with luxury houses?'

'Buh . . . buh . . .' Joel replies, completely discombobulated.

No wonder.

'Just say yes, Joel,' I tell him. 'We were a great team before everything went south . . . maybe we can be again . . . but this time as friends.'

Joel looks at me. That haunted expression has disappeared, to be replaced by something much better. *Hope*.

He nods his head vigorously at me, before doing the same at Ray. 'Yes. Yes, I'd . . . I'd *love* to do that,' he eventually says. 'I'm quite good at selling boats, actually. There was this houseboat that I sold on the Thames, you see . . .'

'Excellent!' Ray exclaims, and claps his hands together. 'Well, that's settled then. I'm looking forward to seeing how you two work together. If you can do for Holland Yachts what you did for Rowntree Land & Home, I'll be delighted!'

I stand up, and put a hand on Ray's arm. 'Are you sure about this? Won't it be hard for you to have . . . to have my ex working for you? With me?'

Ray shrugs and shakes his head. 'I know how much you love me, sweetheart. I trust you.' He turns and looks back down at

Joel, a meaningful look on his face. 'And I can trust you too, can't I, Joel?'

Joel lets his breath out in a short, sharp exhale. 'Are you *kidding me*? You're saving my bloody *life,* Ray!' He cocks his head at me. 'If she won't marry you, I fucking will!'

Which, in the language of Joel Sinclair, is a definite affirmation of trust, I believe.

Ray certainly seems to take it that way, as he laughs and pats Joel on the shoulder. 'Good stuff. Now . . . I'm going to go over to your bungalow to pick your things up, Joel. Why don't you and Amy have a chat about how things will work from now on, while I'm gone?'

Ray's voice is casual, but he clearly wants us both to iron out any lingering animosity or friction before we go any further.

It's something I fully understand and agree with. 'Yeah. Let's go for a little walk, Joel. Down to the end so we can look at the water.'

'Okay,' my ex-husband – and *friend* – replies, looking happy for the first time this week.

Hell, it's the first time I've seen him looking happy for bloody *years.*

I don't want to descend into a trite cliché here, but there's no other way for me to describe the change I see in him. It's like a weight has been lifted from his shoulders (sorry).

I suppose that's mainly down to the fact that Ray has offered him a lifeline out of a job that's obviously no good for him any-more, but I'd also like to think that some of that weight was the ani-mosity between Joel and me. A weight that's been resolutely shifted over on to the shoulders of the person who actually deserves it.

I certainly feel a lot lighter now. You don't know how much something has been affecting you mentally until it's *gone.* The idea that the man I once loved would contribute to my downfall *plagued* me. Knowing that it didn't happen that way is a relief that genuinely makes me feel like I can breathe easier.

I give Ray a kiss on the cheek as he parts ways with us to go and get Joel's belongings. I doubt Carathulhu will put up any kind of resistance after Joel's words to her, but even if she does I feel perfectly happy that Ray can handle whatever she might try to throw at him.

'Come on, you,' I say to Joel, and start to stroll down the wooden walkway, underneath the blanket of stars that has been the most glorious sight throughout this whole holiday – other than the dugong.

I then wince a little when I remember where I'm inadvertently walking towards. The place where I had my little *over the side* evacuation, thanks to Joel's machinations earlier in the week. That seems like it was a lifetime ago – which is just as well, as I can more or less cope with the idea of going to the same place again now.

I make a conscious effort to steer us over to the other side of the widened pier, though. Let's not get stupid here.

As we reach the end of the walkway Joel is looking a little disconsolate again.

'Honestly, Joel, it'll all be okay,' I tell him. 'Ray is as good as his word. You'll be out from under Rowntree's nose before you know it.'

Joel shakes his head. 'It's not that. I do trust him . . . and I trust you too. It's . . . I just . . .'

'What?'

He turns to face me. 'All those *years*, Amy. All that *anger*. All that hate. All a complete waste of time . . .'

I nod. 'Yeah. I know what you mean.'

'It would have all been easier, if Cara hadn't . . . done what she did. Without Goblin Central we might have been more civil to each other. Avoided all the hate and the anger.'

I heave a huge sigh. 'Maybe. Maybe not.'

'What do you mean?'

'Look, we know what happened with Goblin Central was *awful* . . . and it's still taking a huge amount of will power for me not to follow Ray over to your bungalow and throw Cara off the side of it – but to be honest with you, if it wasn't that, it would have been something else, wouldn't it? We would have probably stumbled on even longer in a marriage neither of us wanted anymore, before another incident came along to blow everything up. Cara just speeded up the whole nasty bloody process with what she did to our calendar.'

Joel nods his head. 'Yeah, you're probably right.'

'That stupid mansion – and that even more stupid girl – was the straw that broke the camel's back,' I continue, 'but if we'd been in a better place anyway, we would have worked things out. Don't you think that if we were meant to be *together*, it would have all gone a different way?'

Joel goes to reply, but his mouth hangs open for a moment before he closes it again. There's a lot to digest in what I've just said.

'Remember back, Joel. Remember back to what we were like even before Goblin Central. Sure, we had some great moments – coming here for the first time, for instance – but we argued an awful lot as well. Mostly about work. Because that was our *passion*. The thing that brought us together . . .'

' . . . and the thing that *kept* us together, until it tore us apart,' Joel finishes for me. '*Ugh.*'

'Exactly,' I reply. 'A couple better suited to each other in general would have had more between them to keep them together, even through the roughest of times – like what Cara did to us.' I rub my eyes for a moment, suddenly feeling bone tired. 'Our work both defined our relationship, and was the glue that held it together. I don't think there was really much else. Something was always going to come along to blow it all up eventually.'

Joel stands there for a moment, staring down at the water, letting all of this sink in. He then looks back up at me with a lop-sided grin. 'You always were smarter than me, Ames.'

I shrug my shoulders. 'Not smarter, just *different*. You were the powerhouse in our relationship, Joel. I know that. You knew people better than me. You *got them* better than me. And you knew how to talk to them. I was the details girl.'

'Maybe.'

'No maybe about it. I know what my strengths are, and I know what yours are too. That's why I know we can work together again – this time as friends.'

Joel nods animatedly. 'Yeah. That's right. We can get it *back* again, Ames,' he says with real excitement. 'What we once had? We can sell the shit out of Ray's yachts together!'

I laugh. 'That's what I'm hoping.'

Then Joel does something that would have scared the fuck out of me just a few hours ago. He reaches out and takes my hand. I don't flinch or try to move away when he does this. I just don't feel the need.

'Is it okay . . . is it okay if I say that I love you?' he says, lip trembling a bit. 'You know, as a friend?'

When the tear rolls down my cheek, I don't try to wipe it away. 'Yes. Of course. I love you too, Joel. Always did. Always will.' I take a huge breath. 'That's why this holiday has been such a nightmare.'

'Agreed,' he replies. 'But not anymore. That's all over with now. New chapter, and all that. As friends.'

'As friends,' I repeat.

And when Joel comes in closer to hug me, I happily let him do it, because that's what friends do. Especially friends who have discovered each other again, after a long time of being apart.

When he breaks the embrace, Joel has another smile on his face, this time a cheeky one. It's his best smile, by far and away. 'Ray really is a fantastic bloke, isn't he?' he says.

'Yes, absolutely.'

'I thought he was too good to be true.'

'Did you?'

'Yep. Nobody's that good, I thought. Must be a serial killer in disguise.'

I laugh out loud, even though I know I probably shouldn't. 'I could see you thinking that, yeah. He really is just a very nice man, though.'

'Seems that way. And ironically, it was me who turned out to be with the psychopath.'

'Yes indeed. Carathulhu does seem like she's got a screw loose, doesn't she?'

Joel's eyes go wide. '*Carathulhu?*'

I laugh hard, and put a hand up to my mouth. 'Yeah, that's her nickname now . . . you know, like the creatures in that movie we watched that night in the Premier Inn in Cornwall? The one with all the monsters with the tentacles?'

To demonstrate, I wave my arms around at my sides.

'What are you doing?' Joel asks.

'Tentacles, Joel. I'm doing tentacles,' I reply in a very serious voice. 'These are Carathulhu's tentacles.'

Joel stares at me for second, before doubling over with laughter loud enough to echo around the water bungalows, and out across the gentle Maldivian ocean where the dugongs live.

This is absolutely fine as far as I'm concerned – because if you're going to end a holiday on a good note, it should really be with the sound of laughter . . . don't you think?

ABOUT THE AUTHOR

Photo © 2017 Chloe Waters

Nick Spalding is the bestselling author of fifteen novels, two novellas and two memoirs. Nick worked in media and marketing for most of his life before turning his energy to his genre-spanning humorous writing. He lives in the south of England with his wife.

Did you enjoy this book and would like to get informed when Nick Spalding publishes his next work? Just follow the author on Amazon!

1) Search for the book you were just reading on Amazon or in the Amazon App.

2) Go to the Author Page by clicking on the author's name.

3) Click the 'Follow' button.

If you enjoyed this book on a Kindle eReader or in the Kindle App, you will be automatically offered to follow the author when arriving at the last page.

LAKE UNION
PUBLISHING

Printed in Great Britain
by Amazon